Hallmark
PUBLISHING

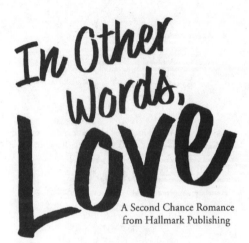

In Other Words,

Love

A Second Chance Romance
from Hallmark Publishing

NEW YORK TIMES BESTSELLING AUTHOR

SHIRLEY JUMP

One

BEFORE SHE EVEN LEARNED HOW to create the curve of a C and the sticks of an L, Kate Winslow was creating her own world of stories in her head. She'd hold the books she brought home from the library, the musty smell sweet and familiar, and imagine her own name across the cover, her picture on the back. When she got older, she'd write little epilogues of her favorite books, just to keep the characters with her, long after the stories had been tucked back into the library's shelves.

She'd dreamed of being an author, but never imagined it would turn out like this.

In the back corner of her favorite bookstore, the self-satisfied smirk of a race car legend stared back at Kate from the cover of *Why I'm a Winner*, written by Gerard Phillips. A *Clearance: 40% Off* sticker covered the last part of the word *Winner*, and a fine layer of dust sat on the stack of a few dozen marked-down books.

"Legend" was a bit of a misnomer, considering Gerard, the Indy 500 winner ten years ago, was more of a legend in his own mind. His mustached grin didn't say that, nor did the inflated story inside that he'd insisted on having Kate craft.

Ghostwriting his autobiography had been a tedious yearlong project. He had been a nightmare to work with, demanding revision after revision, until Kate had considered quitting. In the end, the fact that the electric company really liked to get paid had won out, and Kate swallowed her frustration and finished the job.

For a second, she closed her eyes and imagined *her* name on the cover, *her* face on the back of the book. Her own book—not one she'd ghostwritten and couldn't tell a single soul about because of a non-disclosure agreement. She was thirty-eight, and no closer to her dream of publishing her own novel today than when she'd been little.

Instead, she was living in a second-floor walkup with an overly spoiled rescue cat, writing nauseatingly untrue books for divas. Not exactly the success she'd imagined.

"Kate Winslow? Is that you?"

Kate jerked to attention and turned

around. Behind her stood Loretta Wildwood: tall, blonde and thin, one of those women who excelled at everything she did. They'd been in the same creative writing classes in college many years ago and had even ended up in a critique group that had met in the student lounge twice a week. Kate remembered Loretta being competitive but talented, which had made Kate both try harder and kind of resent Loretta at the same time. After school, their paths had diverged and Kate, busy keeping her head above water and the bills paid, had lost track of her classmates. Partly due, Kate was sure, to the fact that Trent MacMillan had broken her heart five minutes after she'd gotten her degree. So yeah, there was that.

"Loretta, so great to see you," Kate said, because it was the truth. The more Kate worked, the more her world narrowed, and she realized she missed those critique sessions and the energetic exchanges over phrases and plots. "How are you?"

"Wonderful." Loretta beamed, then reached into the pale blue Kate Spade tote bag over her shoulder and pulled out a slim piece of paper. "Here, you can get one early and I can even sign it for you, since we know each other."

"One what?" Kate asked. Then she glanced at the paper in her hands. Loretta's face bloomed on the bright card stock book-mark, right below a book cover for a thriller Kate had vaguely noticed in a face-front display at the front of the store. "This is your book?"

"Of course it is." Loretta laughed. "Thanks for coming to my book signing. It really is so nice of you to celebrate my success."

Kate swallowed hard. "Book signing?"

Loretta shifted her stance just enough for Kate to see the sign behind her. Kate had been so absorbed in the misery of seeing one of her own books on the clearance shelf that she'd failed to notice the banner, a blown-up replica of the bookmark. *Join* New York Times *bestselling author Loretta Wildwood for the launch of her latest book!*

Bestselling author? Latest book? That implied more than one. Kate's chest tightened. Loretta had achieved every one of Kate's dreams, and the evidence of it stood right next to Kate's failure. "I didn't know. Uh, congratulations."

"Thank you." Loretta leaned forward and tapped Kate's arm. She put on a bright, inquisitive look, as if they were best friends. "So tell me, where are your books? I'd love to see what you've published since we graduated."

Kate moved a step to the right, blocking the cover of Gerard's flop, which was kind of silly, considering no one knew she had written it. *I'm writing books that fulfill other people's dreams so I can pay for cat food and rent. Meanwhile, my own novel sits in my computer, unread and unloved.* "I've mostly written nonfiction. I have a few books out."

Loretta turned to the left, then right, scanning the headers on the bookshelves. "Really? Tell me a couple of titles. I'll buy one or two. We authors need to stick together. Am I right or am I right?"

"My books, uh, don't have my name on the cover." Kate swallowed hard and pushed out the truth. "I'm a ghostwriter, and my identity is always kept secret. It's part of the deal."

Loretta put a hand over her mouth and let out a little gasp, as if Kate had just announced the end of the world. "Oh, my. I could never do that. All my hard work, hidden behind someone else's name? That's..." She shook her head. "I'm so sorry."

She said it like she was at Kate's funeral. Given the sinking royalties Kate received every quarter, maybe funeral was an apt description. She glanced at Gerard's clearance book again. Seeing his name as the author—and knowing he hadn't written a single word—smarted, she wasn't going to lie. At least to herself.

"Don't be sorry. I really love my job," Kate

said with a smile she had to fake. In the last couple of years, her job had become more and more frustrating. Her agent had landed her a couple of decent deals, but the income was dropping every year while the workload stayed the same. "It's flexible, and I get to meet lots of great people." *Like diva drivers, snooty heiresses, and overconfident business-men.*

"That's...wonderful." Uncertainty wa-vered in Loretta's face. "Well, I need to get to my signing. Don't want to keep my pub-lic waiting." She placed a business card in Kate's hand. "Let's have coffee sometime. Call me when *your* book comes out and I'll be first in line to get a copy!" Then she spun on her Michael Kors heels and trotted over to the table and chairs set up beside the mystery section.

Kate resisted the urge to stick out her tongue at Loretta's retreating figure. *Call me when your book comes out.* Her own book? Kate was never going to have that. As she watched her ghostwriting income drop, she'd started sending out her resume to marketing agencies and a few struggling newspapers. Writing her own book was a pipe dream that would probably never happen, not unless she met some rich patron of the arts, assuming those still existed.

She loved her life; she really did. It was

quiet and predictable, and gave her time to fuss with her container gardens and read on rainy Sunday mornings. Her dating life barely existed, which meant she spent more time talking to Charlie the Cat than actual humans, but all in all, it was a good life.

It was all going to be okay, she told herself. Another ghostwriting job would come along any day now, and she'd be able to help her grandmother with much-needed repairs on her aging house, plus get caught up on her own bills. Gather a little breathing room.

But as she turned away, she glimpsed *Why I'm a Winner*, looking sad and lonely in the Aisle of Misfit Books, while Loretta's shiny book dominated a nearby stand, and wondered if maybe she should start ghostwriting fiction, because she was getting awfully good at lying to herself.

Trent MacMillan looked out the twentieth-floor glass windows of his offices in Seattle at Get Outdoors Apparel, the eco-friendly outdoor clothing company he'd started right after graduating college. Back then, the business had been about finding a new way to support his passion for hiking, canoeing, cycling—basically anything that kept him in the fresh air and out of the confines of a building.

Beyond his desk, black-and-white orcas slipped through the deep, dark waters of Elliott Bay. Lazy sailboats wove their way in and out of the bay, their sails gleaming in the bright, crisp early spring sun. People dotted the walkways that meandered along the sound, their bodies snug in thick jackets that kept out the breeze. Trent leaned his whole body toward the view, as if he could hop through the windows and put himself on one of those boats, slip into a wetsuit and swim by the orcas, or camp along one of the wooded ridges that cupped the bay.

"You got a minute?"

The voice of his CFO drew Trent's attention away from the world he loved and back into the canned air of his office. Get Outdoors Apparel owned the entire twentieth floor and had been designed to feel as much like being in Mother Nature as possible. Mossy-green carpet, pale-blue walls, communal work spaces with bright tables, and glass walls between the conference rooms and work spaces all gave the office an air of ease and space. A few skateboards were propped against the wall, flanked by bicycles and even a pair of rollerblades. The people he hired were as passionate about the outdoors as Trent, which was great, because they loved GOA like he did. The trouble was, they got to enjoy it while the boss worked long into the night. Again.

Trent pivoted back. "Sure. What's up?"

Jeremy Richards, a tall, gangly man with bright-red glasses and a passion for road cycling, had been with the company from the start. In the office, he epitomized nerd, but outside of it, he was as competitive on the bike as Peter Sagan.

He'd grown up with Trent in the same middle-class, small-town neighborhood where everyone knew their names and what time their dads got home for dinner. Hudson Falls couldn't have been more of a stereotype if it tried. Trent had left that town behind when he went to college and had never looked back. He loved the friendly vibe of Seattle, filled with so many people it kind of seemed like an endless gathering at someone's house. Not that Trent knew anything like that firsthand, considering how long it'd been since he'd done anything other than work.

"Just need a second." Jeremy headed into the office, trailed by Sarah Watkins, the petite, pregnant head of public relations. The two of them sat on the curved burgundy vegan leather sofa that formed the conversational corner in Trent's office. Trent settled into the lone armchair, a replica of one he'd seen on a hiking trip through Tibet. The original chair still resided in a monastery nestled into the side of a mountain, so Trent had hired a local artisan to handcraft the wooden seat, using dowels to fasten the legs and back. The furniture maker had molded cushions to the back and encased them with thick, white wool sheared off Tibetan sheep. Just sitting here made Trent long for the winding roads and steep climbs he'd experienced there.

At the office, things were tense. Soon, they'd have their initial public offering, selling stock to outside investors for the first time. Get Outdoors Apparel had done well in its five years of existence, thanks to the support of a couple of eco-friendly celebrities and a well-targeted social media campaign. Going public with his company baby had Trent pacing the floors at night, worrying about whether he was doing the right thing. It could lead to a big expansion of the business—but then again, if investors were wary, it could mean trouble.

"About the IPO…" Jeremy began, and the room hung on Jeremy's pause. Trent braced himself.

"What about it?"

Sarah was listening to the conversation but waiting until Jeremy had finished the fiscal conversation. Her baby bump sat like a shelf under her notebook.

"The numbers for last quarter were a little soft," Jeremy said. "We expected Christmas to really bump up our sales, but that new line didn't perform like everyone expected."

Trent had designed a brand-new line of winterwear for the holiday season, but with record warm temps in the rest of the country this past winter, they'd had a higher-than-average number of returns and lower spring preorders as retailers tried to make their winter investment back. GOA had launched a fairly aggressive advertising campaign, but the needle hadn't budged, which meant he'd spent more on marketing than he'd made in profit on that collection. Next year could be record snowfall and he could have a run on parkas, but that didn't help this year. "How are the spring orders?"

Jeremy checked his notes and gave a little nod. "After a bit of a slow start, they're going strong. Those windbreakers you designed are really pumping up sales. People love the pockets and versatility of them."

Those were an idea Trent had had on a backpacking trip through Eastern Europe one summer. The weather had been warm but misty, and he'd wished for a flexible but light jacket that could carry his supplies of snacks and water.

That trip had been a solo one, after

Trent and his girlfriend at the time broke up. He and Erin had only dated for a couple of months, and it was probably a good thing he hadn't ended up traveling around the world with someone he didn't know that well, but still...

It would be nice to have a girlfriend who loved the outdoors as much as he did. There had been one woman, once, in college, who he'd thought...

Didn't matter. That was over. What he needed was someone like his PR person Sarah, who had gone on annual Appalachian Trail hikes with her husband until she'd gotten pregnant with their first child. Her face beamed with happiness about her future. A little flicker of envy ran through Trent.

Geez, he really needed to get outside more. This was crazy.

"Of course," Jeremy went on, "we don't have the returns in yet, so we won't know how that impacts the bottom line for a couple more months, and the IPO is right in the middle of the third quarter of this year. However, to the investors, that bumpy few months doesn't look good. We're a startup who came out of the gate and exploded. They get uneasy about that nowadays."

"Because you're only one bad PR day away from a major image crisis," Sarah piped up, reminding Trent how things could go south very quickly. Sarah was a powerhouse in the marketing department. She'd gotten Trent started on social media, posting his trips and adventures. A celebrity client had liked and shared one of the posts, then told her followers to order from GOA like she had, and the company had been on a more-or-less upward trajectory ever since.

"Well, I can't get any bad PR, considering I never leave this place." Trent gave Sarah a nod. She'd been working overtime on his public relations, and keeping up appearances for Trent, at least on Instagram and Facebook. "Thanks, by the way, for making it look as if I get outside once in a while."

"It's all about perception." Sarah grinned. "On Instagram, you're not pushing paperwork and discussing public offerings, you're climbing mountains and discovering trails."

When was the last time he'd done either of those things? It seemed like forever ago. Here he was, pushing forty, and stuck inside an office all day. He'd never thought of himself as a big-business kind of guy—more like a rebel with a surfboard. But then he'd had that idea for eco-friendly outdoor gear and apparel, and one thing led to another. Now here he was, talking IPOs and PR campaigns and longing for what used to be. Was this his future? Spent in an office watching the world go by without him?

He said, "I think I want to live in Instagram."

Sarah laughed a little, then leaned forward, her features sobering. "Here's the thing, Trent. Nothing on social media is real, so you don't want to live there."

True. The life Trent portrayed on the internet was far from his real life. When had that happened? When he'd left Hudson Falls and the garden center business his parents had wanted to pass on to him, he'd vowed to be a free spirit, enjoying life on his own. He had the "on his own" part down, but the rest...

Trent drew himself back to business. "So, what do you suggest, Jeremy? I really don't want to delay the IPO. That looks worse than one bad quarter."

Jeremy propped his leg on the opposite knee, forming a six-foot-five man triangle. As he did with most things, Jeremy paused before speaking, weighing all sides of his answer. "Well, you could, as Sarah said, change the investors' perceptions about GOA."

"How? I don't think your average investor is reading my latest Instagram story."

"There's the book," Jeremy said. Beside him, Sarah gave an enthusiastic nod. "For one, it's a giant advertisement for the authenticity of the brand and the humble roots that formed GOA. For another, those public appearances are a great way to get the message out that GOA is strong and here to stay."

A year ago, Trent had worked out a deal with a publisher to write a memoir. Everyone was interested in how the wunderkind had taken an idea he'd had on a mountain trail and turned it into a multi-million-dollar business. He'd started writing, then set it aside as one to-do after another filled his hours.

He'd kept thinking he had lots of time until the deadline. He searched his memory but couldn't remember what he'd promised the publisher.

"The book? But that's not due until—"

"First week of April." Sarah shared a worried glance with Jeremy. "You remembered the deadline, didn't you?"

"Honestly, I forgot about it entirely. I've been working so much and..." Trent shrugged. "I won't be turning it in by then."

Her eyes widened. "We, uh, thought you were on it, Trent. As it is, the schedule is tight. Like *super*-tight, because normally a book needs months to go through production before it's published. The editor promised to turn it around right away, so we can have that public launch at the end of May. It's a great public relations move right before the IPO, and can get investors excited again."

The schedule was tight because Trent had moved the delivery date. Twice. Every time he thought he had time to work on it, his attention was yanked away. Then he'd forgotten about the book, gotten busy, rinse and repeat. "We can reschedule that, can't we?"

Sarah shook her head. "There's a book tour planned. Several venues rented. You promised last time that you would deliver no matter what, and everyone started putting the publicity pieces in place. Rescheduling would..."

"Look very bad," Jeremy finished. "And the last thing you need is more bad press. Some of the media have speculated that the drop in sales is because the company has become too big for one man to run, and it's losing the personal touch that set it apart. This company was built on you being honest and transparent and *there*, Trent. Your presence and personal touch are important."

Trent ran a hand through his hair and let out a frustrated gust. As if he didn't have enough to do and worry about right now. Why had he thought this was a good idea last year?

"I don't have time to finish the book. I can't make the deadline. We're going to have to cancel and somehow minimize the bad press."

"There is another option," Sarah said. She paused a second, reluctance in her eyes, and when she spoke again, her voice was almost a whisper. "You can hire a...a ghost-writer."

"Hire someone who pretends to be me as the writer? Sarah, our company slogan and the book title is *Be True to Your Nature*," he said, remembering the idea he'd worked out in the publisher's office, something that had seemed easy at the time. "It's supposed to be an honest, unflinching look at how I got here, written by *me*. I have built my reputation on being as transparent as these walls." He waved at the glass that separated him from the workhub of GOA. "A ghostwriter who pretends to be me and writes the book is sort of like lying, isn't it?"

"Well, yes, but..." Sarah shifted forward, in her PR element, running with the idea she'd had and molding it to fit what Trent needed. It was why he'd hired her, and why she was so brilliant at her job. "The ghostwriter signs a nondisclosure agreement. They can't tell anyone ever that they wrote the book. It's entirely secret."

"Forever?"

Sarah nodded. "For-ev-er."

Trent sat back in the chair and considered his options. Well, option, singular. He'd been so busy lately that he'd barely had time to spend five minutes outside, never mind do anything else. A book was a massive, unwieldly project, and just the thought of trying to corral his thoughts and notes into a reasonable manuscript...

He glanced at the big bright world outside his building. A world he might have time to enjoy, if someone else did the heavy lifting on the book. That way he could meet the deadline, go forward with the launch and build goodwill before the IPO. Win-win-win all around. Trent pivoted back to his team. "How do we find a ghostwriter?"

Two

WHEN KATE WAS A LITTLE girl, every Saturday would be a girls-only shopping day with her grandmother. Her parents, who'd worked in a cannery, were either working second shift or putting in overtime, so Kate had spent a lot of time with her grandmother Wanda, who'd become her de facto babysitter.

Saturdays had been Kate's favorite day. The two of them would put on pretty dresses and silly hats, wander through downtown, then go back to Grandma's house with their newfound treasures. Sometimes, they'd stop in the library for a stack of books or linger at a café for a very grown-up-feeling cup of hot cocoa. On the way home, there was always a visit to the bright and busy farmer's market. Her grandmother would take her hand and they'd weave their way through the crowded stalls, past glistening jars of local honey and squat containers of sweet strawberries. If she closed her eyes, Kate could still hear the vendors hawking rhubarb jam and freshly picked tomatoes.

One year, when Kate was five, Grandma had bought her a plant from a wizened and hunched man in a stall at the back of the market. A trio of tiny garnet flowers had peeked up at Kate from a small pot of rich, dark soil. The earthy scent of the dirt had mingled with a whisper of vanilla, all coming from this tiny, delicate life in her hands.

Her grandmother had bent in front of her, her blue eyes crinkled at the corners. She'd tapped a petal, and the crimson flower had quivered a bit. "These are Wandas."

"Like you, Grandma?"

She'd laughed. "Just like me. These are primroses. It's a perennial, which means it comes back every year. They're not named after me, but because they have the same name, they're my favorite flowers. I want to teach you how to grow them, and lots of other things, because when you learn how to tend a plant, you learn how to tend yourself."

At the time, Kate hadn't understood what her grandmother had meant, but in the countless Saturday afternoons of her life that she'd spent at her grandmother's house, seeding, potting, and nurturing everything from tomatoes to marigolds, the lesson had stuck with her. Even now, as Grandma Wanda eased into her nineties, she sprinkled bits of wisdom into every conversation.

Kate loved her something fierce and sometimes hovered over her like a worried hen. In the last year, Grandma had slowed down some, and her older house was beginning to need some expensive repairs, like a new heating system and a plumbing fix for the kitchen. Grandma lived on a limited income, and every time Kate came over and saw the house, she vowed to pay for those things with her next contract. It would have to be a good contract, though, with a hefty advance.

"You are such a good granddaughter," Grandma said when Kate stopped by on Tuesday afternoon, bearing a container of homemade butternut squash soup. A short, spry woman with bright blue eyes and a fondness for turquoise reading glasses, Grandma Wanda's effusive spirit belied her nine decades. Kate stopped by several times a week to check on her and bring homemade food. "You must have read my mind. I was just thinking about your soups today."

Kate laughed. "You're *always* thinking about my soups."

"That's because you are such a good

cook." Grandma patted her cheek. "You need a man who appreciates that."

Over the years, Grandma Wanda had tried fixing Kate up with the cashier at the supermarket, the owner of the gas station on the corner, and her friend Edna's nephew. Most days, Kate was buried under a deadline and didn't even have time to date. She'd fallen in love once—and had learned the hard way that it wasn't a mistake she wanted to repeat. Maybe someday she would again, but that day was not today.

"I don't need a man. I need another book contract." Kate glanced at the darkening sky before she ducked inside the house. She'd forgotten her raincoat again. The predicted thunderstorms and snow showers hadn't come yet. Maybe if she could get in and out of Grandma's house quickly, she could get home before the skies opened up. The early part of spring in Seattle could be anything from cold and slushy to wet and rainy, but Kate still more often than not forgot her jacket.

"Come, come," Grandma said, waving Kate down the hall toward the kitchen. The heating system kicked on, clanking and growling its way to warm air coming out of the vents. "We'll heat up the soup and talk. I want to show you what I'm planting this week, and we'll transplant your seedlings. You should see the tomatoes!"

"That heater is still giving you fits?"

Grandma laughed. "I think that thing is older than me. When your Grandpa Jack was alive, he had it running like a well-oiled machine. But now, it's getting worn out and ready for replacement. I'm hoping to get one more winter out of it. But don't you worry about me. Nothing makes me feel better than some hours in the dirt."

On any other day, Kate would have hurried through lunch to get to the greenhouse at the back of Grandma Wanda's house, but after the run-in with Loretta and two weeks of bugging her agent about needing a new contract, the dark day outside matched Kate's mood. "I'm not really up for all that, Grandma. I was just dropping off the soup."

"Nonsense. Gardening will take your mind off your troubles." Grandma put the soup into a pot, set it to simmer, then ducked out to the greenhouse and returned with a tray of seedlings. "Just look at these lovely little guys."

Kate bent down and marveled at the infant plants, only a couple of straight leaves right now, still too young to form the serrated edges of a mature tomato plant. She and Grandma had sowed the seeds a couple weekends ago, part of Grandma's early start for her garden. "The seedlings need to be thinned."

"That they do." Grandma smiled, as if she knew all along that Kate would say that. She turned off the stove, and a minute later, the two of them were up to their elbows in potting soil in the greenhouse. The small glass building attached to the house was warm, the panes dotted with condensation. Built by Grandpa Jack when Kate was a baby, the greenhouse was a testament to his love for his wife and her love of plants. Pots of delicate orchids lined one shelf, while an army of Wanda primroses in bright blues, yellows, and deep reds marched along the wooden table. The vegetable garden seedlings occupied the space beneath the pitched panels of the greenhouse roof, soaking up all the sun they could.

For an hour, Kate and her grandmother thinned the tomatoes, peppers, cucumbers, and other seedlings they had started in tiny pots a couple of weeks earlier. Soon, it would be time to move them into large pots that would sit on Kate's deck, and the rest into Grandma's half-acre garden. The work was simple and satisfying, with the earthy scent of life hanging in the air.

"I'm glad I stayed to do this," Kate said as she scrubbed her hands in the corner sink.

The two hours of gardening had eased the stress between her shoulders.

"I've always said there's nothing a little dirt under your fingernails can't fix." Grandma leaned over and gave her a kiss on the cheek. "Is something troubling you? You've been awfully quiet."

"Just worrying about my next contract." Kate didn't mention how hearing the groan of the heating system and the steady plip-plop of the leaky faucet only quadrupled that anxiety. "The ghostwriting jobs aren't paying as well as they used to, and it's been a long time since I was hired to do one. I've been thinking of applying to work at a marketing agency or something and put this English degree to another use."

Grandma's pinched face told Kate what she thought about that idea. She picked up the last seedling container, the only one they hadn't separated yet, and held it level with Kate's gaze. "Look at these two and tell me what you see."

"Uh, one big seedling and one smaller one." The twin tomato plants-to-be were spindly stalks with flat leaves and buds of new growth peeking out of the stems. One arched over the other, taller and longer.

"Exactly. And do you know why that is?" Grandma went on, not waiting for an answer. "Because the bigger one is striving toward the sun. See how he's leaning so far to the right, as if he's going to pop right out of the soil and park himself under a ray?"

Kate chuckled. Grandma had a tendency to give her plants personalities and genders. Kate had to admit that every once in a while, she did the same. It was hard not to see something that worked so hard to grow as having a good deal of character. "Well, maybe he was simply angled the right way when you set out the tray of seeds."

Her grandmother tsk-tsked that. "You know I turn the pots so there's an even amount of sunlight for all. This guy—" she tapped the taller of the two seedlings, "—he's ambitious and brave."

"Brave?"

As Grandma talked, she separated the two plants into their own pots, nestling the tinier one into a plastic pot filled with rich, dark earth. "He has no idea what's waiting for him out there, but he keeps on growing, because that's what he does best. He could end up having a nice, sunny life in a rich, earthy garden, or become an early lunch for a hungry rabbit." She shrugged. "Hey, rabbits happen. So do weeds. But you don't see that plant being afraid of all that, do you?"

Here was the life lesson, Kate thought. "It's a tomato plant, Grandma, not Captain America."

Grandma laughed. "And you're a young woman, and not a superhero. Doesn't mean you can't reach for the sun yourself. Don't worry about the weeds and the rabbits. Just keep doing what you do best, and it will all work out."

Outside, the skies began to rumble, dark clouds blocking the sun and hanging heavy and low. "I have to go," Kate said. She pressed a quick kiss to her grandmother's cheek. "I love you, Grandma. See you Thursday."

"With minestrone soup?"

Kate laughed and made a mental note to stop by the corner market on her way home. "With minestrone."

"You are a good granddaughter."

"You said that already." How she loved her grandmother and these quiet afternoons. Kate would make a thousand soups, if only to say thank you for the memories, the advice, and the warmth. Her own parents had retired to Arizona several years ago, which had only doubled the bond between Kate and Grandma.

"Because it's still true." Grandma pressed the small plastic pot holding the newly transplanted tomato plant into Kate's hands. "Now, take him home, and let him remind you of what you can do."

Kate did as her grandmother asked,

knowing she'd bring the seedling back on Thursday to have him join the rest of his budding friends. She started walking back to her apartment, and just as she ducked into the corner market, the skies opened up, releasing a hard, fast storm. Kate hurried through the shopping and lingered after she checked out, hoping the storm would abate. It didn't.

Kate hurried down the sidewalk, clutching the plant to her chest and holding her cloth grocery sack against her side. The rain pelted her hair and clothes, drenching her from head to toe in a matter of two blocks. She yanked the mail out of her mailbox, trudged up the stairs of her building—the elevator was still out of order, according to the sign that had been there for a week—and stumbled into her apartment. She dropped the groceries and mail onto the counter, set the plant in the kitchen window, then swiped the worst of the rain off her face with a kitchen towel.

Charlie meandered over, the tiger cat's long, lean body brushing against every chair leg as he walked. Kate had found him huddled against a dumpster two years ago, starving and skeletal. She didn't know his story, but she did know Charlie was a sweet, loving cat that deserved a better life than the one he'd had before, and so she'd taken him in and spoiled him ever since. Hence the expensive cat food he loved, because Charlie wasn't something she skimped on.

"Hey, buddy. I'm drenched. Can you wait a second to eat?"

Charlie looked up at her with an *are you kidding* glare, then let out a long, plaintive meow. His tail twitched, left, right, swishing against the tile floor.

"I guess not." Kate scratched behind his right ear, his very favorite place for a head rub, then filled his bowl and checked the water dish. With Charlie situated, she could take a second to breathe.

Behind her, she heard a steady plop, plop, plop. She glanced up and saw a spreading water stain on the ceiling that was dripping onto the center of her kitchen table. Great. Just great. Kate grabbed a bowl, set it under the leak, then dropped into a chair. "What else can go wrong, Charlie?"

The cat's only answer was a quick flick of his tail. He kept on nibbling at the salmon dinner in his bowl.

"You know if I call the landlord, it'll take a year to get that fixed." Kate sighed. Given the state of the elevator, she wasn't optimistic about the roof above her apartment. Outside, the storm rumbled and roared, picking up speed and strength. Awesome.

The mail lay in a scattered mess where

she'd dropped it on the counter. Kate sifted through it, ignoring the overdue credit card bill and the Late Payment warning on the electric bill before she saw a familiar envelope. A royalty check. Maybe this would be a good one, and she could pay for the roof repair herself. Take a vacation day and drive down the coast. Pay for Grandma's repairs—

She slid the check out of the envelope, hoping for a lot of zeroes.

Instead, five digits stared back at her, none of them with a hefty comma in between. $137.11. That was all she'd earned in the last quarter. It wasn't even enough to pay for Charlie's food until the next check arrived.

The weight of her responsibilities and the defeat she'd been feeling ever since that day in the bookstore hit Kate hard. A chill raced through her, but she was suddenly too tired to change out of her wet clothes. Charlie finished eating and sauntered out of the kitchen, oblivious to his owner's need for a hug. Or even better, a hug and ten thousand dollars.

Kate dropped her head onto her arms and tried not to cry. She wasn't a determined plant striving toward the sky. She was the smaller one, overshadowed by the success stories, just trying to keep going. A sense of loneliness and despair settled into her chest, and for the first time in a long time, she longed for the very thing she'd told Grandma she didn't need. A partner, a man who loved her and believed in her and who would fix her a hot cup of cocoa when her day fell apart.

But no such man appeared. There was only Charlie, and he was already on the sofa, curled into himself, asleep.

The need for chocolate dragged Kate out of her funk and back to life. She put away the groceries, then climbed onto a kitchen chair and dug in the back of the top cabinet for the emergency stash of Almond Joys. Only one left, but one was better than none. She brewed tea, then took everything over to her "office," really just a corner of the living room with an Ikea desk and an arched lamp she'd had since college.

As she munched on the candy, Kate powered up her laptop, ignoring the funny little whirring sound that spelled impending technology doom, and clicked over to her blog. She'd started *The Secret Life of a Ghost* a couple of years ago as a way to talk about her job without actually talking about it. By keeping the blog anonymous, Kate could vent about clients (keeping their names out of it, of course) and pass on tips for other writers who were crazy enough to walk into the rollercoaster field of being an author undercover, essentially. She had a decent following and enough comments to make her think there were people actually reading what she wrote. But like all the books she wrote, none of this was under Kate's name, either.

Every once in a while, she'd post a picture—without her face in it, of course—of a plant at the market or the silhouette of Charlie. A little rebellious tip of the hat to her real life. No one would ever put the innocuous, mundane pictures together with Kate, but they made her feel as if the blog was more of a part of her.

Today was one of those days when I want to throw in the towel and become a greeter at a grocery store. Something with a steady paycheck and health insurance. Remind me again, dear readers and friends, why I got into this gig.

She hit Post and watched the words fill the screen. A moment later, a comment popped up, posted by Anonymous. *Maybe you should work on your own book instead of someone else's.*

The comment stung, and Kate readied a sharp retort, then drew her hands back from the keyboard. Whoever Anonymous was, they were right. She *should* be working on her own book.

"I hate that they're right, Charlie," she

said to the cat, who didn't have an opinion either way.

Kate clicked over to her documents tab and searched for the file of the novel she'd started back in college. It had been two months since she'd opened it, even longer since she'd written anything. She had a handful of chapters and a vague outline. Not exactly a finished product.

Loretta's smiling, slightly condescending look came back to her. *Call me when your book comes out, and I'll be first in line to get a copy!* Loretta had done it, and Kate had been a better writer than her in college. Maybe Kate should try her hand at fiction again.

"Charlie, want to listen to the opening of my book?" The cat raised his head, then settled back into his favorite sleeping position. "Okay, so maybe I have read that to you a hundred times. Way to be supportive of the person who fills your bowl."

Charlie ignored her. Kate started reading, poring over the first few pages of the women's fiction novel she'd been working on for so long, she knew every word by heart. A story of four sisters, their intrusive but loving mother, and a stray dog who disrupted everyone's lives. Every page gave her that feeling in her gut, that little tingle, that told her this was good, and if she could finish it, this book could be something.

Write a hundred words, she told herself. Just a hundred. Something. Anything. She set her fingers on the keyboard, telling herself that any words would be fine. The second Kate began to type, her cell phone dinged.

Got a new deal offer to discuss, Kate's agent, Angie Greenfield, had typed. *Want to stop by and we can go over the details?*

Just in time. Whatever the deal was, Kate vowed to agree. She needed the money and the work. Taking on a new ghostwriting job meant she wasn't going to have to make that blue-vest greeter job change.

At least, not yet.

Absolutely! On my way. Kate scrambled out of the chair, ran a brush through her damp hair and repaired her smeared make-up. She changed into a clean shirt and a pair of dark jeans, then grabbed her phone and car keys.

Just before she headed out the door, she caught a glimpse of the determined tomato seedling, still yearning for bigger skies. Maybe she was going to get out of the weeds herself too.

Outside, the rain had stopped, the clouds parting for a brief moment of sun. Kate decided to take that as a good sign of what was to come. She got in her car and headed across town. Kate's apartment was far from the water, and visiting Angie always gave her an excuse to see the Sound and sometimes get in a walk along the shore.

Angie's office was in an attached mother-in-law apartment at the end of her one-story ranch on the curve of hilly cul-de-sac, with a partial view of Puget Sound. Kate's agent was petite but brassy, with hair that was a different color every month and a fondness for Grateful Dead T-shirts. As far as publishing agents went, Angie was far outside the expected norm. Which was exactly why Kate loved her. Angie was the queen of the creative deal.

Angie's office faced the partial water view and had a small desk in the corner that she never used. Instead, she favored the twin armchairs and small table where she also held any in-person meetings, as casual as meeting a friend for coffee. Today, Angie's hair was a deep purple, the perfect offset for her normal ebony locks. "Glad you could come in. Have a seat."

That was the other thing Kate liked about working with Angie instead of another agent—the in-person meetings. There was something about the face-to-face interactions that made it feel like they were on the same team.

"I can't wait to hear what you have for me. It's been a long time between contracts."

"I know. I'm sorry about that." Angie

tugged a blue sheet of paper out of the folder on the little table. A deal sheet, with numbers on it that could make a big difference for Kate. "Royalties are down, too, which stinks for everyone. But this deal...you're going to like it. Lots of money."

Kate arched a brow. She liked the financial part, but what cost would she pay? "Lots of money usually means a diva client or a tight deadline. Which is it?"

"Pretty tight deadline." Angie slid the offer across the table. "Memoir of a CEO, all about his travels and eco-friendly approach to life, blah-blah. The kicker is that you have five weeks to produce the book."

Kate didn't hear any of Angie's words, not the money, not the deadline, none of it. Instead, she stared at the name of the author she would be ghostwriting for, and a hundred emotions tumbled inside her.

Trent MacMillan. Of all the people in the world she could end up working for, how had she ended up with the man who'd broke her heart?

"I know him," Kate said, thinking it was sad she could boil a year-long relationship down to three words.

"Oh great, that should make it easier. So if you sign that—"

"No, I mean I used to date him, back in college, before he became this big CEO. He broke up with me." Again, an encapsulated version of what they'd had. The laughs she remembered, the heartache that had followed his surprise breakup.

"Oh." Angie's lips pursed. "Well, that might make things awkward for a minute, but you're both professionals. I'm sure things will be fine."

And Kate wouldn't get distracted by Trent's green eyes, or his crooked smile...or the memory of his hunched shoulders as he walked away from her. She'd forget the picnics they'd had on a rocky bluff overlooking the sound, the time he'd grabbed her for an impromptu dance, or the two of them watching the fireworks cuddled on a blanket on the sand. Almost fifteen years had passed. Long enough? Or nowhere near long enough?

"I don't know if I can take this job, Angie."

"The money is good. I negotiated two and a half times your regular fee because of the time crunch. And it's half down, with payment for the remaining balance on delivery of the final draft."

All Kate could think about was seeing Trent again, and how weird and probably painful that would be. It wouldn't be just one meeting, either. It would be dozens of meetings, like a hundred papercuts every day.

"I can't work with him."

Angie tapped the paper. "I want you to look at that number before you turn this down."

Kate's gaze dropped to the payment details.

Wow.

The numbers seemed unreal, with those zeroes she'd been missing out of that first check. Her heart stuttered, and she blinked twice, sure the amount would disappear. It didn't. Just the first half she would get for signing the contract was more than she'd made in the last six months. The second half would be enough to cover her expenses the entire rest of the year. It was roof repair, and a new heater for her grandmother, and a fix to the plumbing. It was security and comfort and a huge lifting of stress.

"Offers aren't exactly rushing into my office," Angie added. "This is a hot iron, and you need to strike it, regardless of who you have to work with. Besides, how bad can Trent MacMillan be, compared to Gerard Phillips?"

The race car driver had never made her heart race. He'd never made her dream about a future with a dog and kids and a minivan in the driveway. He'd never kissed her and left her thoughts a jumble. Trent had done all those things, and then he'd gone and walked away from her.

She glanced at the fee again. Already, the back of her mind was working through the financial side, adding and spending and seeing what was left over. "It's a lot of money."

"You'll be done in five weeks. That's a little over a month. If you put up with Gerard for a year, surely you can tolerate an ex-boyfriend for a month."

"True." The broken half of her heart wanted to push the offer away and leave Trent to flounder with some other ghostwriter. The other half of her heart, which worried about Grandma's furnace and her own roof, whispered logic and reason. She'd be crazy to turn this down. Who knew how long it would be until another job came along?

Kate was not a risk taker. She liked to know what was coming this month, next month, and all the months after that. Being a freelance ghostwriter was risky enough, but she only had to support herself and a cat, so the semi-regular income wasn't too bad. She should, as her grandmother would say, keep the bird in her hand instead of looking for another one in the bush.

"I'll take it."

"Awesome. I'll let them know right away and get the contracts executed." Angie made a note on the blue paper. "Oh, I almost forgot. Trent's assistant was asking if you could take a meeting tomorrow morning at nine. They're anxious to get started."

"I'll clear my schedule." Kate pushed a smile to her face and wondered if the corner market sold suits of armor. She was going to need something impervious if she was going to resist that man's crooked smile.

Three

TRENT LACED UP HIS RUNNING shoes, pulled on a GOA windbreaker, and darted out of his apartment building, thankful for the overcast and cool morning. After the stormy weather of the last few days, a break in the pattern meant he could sneak a couple of minutes in for a run before he had to get to work. He looped down the street, through the park and onto the Elliott Bay Trail. The paved road gave him a little over three miles in each direction, as it skirted the edge of the water and back into Olympic Sculpture Park. Greg was already there, stretching against one of the park benches.

"'Bout time you showed up for our morning runs." Greg fell into pace beside Trent. Even though Greg was a buttoned-up lawyer and Trent was more of an adventurer, the two of them had been friends for years. They'd done a couple of climbs of Pike's Peak together, and a marathon that had taught Trent he loved to be outdoors but not for twenty-six miles straight.

"Sorry. Work has been insane." Trent pushed the pace a little more. Merely talking about work ratcheted up his stress level. Maybe the endorphin rush would release some of that tension crowding his shoulders. On his long runs with Greg, they could talk for hours about their lives and their jobs. Trent knew all about Greg's wife Virginia and their two little boys, and Greg had heard dozens of stories from Trent's college days and the startup of GOA.

"Gotta say, it's pretty ironic that you own an outdoor apparel company and you're barely outdoors." Greg's long, lean legs had no trouble matching Trent's speed. Already, Trent's lungs were burning and his legs were protesting. That's what happened when he spent too much time behind his desk instead of away from it.

"And that's only going to get worse." Alongside the path, fishing boats dotted the serene, dark water of Elliott Bay. "I've got to write that book."

"That it's-all-about-me book you mentioned a few months ago?" Greg scoffed. "I thought that thing was done."

"Hey, it's a memoir, not a shrine to myself. And it's started...sort of." Trent's breathing was choppy, his words staccatoed by the effort to keep up with Greg, who ran almost every day and was clearly in better shape right now. "I'm...well, I'm sort of hiring a ghostwriter to finish it."

Greg slowed. "Wait, what?"

"I know. I know." Trent pulled his pace back too and tried not to show how grateful he was for the break. "I'm not really sold on the idea yet, because my whole company is about being honest and transparent. This feels like I'm lying to everyone who buys the book."

Those values had been instilled in him by his parents, who'd spent their lives working hard to deliver above and beyond for their customers. Their garden center in Hudson Falls had never become much more than a standard mom-and-pop shop, which Trent had never understood. His parents had the skills and business to expand, but they'd chosen to stay small. Small town, small business, small lives.

Trent had always thought bigger than that. From his first sale, he'd had his eye on expanding nationally, getting his brand into the giants of the outdoor industry, and within a year of that celebrity mention, he'd managed to achieve all those goals. GOA was carried at all the major outdoor retailers and had worked out unique partnerships with other brands.

Greg sidestepped a rock on the trail. "It's your story though, right? So that's not really lying. It's basically paying someone else to type what you say."

They rounded the corner for their turn-around point and started heading back. As much as Trent wanted to get in the full seven-mile loop today, he only had time for three miles. Good thing, because his legs were going to be pretty sore later. "That's true. I can live with that, since it's technically still my words."

A few minutes later, they finished the run with an all-out sprint to the start point. Greg sailed past Trent and slowed to an easy stop.

Trent staggered to where they'd begun and bent over, heaving in deep breaths that burned his lungs. His legs were on fire, and his heart felt ready to explode out of his chest. A steel water bottle appeared in front of him, and he took it from Greg, uncapping it and guzzling half.

"Look at the upside." Greg gave Trent a pat on the back and a teasing grin. "You'll have more time to run if you're not busy writing that book."

"That's an upside?" Trent finished off the

water and handed the bottle back to Greg. "I think I'd rather be writing the thing myself."

"See you in a few days. Maybe then you'll be able to keep up." Greg grinned, said good-bye and headed back to his car.

Trent recovered his breath, then ran back to his apartment, once again pushing himself, as if he was trying to cram months of being stuck indoors into a single run. The three miles was going to have to sustain him for a while, given all that was on his plate.

A plate that would hopefully be lightened by whoever was going to pretend to be him.

Forty-five minutes later, Trent was in his office. He sorted through the emails that had come in overnight, had a quick meeting with the production department, then grabbed the materials he'd compiled for his book and headed down to the conference room. Through the glass walls, he could see a woman standing there, her back to him.

Her long brown hair cascaded in big curls down her back. She wore a dark blue skirt and a crisp white shirt with a pair of red heels that drew his attention to her legs. She had a curvy, gorgeous shape, and was as far from his image of a ghostwriter as Pluto was from the moon. Something twitched in his memory, but he couldn't quite grasp what it was.

"Good morning," Trent said as he pulled

open the door and stepped inside the conference room. "I only have an h—"

She pivoted to face him, and Trent stopped talking. He recognized those big green eyes, the curve of that chin, and the lingering smile that always seemed about to break across her face. He hadn't seen her in at least fifteen years, and if anything, Kate Winslow had become even more stunning. His gut tightened, and a hundred memories rushed by in a blur.

"Kate? What are you doing here?"

"I'm your ghostwriter." She looked hesitant for a second. "Didn't your assistant tell you I was the one she hired?"

"No, she didn't." Though, chances were good that information was in one of the dozens of emails crowding his inbox this morning. Then Trent recovered his wits and strode forward, closing the distance between them. He opened his arms to give her a hug, something he did with pretty much everyone he met, but at the last second, she thrust a hand between them and grabbed his. Detouring his hug into an awkward handshake.

"It's, uh, nice to see you again." She shook with him, a firm, warm grip that sparked awareness in his veins. Her demeanor never changed, as if touching him had no effect. "I'm looking forward to this project."

Already, a wall of distance had been

bricked between them. He stood there a second, uncertain. Trent MacMillan was never uncertain. Why was he letting this woman, someone he hadn't seen since college, unnerve him? *Small talk. A little small talk will get this back on track.*

Except his mind was dancing around the edges of the memory of their first date. He couldn't remember exactly what they'd eaten or what time he'd said goodnight, but he remembered Kate's smile. The way she'd peeked at him beneath the swinging curtain of her hair. The soft blush in her cheeks when he'd told her she was beautiful. The way she'd folded her straw wrapper into an accordion and showed him a trick her grandmother had taught her with a drop of water that had made the accordion inch across the scarred laminate table. Such a simple thing, but it had both softened his heart and intrigued him. Kate Winslow was the kind of woman who always ordered dessert, sang along with the radio even when she was off-key, and couldn't pass a dog or cat without stopping for a hello.

She was also the polar opposite of him in every way. He doubted that had changed in the last decade and a half. Even if she still had the ability to make his heart skip a beat or two.

"I didn't know you were a ghostwriter,"

he said, back to business as he pulled the non-disclosure agreement out of the folder in his hands. He had yet to sign it himself, in case he didn't like the person. He'd never imagined it would be Kate, and now he wasn't sure if he liked that she was someone he knew, or didn't like the inherent familiarity and possible tension. Could she be bitter about the breakup? Would that bleed into the book? "I thought you wanted to be an author on your own. Why are you ghostwriting?"

It was none of his business, really, but that didn't stop him from asking the question. When they'd dated in college, every spare second she'd had she'd spent in her dorm room or at the library, writing and creating. In the beginning, that had been endearing, a trait of doggedness he could respect. He'd ask her to go on canoe trips and mountain hikes, and every time, she'd turned him down. He'd paddled alone and hiked alone and had realized that no matter how attracted he'd been to Kate's wit, beauty, and determination, they'd wanted two different futures. Still, he'd struggled to break the connection, even after he'd graduated and she'd finished out her senior year. Then a friend had offered him and Kate two spots on a six-month backpacking tour of Europe. He'd gone to Kate, sure she'd love the idea of writing in a camp in the Alps, or at a street-side café in Belgium. Instead, a shadow had dropped over her features and before she could turn him down, Trent was breaking it off and walking away.

"I *am* an author," she said. "Just not under my own name." Whatever he'd said had struck a nerve, because the temperature in the room dropped several degrees. Kate pulled out a chair. "Shall we get started?"

So this was going to be all business. Trent should have been relieved, because he'd barely scraped together an hour for this meeting. He had a busy day, a book to produce, and an IPO to save. He shouldn't care what Kate Winslow thought or didn't think about him.

But as he reached for the chair opposite her, consciously avoiding the head of the table and the boss/employee situation that seat implied, he found himself searching her eyes for answers. He set the NDA down on the conference table and tried to read Kate's features. Did she hate him? Blame him? Was she dreading this job? Or had she forgotten the details of their history?

She spoke first. "Generally, when I meet with a new client, I start with an outline, or at least an overview of what the book will be about, so I can make sure it's something I can work with." Kate withdrew a pad of paper and flipped to a fresh page. She clicked her pen and scribbled the title of his book across the top. "So, what was your plan for—"

"Where have you been?"

She blinked. "Excuse me?"

Instead of sitting, he came around the table and leaned against the edge. The unsigned NDA sat on the space between them, neither of them committed yet. "Since we last saw each other. What have you been up to?"

"Oh, you mean since you dumped me at college graduation?"

The sharp tone of her voice told him she hadn't forgotten a second of that day. "I'm sorry about that."

"Are you?" She shook her head and dropped her gaze to the pad of paper again. "Can we just talk about the book, please? I haven't even decided if I'm taking the project on yet."

That was a curveball he hadn't expected. He'd thought her being here meant she was already all in. Maybe Kate was sizing him up as much as he was doing the same to her. "That's okay, because I haven't decided if I'm going to hire you yet."

She glanced at the unsigned NDA. Irritation flashed in her eyes. "And why wouldn't you hire me? I'm a very good ghostwriter."

"I have no doubt you're good at your job, Kate." He shifted closer to her. She'd changed her perfume, he noticed, to one that reminded him of night-blooming jasmine. He liked that. Very much. "It's more because of past history."

Her chin jutted up and she gave him a cool, even stare. "I can ignore that if you can."

"Can you?" A sudden, overpowering urge to kiss her surged in his chest. That would definitely not be the right way to start their professional relationship. That knowledge didn't make the temptation to touch her disappear, though. His brain was short-circuiting all over the place, still rattled by the surprise of seeing her again.

Yeah, that's all it was. The shock of her being in his conference room. As soon as his brain got past that, he'd stop caring if she was married or what she thought about him.

"So...True to My Nature." She underlined the words on her pad, back to business again. "Is that your title idea?"

"It's my company's motto and mine, so yes, you could say the title idea was as well." Once Trent had proposed the initial idea, Sarah had developed the book idea and structure with the publisher. He'd signed off on the project but had barely looked at it since then. For Trent, the book was a branding move, not a literary tome. Well, and something to procrastinate on doing, because he'd done a really good job of that over the last year.

"Interesting." She sat back and clicked the pen. "Because the 'nature' I remember is rather...cold."

"Me? Cold?" That was ironic, given the icy tone in her voice. Yet underneath it all, he could see a spark of the girl he remembered, the girl who'd intrigued him in American Lit class when she'd argued with the professor about the underlying meaning in Harper Lee's *To Kill a Mockingbird*.

"You did break up with me the second I got my degree."

"That might be a *tiny* exaggeration, Kit-Kat." The nickname rolled off his tongue as if he'd last seen her yesterday, not years ago. All the distance between them flooded with memories. The first time he'd kissed her, the little notes inside his textbooks, the sound of her laugh. In that moment, he craved that laugh more than he'd ever craved anything.

What was wrong with him? Why couldn't he seem to focus? They were over, had been over, and the only thing between them now was this book. In a few weeks, that would be done, and he wouldn't have to see her again. That was good, right?

Except a part of him wasn't so sure either way. Not when she was looking at him like that.

Her smile loosened and her eyes warmed,

and his resolve to stick to business wavered. "No one calls me that but you."

"I'm glad." The idea of her dating anyone else sent a flicker of jealousy through him. They weren't together anymore. He shouldn't care who she dated or if she was married—

"Are you married?" The question popped out of his mouth at the same time he dropped his gaze to her left hand. No ring. Didn't mean she wasn't married or engaged or dating. Or that it was any of his business.

She averted her gaze. "That has nothing to do with this book."

Okay, so she was right, but he couldn't concede the point. Maybe because he wanted to know the answer so badly.

"I would disagree," he said, waiting for her to look up at him again. "I should know if my ghostwriter's attentions are divided."

Right. That was his reason for asking.

"While we are working on this book," Kate said, "*you* will be the only thing I'm thinking about." Her cheeks flushed. "I meant your book."

"Of course." He'd flustered her, and a part of him was glad. He'd forgotten how the flush in her cheeks pinked, how deep the green in her eyes seemed to reach, and how much he wanted to coax a smile, a laugh, out of her.

This did not bode well for weeks of working closely together. He would be distracted, his own attention divided. He should tell her to leave, and find another ghostwriter. Just let her go...

Again.

Except Trent couldn't seem to muster the words to do that. He stood there, staring at her like an idiot.

She cleared her throat. "Okay, so what do you have so far? My agent said you'd already started, which is great, because the deadline is so tight."

"'Started' is kind of an exaggeration." He tugged a paper-clipped, very thin pile of papers out of the file folder he'd brought. For a second, he debated showing her anything before she'd signed the NDA. Then he remembered that this was Kate, and what he'd written last year was scant, so there was little danger of her running off and writing an entire book from his scattered musings. He knew her, and he trusted her. "As for pages, I don't have much done yet, but I do have a box of notes, an outline of sorts, and the first couple of pages. More or less."

She took the papers from him. As she skimmed over his words, Trent found himself holding his breath, waiting for her judgment. Which was insane. It was his book. Why did he care so much what Kate thought?

"You weren't kidding. There's hardly

anything here. Didn't you have a plan for getting the writing done? I mean, you've had the contract for a year, right? What happened?"

"I thought it would be easier." When he'd worked out the idea with the publisher, it had sounded simple, fun. Tell some stories and sprinkle them with some advice for budding entrepreneurs. As soon as he'd sat down to write, Trent had quickly realized compiling a book was the exact opposite. He had no idea what was important, what wasn't, what translated into interesting on the page. Given the expression on Kate's face right now, he still didn't know.

Hence the procrastination, the limited amount of words, and the mess he was handing over to Kate. Hopefully she could pull something together out of that.

She kept reading. "But…this isn't too bad. I mean, I know you, so that helps. I think I can work with this, at least to get started."

"Gee, thanks."

"The writing is good," she went on, "but the words—they're not very…honest and truthful. I mean, isn't that the point of the book?"

"What do you mean?" He glanced over her shoulder. Was she reading the same pages he'd handed her? "It's completely honest."

Kate pointed to a paragraph on the

second page. "Right here, when you write about your childhood. You paint it as a little dark and difficult. I met your family. They're lovely."

"My childhood wasn't perfect. It had its difficulties." He and his father had a strained relationship at best. Not that his parents had been bad parents—quite the opposite. It was just that his father had expected Trent to go in a different direction. One that led right back to Hudson Falls and working in the nursery.

"Everyone has some difficulties in their pasts. But that's not what makes you or your company unique, Trent."

It was the first time she'd said his name since the meeting had started. She had this way of extending the syllable when she spoke so that his name ended in a soft whisper. He'd always liked that. He kept getting distracted by her, his attention swiveling back to who Kate was and what made Kate tick. "And what do you think makes me and my company unique?"

All these years apart, and he still cared what this particular smart, beautiful woman in the room thought of him. She'd been the star in English Lit, and he'd barely read the books. She'd been so brilliant with everything she'd done, so impressive. He remembered the first time they'd studied together, and he'd worried Kate would give up on him. She could read a book and find ten different kinds of meaning in a single word, while Trent had gone looking for the CliffsNotes and movie version and hoped he understood it after all that. Trent loved the outdoors, moving and running. Kate loved words and window seats.

She got to her feet and began pacing the room, tapping her pen against her lip as she thought. Her brows furrowed, and her gaze went to someplace distant, while her mind churned through thoughts and words. He'd seen her like this before, back in college, and for a second it was like they were in their twenties again.

"You take risks," she said. "You don't fit into those neat little boxes that society creates. You don't care what people think about your image or your hairstyle or the shoes on your feet. Your clothing lines are practical and conscientious, designed with very specific uses in mind, which is, in a way, a direct juxtaposition to your risk-taker, jump-off-the-cliff personality. I find that...interesting. I think readers will too."

She had come to a stop in front of the floor-to-ceiling windows. A pair of sailboats dotted the dark water with white triangles. Every time Trent came in this room, he noticed the breathtaking view.

Every time but this one. He watched

Kate think and talk, her words so insightful it was as if she'd been sitting next to him all his life. He'd always admired her smarts and how hard she worked, but this was something more. Something that made him feel as if she'd opened up his chest and peered inside at all the gears and pulleys that made up Trent MacMillan.

The soft white light of the morning sun outlined Kate's curves, danced off the curls of her hair, and brightened the gentle angles of her face. The years since college had made her even more beautiful, giving her a polished, charming edge that distracted him. Trent never got distracted, never let anything tear his attention away from whatever mountain he was climbing. Right now, he had a huge mountain of work and responsibilities on the twentieth floor that needed his undivided attention. He'd been doing that, until Kate had come along in his life. The first time, and again, now.

With the stress of a company full of employees counting on him for paychecks and health insurance, a distraction could spell disaster. Maybe he should put the book on hold and find someone else, he thought for the hundredth time since he'd seen her standing in his conference room. That way he could keep his head in the game and not have his mind wandering with thoughts of Kate.

"I'm not sure this is going to work." He gathered up the papers and tapped them into a stack. Besides the distraction, a ghost-writer who knew him inside and out might not be such a good choice, he told himself. Especially if it meant she was going to challenge him on every single word he said. "I'll be sure we pay you for your time today."

She didn't say anything for a second, just watched him reassemble his stack of materials. She crossed her arms over her chest, and her eyes narrowed. "You're scared, aren't you?"

He scoffed. "Honey, I've climbed some of the highest peaks in the world. I'm not scared of anything." *Honey?* Where had that come from?

If she heard the endearment, she didn't show it. Kate crossed the room and put a hand on the pages he'd written last year, pushing them gently back onto the conference room table. "You're scared to be honest. Scared to open yourself and your life up to the world. Maybe scared it won't be as interesting as the publisher told you it will be. Or maybe you're still scared to be vulnerable to other people."

"I've changed since college." Even as he said it, he knew she had a point. One of their arguments had been about how he'd kept his feelings close to his chest but lived every other part of his life out loud and by the seat of his pants. He wasn't going to admit that now, though. He wasn't going to let Kate know that she'd gotten to him, that her peek inside him had been like an X-ray. "I've been in mud slides, avalanches, raging storms. I almost had my leg torn off by an alligator in the Everglades."

"But when it came to me, you kept your distance. Emotionally, anyway. I always felt like you were on the other side of a hill. I could see you, but you never moved closer to my side."

Her voice was soft, almost sad, and he found himself wanting to apologize for breaking up with her. He'd had very good reasons for doing it back then. He'd seen the inevitable end of their relationship, years of arguments and resentments later, and had pulled the chute before she could. It had been the right decision, Trent reminded himself. Hadn't it?

"That's because I was climbing those hills, and you weren't. We had two different personalities, Kate. We wanted two different things out of life."

That old saying about opposites attracting had been true in every sense of his relationship with Kate. He'd thought she would balance him, or maybe complement him, but as his world had taken him farther from hers, it had become clear that the adventurer and homebody love story wasn't going to end in a sunset and a kiss. She was "home by five, supper on the table at six." He was "grab a backpack and head for parts unknown."

Kate didn't answer. She took a step closer, and it seemed as if her gaze saw inside his brain. "Everything about you now is a carefully crafted image. The picture-perfect poses on the water or in the woods. The long, searching gazes you give to the camera when you're on a hike, as if you're spying some horizon no one else can see. Where in all of that is the real you, Trent? The guy I knew in college?"

So she'd looked at his social media. That flattered him and made him wonder if she still thought about the past. Then he realized she was a professional and had probably only done it to research her client. Ouch. "I'm the same guy. Just because I'm not some touchy-feely, pour-out-my-feelings-on-a-psychologist's-couch kind of person doesn't mean—"

"This book is about honesty, Trent. If we're going to write this book together, you have to be honest with me. I can't work with another grandstander who thinks he doesn't have a single fault."

Maybe she didn't know him that well. Or maybe she'd forgotten the person he'd been in college. "That isn't me."

"Oh, yeah?" She clicked her pen and held it out to him, above the blank nondisclosure agreement. "Then prove it."

Four

K ATE MANAGED TO WALK OUT of Trent's office building with her spine straight, but soon as the elevator hit the ground floor, her legs shook and the confidence evaporated. She'd held it together during the meeting and had managed to feign a self-assurance she didn't feel. Everything about being around him again set her on edge, made her heart stutter and her thoughts jumble.

Why did he have to look so good, anyway?

Trent had been the boy in the back of their American Lit class in college, hardly paying attention, only there to fulfill his English requirements. She'd been the one up front, asking questions, turning in assignments early. He'd usually strolled into class a few minutes after it had started, which made

Kate's brain short-circuit for a minute or two. With his mop of light brown hair that had a stubborn habit of dusting across his eyebrows, and his irresistible grin, almost every girl in class had paid attention when Trent had walked by.

The day before the first big test, Trent had pulled her aside after class and asked her to help him study. Bookworm Kate had been shocked the handsome athlete had noticed her, much less talked to her. She'd stuttered out a yes, and he'd asked her to grab a bite while they cracked the books. They'd gone to Chick and Cheese, and she'd fallen in love with his humor, his smile, and the way he didn't even pretend to have it all together.

Now he was all grown up and the owner of a multi-million-dollar company about to go public. She was still a bookworm, but now being paid for her love of words. And her heart still stopped every time he looked at her.

Geez. She really needed to wear a lead shield or something next time she was around him, because her brain still short-circuited at the sight of him. His hair was shorter now, sandy brown wayward waves above eyes as blue as the deepest regions of the Pacific Ocean. Instead of a suit, he'd worn a pair of GOA khakis and a T-shirt that had hugged his muscles in all the right places. She was surprised she'd managed to string together a bunch of coherent sentences this morning.

Writing a book with Trent would be cramming for a test all over again, and she knew deep down inside the little dregs of bittersweet regret about the ending of their relationship could open a door in her heart again. Because she was a weak woman who couldn't resist a crooked grin and a pair of blue eyes.

Kate slipped into her car and dropped her head onto the steering wheel. "This is a mistake," she told herself. "A huge, huge mistake."

And one she couldn't afford to turn down.

She pulled out of the lot, drove across town, then ducked into a coffee shop just as it started to rain—one of these days, she'd remember to grab her raincoat—and sat down at a table by the window. Even though it was miles away, her masochistic self stared in the direction of Trent's building and wondered what he was doing, if he'd been as upended as she'd been by seeing each other again.

Kate jerked her attention back to the present. She needed to work, not daydream about the past. She ordered a cappuccino, sprinkled the drink with extra cinnamon, and opened her laptop. Trent had promised to email the handful of pages and the beginnings of his outline. The email popped into her inbox. No message, no words from him, just the attachment. Disappointment flickered inside her.

What did she expect? Some rambling love letter about missing her and wishing she was back in his life? That would only complicate things and add a level of awkwardness she didn't need on a job. He was a mistake she'd put in her past, which was where her feelings for Trent would stay.

She sipped her coffee and took a closer look at the file. What he had could barely be called a chapter. Snippets of thoughts strung together— nothing concrete. The outline was a list of bullet points. Okay, so this was going to be a lot of work in a very short period of time.

Which meant spending a lot of time with Trent. When he'd stood so close to her today, it had taken everything she had not to lean forward and kiss him. Somehow, she needed to slot him into the Client section of her mind and get him out of The Man I Used to Love section. Doing that was going to take some chocolate. A lot of chocolate.

The bell over the coffee shop door jingled as a woman stepped inside, closing her umbrella, giving it a little shake, then setting it against the others on the wall. Loretta again, like a stray cat following Kate everywhere she went. "Kate! I'm so delighted to see you again!" Loretta pulled out the second chair and plopped into it. "We must have coffee together and catch up. We didn't have time in the bookstore, and I've been dying to hear more about how you do that ghostwriting thing."

Kate swore she saw Loretta shiver in revulsion when she said the word "ghostwriting." "Actually, I'm kinda working right now."

Loretta waved that off. "Work, shmerk. You have time for a cup of coffee. Everyone has time for that. Let me order, and I'll be right back."

Kate started to protest, but Loretta was already at the counter, handing the cashier a bookmark as she ordered a caramel latte. She heard Loretta telling the poor barista all about her new book, but Kate tuned the words out and refocused on her computer. She started a new file for Trent's book and began filling out the outline with some thoughts. She was about to title the first chapter when she heard her name being called.

"Kate! Kate!" Loretta waved at her. "I was just telling Carl here that you're an author in the making. He didn't know you wrote. I told him you have a novel in you that's waiting to come out, like a butterfly in chrysalis."

"Cool, dude." The aforementioned Carl nodded. His bleached hair hung in shoulder-length dreads, topped by a rainbow beanie. "I wanna write someday too. Poems, mostly. Like dark stuff about the moon and planets."

"Uh...that's great." Kate didn't want to have this conversation, because all she had was a caterpillar of a novel, languishing in a dusty drawer of her desk. Three chapters that hadn't grown by a single word in years.

Loretta grabbed her order and hurried over to the table again. Kate would've told her to leave, but Loretta had also ordered cookies, and if there was one thing Kate needed right now, it was sugar. "Are these chocolate chunk?" Kate asked.

"Of course. Us girls need to have our chocolate. Am I right or am I right?" Loretta nudged the plate in Kate's direction.

They weren't just chocolate chunk cookies, they were warmed chocolate chunk cookies, with ooey goodness in every bite. Kate ate a third of the first one in a single chomp. The sugar hit her palate, and the tension in her shoulders eased a degree.

"So, dish," Loretta said, her voice all high and friendly. "What has happened to you since college? Did you get married? Buy a minivan? Have five kids?"

Kate let out a little laugh. She loved her quiet, predictable life, but deep down she wondered if she was missing out by being alone and almost forty. "No to all of the above. I've done some freelance magazine writing, and the ghostwriting. That's pretty much it. Nothing too exciting."

"Oh, well." Loretta's long, dramatic sigh had a distinct pity ring. "As long as you're happy."

Kate was happy, wasn't she? Sure, her life revolved around her cat and her grandmother, but there was nothing sad about that. Exactly. She ate another bite of cookie. "I'm just happy to be paid to do what I love to do."

"Which is write other people's books." Loretta's face pinched. "I gotta tell you, Kate, I don't know how you do it. Isn't that terribly… dull?"

"Sometimes. But some clients are a challenge, and I love that. The project I'm working on now will be a challenge, to be sure, which will keep me on my toes." An understatement of epic proportions. Trent was unlikely to be the diva Gerard had been or the dictator the actress from last year had been. The challenge was entirely on Kate's end to stop thinking about how tempting he looked and whether his kiss would be as amazing as she remembered.

Now the first cookie was all gone, and Kate's nerves were still a jumble. Loretta hadn't touched so much as a crumb, and Kate had had a very bad day thus far, so she justified nibbling—okay, biting deep into—the second cookie.

"Oh, do tell." Loretta lowered her voice to a whisper and leaned in. "I won't tell anyone. I swear."

How Kate wanted to unburden the entire insane story to someone. Just vent about her complicated feelings for Trent and how her heart tripped at the thought of working closely with him. How part of her wanted to run away and avoid him, and how seeing him again had aggravated a scar she'd thought healed long ago. If not for the things she wanted to do to help Grandma Wanda and the need for extravagant things like shelter and food, she would have walked away from the contract.

"I really can't say anything," Kate said, while the complex truth bubbled at the top of her throat. "Nondisclosure and all that."

Loretta sipped at her latte and peered at Kate over the rim. "It sounds like a spy operation when you put it like that."

"It's nothing that sinister." Kate laughed. "Only business."

"Well, darn, because then you could write your own mystery novel." Loretta looked down at the empty plate. "Well. Someone's having a rough day."

"Sorry." Kate tried to give Loretta an apologetic smile around the last bite. "I should have shared."

Loretta waved at her. "You go on and have all the cookies, Kate. Sometimes us girls just need a little sugar."

A little? Kate would have eaten every single dessert in the glass case if she could have. Maybe after Loretta left, she could order another cookie. Or five.

"Oh! I forgot to share about me," Loretta said, her loud, excited voice startling Kate and the guy at the next table. "I have two wonderful children and such a supportive husband. He's an orthodontist, isn't that great? We just bought a second home in Maui, in fact, although we can't get there very often because the children have school."

"Gee, what a bummer." Kate gave herself a mental pat on the back for not rolling her eyes. Darn it. She'd eaten every last crumb of chocolate. "I really need to get to work, Loretta. So if you don't mind..."

"Oh, of course not. We authors have to take every opportunity we can to hone our craft. Am I right or am I right?" Loretta gathered her things and got to her feet. She turned to go, but before Kate could breathe a sigh of relief, Loretta pivoted back. "Oh, before I forget. Are you going to the writers' conference in town this weekend? It's at the Hyatt."

A vague memory of seeing something in her Facebook feed came back. As much as Kate loved writers' conferences and wanted to go, the registration fee was something she couldn't afford right now. And not because she'd bought a second home in Maui. *Ugh.* Why had she talked to Loretta at all? "No, I don't think so. I have some work to get done."

"All work and no play makes for very dull books and very reclusive authors." Loretta smiled. "If you can't make the conference itself, why don't you come to the VIP cocktail party on Friday night? I have an extra ticket and would love to bring a friend along. You can hobnob with all the agents and editors."

Kate started to decline, then thought of the networking opportunities and the unfinished novel sitting in her computer. Maybe chatting about fiction with agents and editors would jumpstart her writing. She might even nab a request to see it from one of the publishing professionals. Either way, it was a great opportunity she couldn't afford to pass up. "That would be wonderful, Loretta. Thank you."

"Anytime. As I always say—"

"Us authors have to stick together," Kate finished with her. Maybe, just maybe, this would be the first step toward finally being able to legitimately put the word "author" beside her name.

If not, there was still a platter of cupcakes on the counter of the coffee shop. And a memoir she didn't want to write that could pay the bills. Assuming she could keep her heart out of the whole complicated mess.

"This is even worse than I expected." Kate shook her head. "Impossible" didn't even describe what she had in front of her.

The day after their first meeting, Kate had agreed to meet Trent at his apartment after he got home from the office. They'd discussed different places to meet, and in the end, they'd decided his apartment would offer the quietest location to work. Curiosity had nudged her to offer to walk into the lion's den, which put her altogether too close and too alone with him. She could have insisted on her apartment, or somewhere public, but a part of her really wanted to know the Trent of today. All grown up, successful…unmarried?

She shouldn't care if he was single too. But it mattered to the part of her that had never quite forgotten him or the sweet, slow way he used to kiss her. So many years ago, but right this second, it seemed like yesterday.

As she parked in the lot and rode up in the elevator, all Kate could think was how alone they would be. Just her and Trent.

Of course, they were adults, so being alone in the same room for hours on end didn't mean anything would happen. Even if everything inside her yearned for a touch, a glance, a smile.

She'd opted for jeans and a T-shirt this time, with a cute pair of low dark brown boots she'd found on sale last month. Epitome of writer at work, not woman who still got butterflies in her stomach whenever she was around him.

All business. No flirting. No getting caught up in memories.

That hadn't stopped her from trying to puzzle together the man he was now, using his spacious, modernist apartment as a guide. Clearly, Get Outdoors Apparel was doing well, given the penthouse apartment with an expansive view of Elliott Bay. She could see the edges of Olympic Park and the trail that skirted the bay across the street. His apartment was warm but minimal, filled with eclectic treasures he'd picked up on his world travels. A pair of bikes hung on the entryway wall, and a small wooden shelf held a dozen pairs of running and hiking shoes.

His paddleboard leaned against the far wall, a bright white slash in the soft gray décor. The rich scent of freshly brewed coffee filled the air, undercut by the warm notes of cinnamon and apples coming from a candle on the entryway table. No signs of a woman living there, nor any pictures of anyone other than his family.

Trent had set up a work area for them on his dining room table, an oval polished hunk of wood carved from a felled Sequoia, he told her. The swirled concentric rings echoed a fingerprint, with their ridges and whorls honed from an imperfect life. Thick repurposed branches formed the mighty legs supporting the heavy wood. It had to be one of the most beautiful things she'd ever seen, and so evocative of the Trent she used to know. Sitting at the table almost felt like being inside a treehouse.

On the table sat a shoebox he'd filled with notes and scribbles, the extent of his "research" for the book. He'd taken off the lid, unveiling the contents as if it were a prize to behold. Not so much.

"That's what I have so far. I figured maybe you could piece something together from my notes." Trent had opted for casual too, with a pale green GOA T-shirt and a navy company-branded fleece jacket. He looked like a magazine ad for relaxed and comfortable—as if she could curl up against him and nap for days. "Can't you cobble my story together out of that?"

She held up one of the dozens of Post-It Notes crammed into the box and looked at him askance. She'd worked with lots of clients over the years, but none of them had been as ill-prepared as Trent. Coupled with the tight deadline, Kate worried she wouldn't be able to pull this book off in time. "I'm not even sure I can decipher what this means, never mind figure out how it goes into the book."

Trent took the paper, his fingers brushing against hers for a second and sending a tremor through her veins. He turned the yellow scrap left, right, his eyes squinting. "Oh yeah, I remember now. This is the story of my climb in Machu Picchu. It's where I came up with the idea for GOA."

She rose and peered over his shoulder. Why did he have to wear such tempting cologne, anyway? The scent reminded her of a deep forest at night. Alluring and dangerous. "There's something that looks like a triangle and three words, Trent. That's not a story. All it says is 'Trash. Get Outdoors.'"

"Exactly. When I stood at the top of Machu Pichu, I saw beauty and amazingness. And a pile of trash a few yards away, left by some uncaring tourists. I thought of how the environment needed less trash, and people needed to go outside more often and appreciate the world. Hence, eco-friendly Get Outdoors Apparel."

It was a great story about the foundation of the company, and Kate could already see how she'd spin it in the book. She had no doubt the rest of the paper scraps held similar nuggets—if she could dig them out of Trent's brain. "And I am supposed to get all that from three words?"

"Well...yeah."

"Ghostwriter isn't some fancy code for 'miracle worker,' you know." She blew her bangs out of her face and dropped into the chair. She rummaged through the box more, hoping for a diary, a journal, anything with actual words she could use. She'd have better luck panning for gold in the bathtub. "You've got printed PowerPoints here about the company with notes scribbled on them. Is that a...keychain? Some kind of hand-carved pencil? How am I supposed to create a book in five weeks out of this?"

"The gems are there, KitKat. It's just going to take some digging."

The nickname whispered a memory, but Kate ignored it for now. If she let the past intrude, she'd never get anything done. *Focus on the book, the deadline. Not him.* "Trent, this isn't digging. It's mining from the center of the earth. I'm not Jules Verne—"

Trent gave her a blank look.

"The guy who wrote *Journey to the Center of...*" She waved it off. In college, Trent had teased her about how much trivia she remembered about books, while he could name nearly every tree and plant on the side of a mountain. Opposites, in every sense of the word, something she needed to remember. "Never mind. It's not important." She gathered up her laptop and began putting it back into her tote bag. "I'm going to need more than that, Trent. *Much* more. We don't have enough time, and you don't have enough material. I don't think I can do this."

"You have to, Kate. I don't have another option."

She scoffed. "Gee, thanks for making me feel wanted."

"I didn't mean that." He ran a hand through his hair. If anything, the displaced sandy brown waves made him even more attractive. Her resolve softened and she lowered back into the seat, clutching her bag in her lap. "I meant you're good at your job and you know how to do this, and I don't."

Trent had always been reluctant to admit he was out of his depth. The fact that he'd acknowledged it now was endearing. Well, it would be endearing if she still cared about him, which she didn't. Not even a little.

His admission didn't change the dearth of material she had to work with, though. Even Gerard had had a stack of newspaper and magazine articles to help her get started before he'd launched into his self-celebrating monologue. Trent had a shoe box and a keychain.

"I'm sorry." She shook her head. All she saw before her was countless hours of work. Hours spent with Trent, which only filled her with what-ifs and regrets. The deadline was so tight, and barely manageable, even if Trent was at her beck and call and she wrote like a crazy person. In all reality, Kate could probably make it work, but did she want to? All that time with Trent and her indecisive heart? "This is a much bigger project than I anticipated."

"What's it going to take to get you to stay?" He narrowed the distance between them, and a smile tugged at the edges of his mouth. "How about if I throw in a guacamole grilled chicken club?"

Her stomach growled, a Pavlovian response to one of her all-time favorite sandwiches. He remembered that? Remembered "their" restaurant? Okay, so maybe that did make him even more endearing and warm a little of the icy wall she was having trouble keeping between them. "From Chick and Cheese?"

He grinned. "Yup. If I remember right, that was your favorite. We can grab a bite to eat there, and I'm sure it will trigger some memories for me."

Of their first date? Of the first time he'd made her laugh? The first time she'd fallen in love?

The man knew her weaknesses, that was for sure. Just the mention of the sandwich made Kate's own memories tumble back in a rush. That night, sitting in a booth at Chick and Cheese, talking and laughing until the restaurant had shut down for the night. They'd gone back many times, so many the owner knew their names. Chick and Cheese had become their Sunday night staple for dinner when they were cramming for finals and no one wanted to cook. A picnic on the water, when Trent had picked up all the dishes she loved and surprised her for her birthday.

"I love that place."

"I know." His gaze met hers and held for a moment. She could see the depths in his dark blue eyes, the parts of Trent he never showed to anyone, certainly not her and maybe not even himself.

She knew this man. She knew his history, how hard he worked, and how his story should be told. Her heart softened, and her resolve to leave melted. Maybe she could help him. For old times' sake, if nothing else.

"Make sure you order a slice of Tres Leches cake too," she said. "You know me and dessert."

His grin widened. "I'll order ten slices if that's what it takes to keep you here."

She knew he meant something other than her being with him, but her silly, traitorous heart skipped a quick beat before reality crashed. She was here to work on a book, to earn money for the repairs on her grandmother's house and her own bills, not to fall in love.

Especially not that.

Five

THE SPICY SCENT OF CHIPOTLE filled the air of the small, cozy dining room of Chick and Cheese. The restaurant was tiny, tucked between a bank and a law firm and decorated in bright oranges and yellows. A steady crowd of college students and millennials filled the place and kept the register ringing. Every so often, a bike messenger would hurry in, grab an order from the kitchen, then pedal off to his next delivery destination.

Trent had ordered them almost everything off the menu, plus an extra slice of cake, just in case, but he wasn't sure either of them had any room left for dessert. The table was crowded with colorful dishes and heaping bowls of Spanish rice. Trent and Kate passed the dishes around, trying a bite

of this, a bite of that, some spicy, some sa-
vory, some sweet.

"Verdict's in," she said as she put down
her fork and sat against the bench, a hand
on her belly. "This sandwich is the best thing
on this menu."

"As always." Trent groaned and shifted
his position. He hadn't eaten that much in
forever. Maybe since he'd last been here with
Kate. "I'd forgotten how awesome it is."

When they'd been in college, they'd come
to this restaurant almost every week. And every week, they'd try one new dish as a contest
against their shared favorite. Hands-down,
the grilled chicken sandwich with guacamole
and bacon won every time, then and now.

It seemed as if no time at all had passed
since they'd dated. As they ate and talked,
laughed and teased, Trent couldn't quite remember what it was about Kate that had led
to their breakup. She was smart and witty,
beautiful and thoughtful. An edge of shyness
only added to her appeal and the whisper
of mystery around her. He wanted to know
everything that had happened in their years
apart—every achievement, every loss, every
heartbreak, every hope.

Might be a bit much to cover over one
dinner, but he was going to try.

"How are your parents?" he asked. He'd
met them once, when they'd come up to

visit Kate at college on a rare weekend off. He knew they'd both worked a lot of hours, leaving Kate with her grandmother when she was young.

"Good. They retired to Arizona, because it's sunny and dry there. They live in a little apartment in one of those retirement communities and are finally getting to do all the things they put off when they were working so much."

"That's good. I'm glad."

"And yours?" she asked as she forked up a tiny morsel of chicken. Their plates had been, as usual, full of deliciousness that was enough to feed ten people. "Ugh, I really shouldn't eat more but I can't resist."

"It's addictive, isn't it?" Trent said with a grin. "There's nothing like this dish. I've eaten in some fancy restaurants and honestly can't remember a meal as perfect as this one."

Kate put down her fork and place a hand on her stomach again. "I am so full. I don't know if I can move again, never mind write anything."

"Then let's just talk for a bit." Trent liked how happy and light Kate looked right now, like the girl he'd dated in college. Bringing business into the equation would change everything and erase the look in her eyes. A few minutes of lingering at the table wouldn't make any difference in the work or the deadline. Would it? "We can talk," he went on, "while we share a bit of cake, and get back to fleshing out the outline later."

"Cake? Oh, I don't think I have enough room. But it is dessert..." She flexed her arm. "I'm up to the challenge."

He laughed. "A little sugar makes everything better. Afterward, we can get a little exercise while we let the food digest and then go to work."

Kate arched a brow. "Please tell me you aren't thinking of making me scale a mountain tonight."

"Well, maybe not tonight. But in the daylight, it's a great way to get the endorphins flowing, which should help creativity and all that." He gave her a grin, but she let out a groan. "Still not much of an outdoors girl?"

"Let's just say every time I'm outdoors, a disaster happens. Maybe because it rains here all the time and I never seem to remember my raincoat, but still...no I'm not much for the outdoors."

Their two different lifestyles had been a large part of what had broken them up, because it had created a chasm that had only widened the more time they'd spent together—and apart. Trent couldn't imagine a life spent indoors, and Kate didn't want one spent outdoors. Now, ironically, Trent was behind a desk far more often than away from it. "There's a beautiful world out there, Kate, if you explore it."

She picked at her last bite of chicken. "Maybe. I'm pretty happy in my little apartment with Charlie."

Trent's attention perked at the name. "Charlie? Is that your boyfriend?" And why did he care? He wasn't here to date Kate. The meal at Chick and Cheese had awakened some kind of odd sentimental feelings. That was all. Uh-huh. *Right.*

"Charlie's not my boyfriend." She laughed. "He's my cat. He's a rescue."

The wave of relief that swept over Trent was ridiculously strong. It had to be due to returning to one of their favorite haunts, because he had no time for dating and no interest in revisiting the past.

Then why was he sitting in his favorite restaurant in college, with the woman he'd once loved—and whose heart he'd broken? For the book, he reminded himself. A mountain he couldn't climb on his own. He didn't have enough time or experience, and not for the first time, Trent was going to have to rely on Kate's experience and expertise. It was the *To Kill a Mockingbird* test all over again, but with much bigger stakes.

"Why am I not surprised you have a rescue cat? You were always helping strays when I knew you." There'd been a family of

cats that had lived behind one of the buildings on campus, and Kate had fed them
every day until they'd trusted her enough for
her to bring them to a vet and then find them
homes. He'd never met anyone with a heart
as big as hers. If she wasn't a writer, Trent
had no doubt Kate would have become a vet
or a shelter operator. She was the kind of girl
who saw the need in others, even when they
didn't see it themselves.

"Including you." She dipped her head.
"I shouldn't have said that. That's all in the
past, and right now, we're in the present,
working on the book. What happened between us has no bearing on that."

He wanted to travel down that conversational path a little more. To ask her what
she remembered, why she'd lumped him in
with the strays she'd rescued. That conversation would undoubtedly lead to a recap of the
breakup, which had been callous on his part,
but necessary. They never would've been
happy together in the long run, not this outdoorsman and the homebody with a rescued
cat.

"Kate, can't we—"

"So we had a few minutes to digest that
excellent meal. Let's get back to the book,"
Kate said, cutting off the personal line of
questions before they could restart. She
shoved some of the dishes to the side, then

pulled out a pen and pad of paper from her tote bag. "Start at the beginning. Tell me about your childhood."

He admired her determination, but she wasn't the only stubborn one sitting at the table. "On one condition."

"What?"

"You share your story too." *Like who you're dating. If you thought about us since college. If you're happy.*

Kate was already shaking her head. "You know me, Trent. We dated for almost a year."

How well had he known her, though? He knew her favorite food, knew she'd tried to find the Big Dipper every night before she'd gone to bed, and knew she was close to her grandmother. But he'd be hard-pressed to name anything more about Kate's history, or her dreams for the future. Had he really been that bad of a boyfriend? Or just a typical twenty-something, more self-involved than aware?

"True, but we were college students. Most of our conversations revolved around music and homework. Not each other. I want to know more about you."

"Why?"

"You're writing my memoir. I think it's important to know the real author." Right. That was his only reason.

Something flickered in her face, but she

dropped her gaze to the notepad before he could figure out what that something was. "Where did you grow up?" she asked, ignoring his questions about her. "And you have a sister, right? I know all this, but want to be sure I have the details correct."

Clearly, she didn't agree with the quid-pro-quo information deal. Somehow, Trent would circle the conversation back around to her. The curiosity nagged at him, danced on the edges of his thoughts. "I do. She's three years younger than me. We grew up in Hudson Falls, which is about an hour north of here."

"I remember. It's a gorgeous place."

"You came to Sunday dinner once." His mother had insisted, and Trent had finally caved. They'd made the trip north on a sunny spring day, and when they'd rounded the corner to the gardens, Kate had begged him to stop the car. *I want a moment to take it all in,* she'd said. He'd watched her gaze skip from the lilacs to the azaleas, over the thick evergreens and newly budding cherry blossoms bursting from the seams of the nursery. A cacophony of color and life that had never seemed so beautiful until he'd seen it through Kate's eyes.

His parents had welcomed her warmly. In those days, Trent and his father had gotten along pretty well. Marla was out of high school but still trying to decide what she wanted to be and taking a few classes at the community college. Trent's mother had been, and still was, the glue that held the entire family together. She'd welcomed Kate into the MacMillan home as if she'd always been part of the family.

"Your family was wonderful. And your mom is a really great cook." She stopped writing and plopped her chin in her hand. "She made a roast chicken, remember? With those fingerling potatoes, tossed in an herb butter sauce. Oh, and a cherry pie that was still my very favorite dessert in the world."

"Better than the Tres Leches cake?" Why was he jealous about his mother's desserts? Maybe because he wanted to see Kate look at him like that, and for her to remember being with him in that same wistful, sweet tone. Trent hadn't remembered the meal, but then again, he'd lived there for the first eighteen years of his life, which had made for a lot of awesome meals made by his mother. "That's the pie she makes my dad for his birthday and, once in a while, a special occasion."

Kate grinned. "So was meeting me a special occasion?"

For his parents, it had been, especially when they'd found out he and Kate had been dating for close to a year at that point. They'd expected him to bring a girl home, marry her in the church down the street, then take over the house and the gardens and continue the business for another generation. Trent had never intended to do that, but they'd seen the first long-term relationship he'd had as a prelude to a chapel and a preacher. "They thought so."

"And you did not."

Geez. Why had he gone down this road? "I thought you were special. They wanted me to settle down, and they thought you were the one."

"And I wasn't."

"I was twenty-one, Kate." For a millisecond, he'd thought about marrying her, then had seen a future spent on the sofa instead of in the mountains, and he'd broken it off. They were like the proverbial bird and the fish, never destined to live in the same place. "I wasn't thinking beyond my next pizza, never mind the next year."

He'd said the words to soften the reminder about their breakup, but he could tell Kate wasn't fooled. She nodded, but her hair had dropped in front of her eyes. The distance between them increased. "So did you ever settle down?"

Trent had dated over the years, but the time he'd spent working, and then on treks, had been detrimental to any relationship he tried to have. He'd dated outdoorsy girls and businesswomen, but none of them had had that special...something that would have encouraged him to linger instead of leave. "The only thing I ever married was the company. In the first couple of years, it was because I was doing almost everything myself. Then GOA exploded, and all of a sudden, I was juggling more than I knew how to." He went on to explain how he had built global brand awareness for targeted, specific expansion of GOA.

If she was impressed by the growth of his business, she didn't show it. This was work Kate—all business and no emotion. She took notes as he talked and used her phone as a backup recorder for the conversation.

"Tell me more about your childhood," she said, as dispassionate as a stranger. "How that impacted you and your business model. Your parents are entrepreneurs. Surely you learned something from them."

Trent bristled. How many times had a reporter asked him the same thing? Assuming that because his parents ran a mom-and-pop garden center that he'd learned everything he knew from them? If anyone asked Trent's father, he'd say his eldest son had learned nothing from the family. It had been a long time since Trent had asked his father anything. "My business model is different."

"How so?"

"I'm global retail. They're small-town sales." Those two sentences didn't begin to cover the gap between his vision and his parents'. They loved that tiny nursery and couldn't understand Trent's ambition. Or at least his father couldn't. Mom didn't care, as long as her kids were happy.

Kate's gaze met his. "But in the end, isn't it all the same thing? You're helping customers find what they need, and then providing that. That's what your parents do, only with plants instead of gear."

"I disagree." His parents had never thought, or even wanted to think, beyond Hudson Falls. Their customer base extended a few miles in either direction, and they were fine with that. It was only in the last year or so that Mac's Nursery had added a website and social media component, mainly because Marla had insisted. She'd ended up with a degree in landscape design and was the one who'd come home to help out and take the business into the twenty-first century.

Trent had given up on trying to help his parents think bigger. His father didn't like change, and Trent didn't like butting his head against a stubborn wall. "I utilize multiple channels to reach customers all over the world. Part of our strategy in smaller, struggling countries is to source materials and labor locally. The customers in countries like

Sri Lanka, for instance, take pride in knowing what they bought directly supports their friends and neighbors. As opposed to my parents, what I'm doing is targeted—"

"When did you become so boring, Trent?"

He sat back in the seat. "Me? I'm not boring."

"We have sat here for ten minutes straight—not eating dessert, which in itself is a capital crime—discussing global sourcing and selling." Kate shook her head. "The Trent I knew could barely sit still to discuss a chapter of *Anna Karenina*."

"Those chapters were huge. And that book was the epitome of boring."

She laughed. "You have a point there. But still...aren't you tired of being the businessman all the time? That's not who you were in college. It's like it's not even the real you when you're talking like that."

And this was the problem with working with a ghostwriter who knew his history—she could see through the charade, the marketing spin, and bring him back to reality. She'd nailed a part of himself that even Trent hadn't recognized until now.

Somewhere along the way, Trent had shifted from being active and engaged to being the one behind the desk ten hours a day. She was right—that wasn't the man he'd been in college, and it wasn't the man he wanted to be. The only one who could change that, though, was Trent himself.

The waiter came by and bussed their table, boxing up the Tres Leches cake and handing the cardboard container to Kate. Trent paid the bill, and as he did, he glanced out the window of the restaurant at the bright lights across the street. A flashing neon sign beckoned, the letters dancing in the window.

Maybe it was time he stopped being the corporate man and went back to the person he used to be. "Let me show you just how boring I can be." Then he threw some bills on the table for a tip, grabbed her hand, and they dashed out into the rain.

"I look like a clown." Kate tied the last shoelace and tucked her own shoes under the plastic bench. Around her, there were rumbles and crashes, like being in the center of a storm. "I swear my feet aren't this big in real life."

Trent shot her a grin. "I think you look adorable."

She parked her fists on her hips and shot him a glare. Why had she let him talk her into this crazy idea, anyway? "You might want to reread *Wooing Women 101,* because 'adorable' is the last thing any woman wants to hear. It makes me sound like a six-year-old."

He shifted closer. Around them, a steady hum of activity, punctuated by thuds and crashes, and an undertow of top-forty music on the sound system. It was loud and bright and busy, but it didn't matter. The rest of the world disappeared until all Kate heard and saw was Trent, and the hurried pace of her own heart. "Am I supposed to be wooing you right now?"

"Well, no...but..." She tipped her foot to the side, if only to look away from those hypnotic blue eyes that still had the power to trip her pulse, even after all these years. "I'd like to know you think I look like a grownup."

"Even with the clown shoes?"

"Especially with these shoes." She frowned at the clunky leather bowling shoes, half white and half red, with bright white laces and rubber soles. If she was trying to look pretty for Trent, bowling shoes was the last place to start.

Except she wasn't trying. Exactly. Okay, maybe she was. A little.

Trent put a finger under her chin and tipped her attention toward him. His dark blue eyes were a stormy ocean of questions and messages she couldn't read. A soft shadow of stubble gave him a rough-and-tumble edge, like some kind of bad boy in a romance novel. Her breath caught in her throat. "You're the kind of woman who can make those shoes look gorgeous."

The sentence melted all of Kate's resolve to stay far, far away from a mistake she'd thought she'd left in the past. "Thank...thank you."

He held her gaze a second longer, then a grin tipped one side of his mouth. "Now, let's make it interesting."

Was he talking about kissing her? Or was she simply hoping he was? "Uh, not sure what you mean by that."

"I meant with a wager. If I remember right, KitKat, you are a tiny bit competitive."

Her face heated. She'd completely misinterpreted him. All she wanted to do was back up, put distance between them, and forget she'd gotten wrapped up in Trent MacMillan's words. Again. "Oh, yeah. A competition. That'll make the game more fun."

This was bowling, not a romance. He wasn't interested in her that way anymore, and she wasn't interested in him, either. Not one bit.

The real world came crashing into their space when a stray bowling ball rolled past the bench and came to a stop against Kate's foot. A little girl dashed over and grabbed the bright pink ball. "Sawwy," she said.

"It's okay." Kate smiled at her. "Are you having fun bowling?"

The little girl nodded. She was maybe five or six, and kept standing there, staring at Trent and Kate with the ball clutched against her stomach. Long blond ringlets framed her face and dusted her black and pink T-shirt, decorated with tiaras and princesses. "I'm bowling with my grandma. She says Imma gonna beat her."

Kate bent down until she was eye to eye with the girl. A few feet away, the girl's grandma watched them talk, a little cautious, but also amused. "Do you like bowling?"

The little girl nodded. "I gotta use two hands. 'Cuz I'm little. But Grandma says that isn't cheating."

Kate laughed. "Not at all. I use two hands too, because I'm really bad at bowling. But don't tell him—" she thumbed over shoulder in Trent's direction, "—because I'm going to try to beat him."

"Grandma says use the dots." The little girl nodded in the direction of the black circles painted on the start of the alley. "'Cuz they help you go the right way."

"Good tip, thank you." She stuck out a hand. "I'm Kate. What's your name?"

"Lizabeth." The little girl spared two fingers for the handshake, then hefted the heavy ball in her arms. "I gotta go. It's my turn."

"Nice to meet you, Elizabeth. Good luck with your game."

"T'ank you!" She spun away and joined her grandmother in the next lane. Kate could hear her telling her grandmother all about the nice lady she'd met. Kate gave them a friendly wave, then slipped behind the small desk and started typing in hers and Trent's names on the game sheet.

"You're good with kids. I'm impressed. Every time I have to talk to a kid, like at an event or something, I always end up running out of things to say. Maybe I'm just not parental material."

Kate glanced up at Trent. "Kids are easy. The key is to not treat them like they're kids."

"What do you mean?"

She turned on the stool and faced him. Trent made those silly bowling shoes look good, with his dark jeans and soft T-shirt. Of course, Trent also made paddle boards and scuba gear and anything he wore look good. He'd asked her a question. It took a second for her brain to refocus. "My grandmother and I volunteer at a co-op garden every spring. There are lots of families that come and plant, and we all take turns weeding and tending the seedlings. In the summer and fall, we work together to do the harvest, and then we all share the bounty. When Nana and I realized most kids had no idea how seeding and growing worked, we started a little class just for them. They pay attention if you don't dumb it down and give them some responsibility."

Trent sat on the bright orange bench and draped his arm over the plastic seat. Respect and admiration shone in his eyes. "Wow. You surprise me."

"Because I can garden?" Kate chuckled. "I've always liked doing that. Didn't I tell you how much I loved gardening when we were dating?"

"You did. But I meant about the kids and the community. That's...really great, Kate."

The compliments warmed her. In their college days, the roles had been reversed. Trent, the dashing, exciting outdoorsman who'd impressed everyone with his reckless adventures and crazy stories. Now, he was looking at her the way she had once looked at him. It was...nice. Very nice. Even if it did embarrass her a little to be under that laser focus of his gaze. "I'm not creating world peace here. Just teaching some kids how to grow tomatoes."

"In the end, isn't it all the same thing?" he pointed out, echoing her words from earlier. "You teach kids to work together in a community garden, where everyone benefits from the hard work, and you teach them to get along. To tend and nurture each other."

She rolled her eyes. "Who's the writer now? It's a garden, Trent. Nothing more." She jumped to her feet, grabbed a nine-pound ball and balanced it on one palm. Far easier to do that than to take his compliments to heart, because then she'd have to do something with them. In her head, she had Trent firmly slotted into the "Client" category. Listening to his kind and poetic words would nudge him into some other category she was sure would end badly. "Now, what's our wager?"

He thought a minute. Amusement danced in his eyes, toyed with the edges of his smile. This was the Trent she remembered—spontaneous and clever and tempting—the one who had seemed to disappear in the busy-ness of his business. "If I win, you tell me as much about you as I tell you about me."

"You tried that once back in the restaurant, and I didn't fall for it then." In fact, she'd hoped he would forget all about that silly quid pro quo. Opening up, even if it was only about her life since college, would invite Trent back into her world, and maybe even her heart. Kate had no intentions of doing that again. "I'm here for a job, Trent, not... whatever that would be."

"And this—" he waved toward the bowling alley, "—is this part of your job?"

Coming to the bowling alley had been a crazy, impromptu idea. One that was far afield of how Kate usually lived her life. She liked her world to be predictable, comfortable. The clown shoes and the way Trent was looking at her were the exact opposite of comfortable. "A, it was your idea, and B, as a ghostwriter, I have learned that the best way to get the client's story is to be on his or her turf and ease into the conversation." She shrugged. "I've met clients on the golf course and at wine bars, and once, in a cigar bar."

"That I'd have to see." He laughed. "Did you partake of the cigars?"

"No, but I did have to get my dress dry-cleaned and wash my hair twice to get the smell out. Either way, I got the story, and finished the book."

"So you're saying..." He pushed off from the bench and closed the gap between them. Her heart stuttered when Trent leaned in— *what is happening here? Why can't I think straight?*—then moved past her to grab a bowling ball. Disappointment sunk in Kate's stomach. "That whatever the client wants to do, whatever helps him open up, is part of the job?"

"Yes, but—"

"Well, I'm telling you I'm a relationship

guy," Trent said. He shifted the heavy ball between his palms, making it look like it weighed no more than a feather. "I like to know my customers, my employees, my vendors. And now, my ghostwriter."

She scoffed. "You. A relationship guy? You weren't in college."

"Back then, I was young and dumb. Now I'm older and, presumably, wiser." He turned, took three steps, then sent the ball flying down the waxed lane. It collided with the pins, knocking eight to the ground before disappearing into the catcher at the back. "So, if I win, I get to learn as much as I want to about you."

She bit her lower lip and thought about his deal. Would it be such a bad thing to give Trent a peek—a tiny peek—inside her own life? If it got him to open up and meant she could make the deadline, then how was it a bad idea? "Okay, but I have a condition of my own."

He shifted a couple of inches to the right, lined up for a curve ball, and released the heavy black bowling ball again. It whistled down the alley, hitting one pin, then the other, giving Trent a spare. "Considering I'm already winning, I don't know if I have to accept your condition."

"I haven't even taken my turn yet. You have no idea how good of a bowler I am."

"You just told our new friend there—" he nodded toward Elizabeth, who was giving her pink ball a push toward the pins, "—that you were really bad at bowling."

That's right. She had said that. As he approached, noted his score, then stood beside her, she feigned indifference. She had control of this situation. Yep, she did. "Well, either way, don't be too confident in your victory. Because if I win, I want your undivided attention all day Saturday."

A slow smile spread across Trent's face. "You already have that now, Kate."

The room felt a hundred degrees warmer. She opened her mouth to speak and couldn't think of a single word to say.

It had been over fifteen years since she and Trent had been a couple. Plenty of time to get over him, move on, have closure, whatever it was in the magic formula that ended a relationship in a woman's mind and heart. But right now, staring into a face as familiar as her own and hearing his deep voice utter things she had wished for in those long, lonely months after graduation...

She was torn between wanting to run far, far away, and wanting to never move from this spot. Instead, she opted for a distance-increasing middle ground.

"Well, there's only one way to find out." She spun on her rented shoes, then stepped up to the desk and pushed a button. There was a whirring and clanking.

Trent burst out laughing. "Bumpers? Isn't that cheating?"

"Should have set the rules before you made the bet." She tossed him a grin, then sent the ball sailing down the maple alley. It careened off the right bumper, then the left, before finding the center. The dark green ball sailed down the middle, slammed into the pins, and all ten tumbled down. "Well, well. That would be a strike, wouldn't it?"

"I would have to agree," Trent said with a little laugh. "You are creative, Kate, very creative."

"Yay!" In the next lane, Elizabeth jumped up and down, cheering as if she was the one who had gotten a strike. "Good job!"

"I had some help." Kate shot her enthusiastic cheerleader a big smile. "You're doing pretty good too, Elizabeth."

"Watch me!" The little girl hefted another bowling ball into her arms, teetered to the line, then gave the heavy ball a hard shove. Her grandmother stood close by, watching with amusement and pride. The ball did a turtle-slow roll down the alley and hit three pins.

Kate cheered. "Great job!"

Elizabeth grinned. "T'ank you!" Then she ran up to her grandmother and recounted every move she'd seen Kate make, bragging about her as if Kate was Elizabeth's new best friend. The whole moment was adorable and sweet. Maybe someday Kate would have a little girl like that.

Someday. In college, she had hoped the man standing beside her would be the one she'd marry, the one she'd raise a family with. Then their paths had diverged, and Kate put that future on hold.

"She could be me," Kate whispered to Trent as she watched Elizabeth's grandmother fold the little girl into a hug and saw an echo of the afternoon at Grandma Wanda's, with the soup and the plant and the wisdom. "My grandma has always been the one who was there for me. She taught me pretty much everything I know."

"I always liked your grandma. She'd send cookies back to school with you for me." Trent chuckled. "Everybody needs a grandma like that. How is she?"

It had taken a couple of years after the breakup for Grandma to stop asking about Trent. She'd always called him "that nice young man." When Grandma had put her stamp of approval on Trent, Kate had taken it as a sign they were meant to be together. In the end, she'd been wrong, and grateful her grandmother had been there to help her through those first few devastating weeks.

"She's getting older," Kate said. "But she still lives on her own and still gardens. Her house needs some repairs she can't afford, so I've been helping her." She shrugged, the gesture belying the worry that undercut every word.

"Kate to the rescue again." He chuckled.

"You say that like it's a bad thing."

"It's not. Not at all. I wish…" He shook his head. "I wish I had some of that spirit in me. That generosity, and that attention to the people around you. You've always been so good at that, Kate."

She wrote down her score, then stepped back, giving him room to grab the next ball. "You have to stay in one place long enough to find a way to give back and to give attention to people, Trent."

"What are you talking about?" Trent balanced the ball in one hand. "I've lived here for twenty years, ever since I started college."

"But you've never been…grounded. Even in school, you were always gone, riding some trail or climbing some mountain. Taking advantage of a sunny day to kayak. Or a windy day to sail. There was always another place to be, and almost always you were at that place alone." A trace of bitterness lingered on the edge of her words. Their relationship had been as hard to pin down as Trent. Just when she'd thought she could count on him, he'd been gone again.

"I was in school a lot more than you think. You saw me, in Mr. Lipman's American Lit class every single week."

Clearly they had different perceptions of the past, because she was the one who had never missed a class or an assignment. "Trent, you missed so many, Mr. Lipman drew a smiley face on a piece of cardboard and sat it on your desk."

"Okay, I might have missed one or two classes."

"Try seven." Not that she'd been paying attention and counting or anything like that. Once she'd noticed Trent MacMillan, it was all she could do *not* to keep noticing him. "You're lucky he gave you a passing grade."

"That's because you helped me write my essays. And study for the tests." He grinned. "I bought a lot of those sandwiches to thank you. I tried to take you out on the water before the end of the semester too to give you a little break."

"Someone had to stay in her dorm room and study, instead of embarking on another adventure." There had been weekends when she'd been stuck doing research or working on papers, and had resented him a little for having fun in the sun. He'd asked her to come with him a dozen times, but instead of finding a middle ground when she'd said no, Trent had gone on his own. More and more, she'd begun to resent him and to wonder if they were meant to be together, until they weren't, the abrupt ending expected but painful.

Trent curved his wrist and pressed the ball to his chest. "All study and no adventures makes for a very boring college life."

"I was there on scholarship, Trent." She let out a long breath. How did he not understand that things had been harder for her? That her parents hadn't been there like his had been, and that she couldn't just abandon her responsibilities? Not then, and not now. "I couldn't afford to take days off, and risk my grades dropping. You...you had a different life."

"We're not so different. Like..." he pointed at her, his finger wagging as he thought back, "we both did that, uh, environmental thing. The protest."

"The fundraiser for the sea turtles? Yeah, we did that, but not together, because you were gone before we finished setting up the table." Again, their versions of history differed. Maybe it was because Kate paid attention to details, logged the long hours. The responsible one who stayed put and, yes, rescued dogs and cats and turtles.

"No, I wasn't," Trent said. Two lanes

away, someone got a strike, and the whole group cheered. "I remember helping you."

She put a hand on her hip. "Then tell me one fact about the turtles we were trying to save. Do you even know what kind they were?"

"Uh..." He thought for a second. "Snappers? Who have shells?"

Kate rolled her eyes. "For a guy who spends so much time outside, you'd think this would be something you would pay attention to. Olive Ridley sea turtles. They're at risk of being endangered, and every single nest matters so they can have their babies and live a happy life in the ocean. That's why I got involved in it with you. I thought..."

"Thought what?"

She shook her head. "It doesn't matter." The thunder of balls rolling down the lanes, punctuated by the crash of the falling pins and clunking of the machinery was a steady beat under a peppy Taylor Swift song on the sound system.

"Yeah, it does," he said.

"It was a long time ago." Why had she brought this up? Opening a door to the painful parts Kate liked to ignore wasn't getting her any closer to finishing this book. Neither was standing here bowling with Trent, or getting dinner with him, or debating American Lit class again. She needed to get back on track and maybe put some mental bumpers around all this reminiscing.

At that same moment, Elizabeth and her grandmother walked over to Trent and Kate. Elizabeth had a pair of light-up sneakers on, and her bowling shoes dangled from one hand. "It's my bedtime." Elizabeth pouted. "I gotta go, Kate."

"Thank you for being so sweet to her," her grandmother said. "Elizabeth can be a bit...effusive. Like a bottle of champagne that's been shaken a little before you open it."

Trent laughed. "I was like that as a kid. Kept my parents running."

"Well, you look like you've done well for yourself." The elderly woman gave them a smile. She had light blue eyes, a paler shade of Elizabeth's. "You two make a lovely couple. Do you have kids of your own?"

Kate flushed. "Oh, we're not, we aren't...."

"Well, you should." The woman wagged a finger at Trent, even though she was a good twelve inches shorter than him. Elizabeth stood there, watching the whole encounter with wide eyes. "If you're a smart man, you'll scoop up this treasure before some smarter man beats you to it."

"Yes, ma'am," Trent said.

"I was married for fifty-two years, God rest my husband's soul. We had our ups and downs, like everyone does, but we made it work. I know you didn't ask for it, but I'm going to give you my advice anyway. If the two of you want to make this last, just remember that arguing about the little things is a waste of the time you have together. You have to learn to let go more often than you hold tight."

"That's good advice," Kate said. "My own grandmother would undoubtedly say the same."

"That's because we have age and wisdom. The wrinkles are proof of it." Elizabeth's grandmother smiled. "Good luck to you both." Then she took Elizabeth's hand, and the two of them said goodbye. Elizabeth chattered the whole way out the door about bowling balls and pins and the new friends they'd made.

"That was...odd." Kate shook her head. "I have no idea what gave that lady the impression that we're together." Or what would inspire her to give marital advice to two people who weren't a couple.

"Maybe it's the bickering about the past." Trent grinned. "Speaking of which, you didn't answer my question."

"I didn't?" Although she knew full well what Trent was talking about. Maybe if she played dumb, he'd move on, and she could skirt around that painful bump in their history. "You do know you're supposed to roll the ball, not hold it, when it's your turn, right?"

"KitKat..." He waited until she looked at him. "What did you think would happen when you and I got involved in that sea turtle thing? Excuse me...the Olive Ridley sea turtle rescue program?"

Kate shifted her weight and glanced away. Darn him for getting the name of the project right this time. Why couldn't he have been this invested years ago? And if all this was in the past, why did it still sting so much? "I thought...I thought it would be something you and I could do together. Saving the sea turtles was something to do with the outdoors, and something to do with the environment. A middle ground between us, and between the things we were each passionate about. I thought you'd like that. But you were gone, Trent. You were *always* gone."

He considered her for a long moment, then set the ball back into the return. Trent took her hand and pulled her down to the bench. They sat across from each other while pins fell and balls rolled and people cheered. "Then tell me now, Kate. Tell me everything I should know about those sea turtles."

"Trent, you don't care—"

"I do, Kate. I care, right now." He touched

her hand and met her gaze. As much as she wanted to look away, to leave, Kate was transfixed by his blue eyes and his touch and his honesty. "Tell me everything I missed. Because I think I missed an awful lot."

Six

T RENT WISHED HE HAD AN excuse for
how distracted he had been at dinner
and the bowling alley. Lack of sleep,
malnutrition, a bout with malaria. Truth be
told, it had all been Kate. Something about
Kate had captivated him tonight, just as
it had that day in American Lit when she'd
argued that Scout's depiction as a tomboy
was a rebellion, not just against dresses, but
against the societal norms of the time that
silenced female voices. Kate's spirited dis-
cussion of Harper Lee's classic novel had so
intrigued Trent, he'd gone back to his dorm
and read it that night. He'd made sure to
stop Kate in the hall after class so he could
meet the girl who had ignited his curiosity
in a course he'd intended to skate through.
From that day forward, he'd started to pay

attention and listen to Kate's passionate arguments.

That passion had ignited again tonight when she'd sat across from him in the busy bowling alley and told him about the turtles. How the Seattle Aquarium was the only recognized sea turtle rehabilitation facility in the state of Washington. How the shifting ocean currents and the cold water of the Pacific Ocean stranded the turtles, stunning them into immobility with the sudden drop in their body temperature.

"The aquarium rescues the ones that get stranded," she said, continuing her story as they bowled a few more strings. "They give them medical care, then release them back into the wild. During nesting season, the Olive Ridleys make these deep circles in the sand, lay their eggs and cover them before heading back out to sea. The aquarium has volunteers who patrol the beaches to mark off the turtle nest and protect it from curious people. When the hatchlings are born, volunteers watch to make sure the little guys make it into the water. When you see one of them struggling so hard to get over a divot in the sand, or to battle against an incoming tide, you just..." Kate sighed. "I guess you feel like saving that turtle is the most important thing in the world. The little guy is working so hard just to live, and he deserves that chance."

"You've been there?" He knocked down eight pins, then waited for the pinsetter to reset. "When the babies hatched?"

She grabbed a ball and threw it down the lane. It careened off the bumpers and hit nine pins. "Every single fall. The mamas use the flippers to hollow out a nest in the sand and lay about a hundred eggs. About two months later, the babies hatch, and if we're very lucky, we are there at just the right time to help them get to where they need to go."

"That's amazing." He watched her take her second run at the pins, seeing Kate with new eyes and a renewed curiosity in this self-proclaimed bookworm, who was also one of the most multi-faceted and interesting women he had ever met. "I never knew that. About you or the turtles."

She took his hand and opened his fingers, then drew a circle on his palm. "They're so tiny when they're born. They can fit right there, in the center of your palm. They are the cutest little things, with big front flippers and a shell that looks like dozens of itty-bitty blue-green bricks. They dig into the sand and push themselves forward, because somehow they know the ocean is where they need to be." A second later, her cheeks flushed as if she'd just realized she had touched him.

"I imagine that something as small and simple as someone's discarded soda can or a moat for a sandcastle can spell doom for the little guys?"

"Exactly. The volunteers try to keep the pathway as clear as possible, and we monitor the nests so we can try to predict when the hatchlings will be born, but every once in a while, there's a nest that hatches when no one is there. So many hatchlings don't make it." She released his hand, and a flicker of disappointment ran through Trent. "It's so sad to see, because you know they tried their hardest."

Despite the odds and the tragedies and the challenges, Kate kept on volunteering. With that community garden, with the turtles. He liked that about her. Liked it a lot. "But it's also what makes you come back year after year to patrol the beach and fill in the moats."

"What can I say? I'm a softie for turtles." She glanced at her watch. "It's late, Trent," Kate said as she grabbed her shoes from under the bench. "I really need to get home and start working on the book."

Trent wanted to stay longer, but knew his phone was already blowing up with emails and texts about doing something to get good publicity and better buy-in before the public offering. With the IPO a few months away, Jeremy was panicking and telling Trent he needed to somehow boost spring and summer orders even more, to offset the losses from last quarter.

Yes, they'd had a misstep last season, one no one could have predicted, but there was no sense dwelling on it. Just like when he hiked, Trent believed that looking forward was the only option. Looking back would mean a stumble, maybe even a fall.

Which was why he should focus on the book, not the fascinating details about Kate he had yet to uncover. She was part of his past, not his future, and all this stuff about bowling and sea turtles was pulling him off that path he should be following. "Do you have enough material to write the chapters?"

She laughed. "No. But I can work with what I have, then fill in that outline some more, so you'll know what other areas we need to expand upon. I'll email the updated outline to you so you know what I'll have questions about for the next time we meet."

"Sounds like a plan." They exchanged their bowling shoes for street shoes and headed out of the bowling alley. The skies had opened up while they had been inside, and a steady rain was falling. Trent and Kate hovered under the building's overhang for a while. As much as he knew he should leave her to her work, and he should return to his own, a reluctance to leave kept him rooted to the spot. "I just realized we never decided who won."

"We tied, one game each. I guess we call that a draw." Kate looked out at the storm and made a face. "I really have to start remembering my raincoat."

"Here." Trent shrugged out of his fleece jacket and draped it over Kate's shoulders. The thick jacket swam on her, but the pale green material made her eyes seem even darker and richer.

"Won't you need it?"

Trent grinned. "I know where I can get another one."

"Well, thank you." She pointed a couple of lanes up in the parking lot. "My car's over there. I can run and get it and drive you to yours."

"KitKat, let me be the gentleman tonight." He shifted the jacket to cover her head, then drew it closed. "Maybe it'll make up a little for all the sea turtles I haven't saved yet."

She gave him a smile that was almost... bittersweet. "Maybe." Then Kate darted across the parking lot toward her car. A second later, she was gone. Trent walked out to his Jeep with the rain pelting on his head and shoulders, not caring about the storm whirling around him.

The next morning dawned with a speck of

sunshine and a whole lot of regrets for Trent. If there was ever a time GOA needed his undivided attention, it was right now. Every element of the company needed to be ready to launch the next level of success. He had employees to worry about, customers to take care of, and investors to soothe. Even as he brainstormed ideas, Trent's mind kept skipping back to the night before and the conversations with Kate.

Just a few days ago, he'd been here, in this same conference room, with Kate. She'd walked back into his life, and already he couldn't imagine her walking out again. When all this was done, maybe there was a way they could at least remain friends.

Friends? Was that what he wanted? Or was it all he was capable of right now?

He cleared his throat and drew his attention back to the people in front of him, refocused on things he could control. "So, about the IPO. How are things looking? What's the mood from the investors?"

Jeremy smiled. "So much better than a week ago. Sarah's PR push on the book, and the rapid boost in orders, will definitely ease the investors' fears. That buyback idea you had in the middle of the night was great. Sarah dashed off a press release, and we've already got traction. CNBC did a short segment on it this morning."

"That's the kind of PR you can't pay for," Sarah said. "Everyone loves the idea of the unsold inventory going to needy people."

"Glad to hear it." The overstock of last quarter's inventory had made his customers wary of investing in new orders. Understandable. On the way home from the bowling alley, with the conversation about the sea turtles still lingering in his mind, Trent had had the idea for the buyback. He'd called Jeremy—waking the poor man up—and had him send an email right then and there. Jeremy had called Sarah and, together, they'd gotten the word out before the sun rose. Already, a dozen customers had taken advantage of the program, then increased their spring orders to restock. "And the plans for the book launch party?"

Sarah slid a sheet across the glass table. "Caterer is booked, and the hall ordered tablecloths in the company colors. We hired a video production company to create a montage of GOA's history, from the germ of your initial idea to its amazing expansion in the years since. I won't get into all the A/V details, but it should be pretty impressive. We'll set up for a podium for a speech from you at the beginning of the night—"

"No. No speech from me." In the early days, Trent had run GOA solely on instinct. When he'd had to make a decision to turn right or left, he'd gone outside, spent some time in the stillness of the world, and waited for his gut to whisper an answer. It had been a long time since that had happened. Until last night, when he'd shed the corporate mantle for a few hours and let his brain clear the clutter. "Instead, I want to bring in some of the customers who have bought our products and celebrate their journeys. Without them, I wouldn't be here."

Sarah leaned forward, her eyes bright. "I like it, I like it. It's different, engaging, and memorable. There are so many who have tagged us on social media after completing their first marathon or finishing a family hike."

Trent nodded. "That's who I want. Average Joes. Find a diverse group of stories. From the guy who bought our running shorts to do his first 5k to the long-distance cyclist riding the hills of Tennessee. I want the stories to be ones everyone can relate to."

Jeremy fiddled with his pen, a nervous tic that said he was still thinking through the wisdom of Trent's idea. "And the goal of these is...?"

"To show the investors what GOA is all about. There will be press coverage of the book launch, and I think we should start laying that positive press track as soon as possible. The message is easy: the investors might be about the bottom line, but we here at GOA want more out of our business and out of our lives." Something Trent had forgotten in the last few months, but vowed to change going forward. The bowling had been a departure from the mundane sunrise-to-sunset days in the office, and he needed to do more things like that. The ideas his brain had generated after he'd gotten home were proof enough that getting out of the office was good for him and the company.

Of course, some of that residual excitement could have been because of spending time with Kate. Her smile. Her words. The way she'd traced a baby sea turtle in his palm. He could still feel her hand there, and the outline she'd drawn.

"I'm not so sure the investors are going to be all touchy-feely, you know," Jeremy said, drawing Trent's attention back. "Like you said, they're only going to care about the bottom line."

"Sometimes people need a reminder that there's more to life than business." The first person who needed that was himself. Outside this building, a big world waited, a world Trent had spent far too little time exploring lately.

"I'll put it in motion," Sarah said. She made a note, then reached into the folder beside her and pulled out a stapled pile of papers. "By the way, the results of the employee survey are back from HR."

"Let me guess. They want more vacation time and less work hours?" Trent chuckled as he flipped through the report. "I would vote for that."

"Actually, the number-one suggestion was getting rid of the glass walls."

Trent looked up. "What? Why?" He scanned the open space beyond the conference room. In a single glance, he could see every one of his employees at work. He could wave to George in Sales, or give Leslie a thumbs-up for her great customer service. The entire floor had a light, airy, cooperative feel to it, just as Trent had planned.

"Well, they say that the glass walls make them more distracted and reduces privacy. If someone's having a bad day, they don't exactly want the entire office to know about it."

Trent's brow creased. "The entire purpose of the glass walls is to build a cooperative, supportive environment. Switching to traditional partitions would erase that."

"Maybe not. The employees—"

"Need to get used to the environment I created. Being open and honest is the first sentence in our mission statement, and that includes the glass walls." Trent set the survey aside. He didn't want to argue this, not when he had so many other things on his mind.

"How about we try a middle ground?" Sarah suggested, unwittingly echoing Kate's words from last night. "We could let them hang some posters in their spaces or put up a curtain or—"

"No." Trent was rarely curt with his employees. For some reason, the whole idea of a middle ground irritated him. Maybe because he'd never found one with Kate, and she'd reminded him of that last night. Maybe because Kate kept questioning how open and honest he was really being in his life and in his book.

It didn't matter. They were over, and whatever happened after they were done working together would be a friendship at best. "I want this company to have the look I planned and created when we do press about the IPO—"

"And the book," Sarah added.

The book. Trent both dreaded it and couldn't wait to work on it again, because the book came tangled with Kate. And everything to do with Kate seemed to become more and more of a mess every day. "The glass walls aren't going anywhere. I want that clean, open aesthetic for any photos and interviews with the media."

"You're the boss." Sarah got to her feet and gathered up her files. "Oh, about the book launch party...I think it might be good to invite members of the press. We can talk up the buyback program, tie it in with a preview of next season's designs. I think it would give GOA some much-needed positive press."

Trent still wasn't sure the IPO would work out. Investors could be fickle, and it could all backfire. He'd built GOA from the ground up, and going public with stock options and all that entailed was like putting his baby out in the world to be judged—or rejected. He'd always told himself he'd be content running a small, profitable company. Until GOA became a huge, unwieldy thing that kept him away from the very activities that had formed the basis of his approach.

Either way, too much was riding on this to have doubts. "Invite the press," Trent said. "Let's show everyone how amazing Get Outdoors Apparel is, and will be."

Three days of basically chaining herself to her computer, and only communicating with Trent by email and short phone calls, had resulted in fifty pretty decent pages. Kate built on what she knew about Trent from college, because he still hadn't opened up much about his childhood or his life in the last few years. Everything he'd emailed her had been corporate—press releases, media articles, end-of-year review reports. None of it was personal, and none of it fit the theme of the book. Somehow, she needed to get him to open up more and give her that true, unvarnished look at himself and the company.

Well, sort of true and unvarnished, at least when it came to the college years. She'd left a gaping hole in Trent's history—a Kate-shaped hole of truth. Putting herself in the book seemed weird, because she had no idea how Trent felt about the year they had dated or how their relationship had impacted him. In the end, Kate decided that meeting her hadn't changed anything when it came to GOA, so she left out that part of his personal history. But when she read the pages over, the paragraphs seemed as hollow as a half-filled bottle.

Charlie came over, slinking his body against her leg. He let out a plaintive why-are-you-ignoring-my-not-even-close-to-emp-ty-food-bowl meow.

"You have plenty of food, silly cat. I filled your bowl an hour ago."

Charlie vehemently disagreed. His tail flicked along her calf, and his meows became louder.

Kate gave him a head rub. "Silly cat. Dinner is at six. You can wait."

Charlie purred for a second, then walked off in a picky-cat protest. The clock chimed three, which meant Kate had just enough time to run over to Grandma's for a quick visit before she met Loretta at that party. She'd almost forgotten about it until Loretta had texted her the invite a few hours ago.

She checked her phone for the hundredth time since she woke up. Nothing from Trent today. No *How are you? Had a great time bowling. Thinking of you.*

Of course there wouldn't be anything personal from him. They weren't dating. They weren't even technically friends. They had a working relationship, and working-relationship people didn't send *thinking of you* texts.

As she threw on some shoes and brushed her hair, her gaze strayed to the phone at least a half a dozen times. On the short walk to her grandmother's house, she checked it another three times. Not a word.

Kate didn't feel so much as a smidge of disappointment. Nope, not at all.

"I made cookies," her grandmother said as soon as she opened the door. Grandma Wanda's bright orange shirt burst like a flower over the long, pale green skirt she wore. On rainy days, Grandma always seemed to bring something sunny in exchange. "I had a feeling it was a cookie-needing day."

Kate laughed. "I swear, you can read my mind."

"No, dear"—her grandmother cupped

her cheek—"I can read your face. You've been looking like something is troubling you lately."

Kate used the excuse of hanging up her raincoat and umbrella to avert her gaze. Talking about Trent would only make her think about him more often. If there was such a thing as more often than ten thousand times in the last six hours. "A little stressed about work, that's all. You know how I get when I have a tight deadline."

"Or a difficult client." Grandma led the way into the kitchen and started filling a kettle to make tea. "Another overly-in-love-with-himself race car driver?"

"No. Worse." Kate sighed and dropped into a kitchen chair. Who was she kidding? Not talking about him wasn't going to make any of this any easier. Her brain circled back to his sky-blue eyes and that mop of hair that never seemed to be perfectly parted either way. "Trent MacMillan."

Grandma spun away from the stove, still holding the kettle. "That nice young man from college? The one who broke your heart, and so now I don't think he's such a nice young man?"

That caused a little laugh on Kate's end. Grandma, always defending those she loved. "He's still a nice young man. And a very successful one. His company hired me to write his memoir. Which means spending a lot of time with him."

Grandma put the kettle on a burner and turned on the flame. "And that's hurting the heart you thought had healed?"

"Does it show that much?"

Her grandmother nodded and slid the platter of cookies across the table toward Kate. "It's a good thing I made cookies."

The warm, rich scent of chocolate and peanut butter filled the air. Kate picked up one, fresh from the oven, and took a big bite. They were a blissful treat that might ease some of this constant ache in her gut.

The sugar hit her palate with an immediate rush of ahhhhh. Cookies might not be the healthiest way to stop thinking about a man she shouldn't be thinking about, but she didn't care. "These are awesome, Grandma."

"I'm glad you like them." While she waited for the water to boil, Grandma sat at the table and fussed with the linen napkins, folding and refolding the edges. The nervous gesture spoke volumes about how Grandma worried, even though Kate was well into adulthood. Kate's mother had always said Grandma Wanda could do enough worrying for an entire country full of Mother Teresas. "So, what is happening with Trent, dear?"

"I'm supposed to be working on his memoir, and I am, but then we somehow ended up going out to dinner and bowling and..." Kate sighed. "It felt like a date, and even though I know that even *entertaining* the thought of dating him again was crazy...."

"You did." Grandma's soft hand covered Kate's. "You used to be in love with him, honey. That's to be expected. And chances are, he still has some feelings for you."

That night, Trent had stood so close to her, close enough to kiss. He'd touched her, a brief, whisper of a touch, but every time, Kate had felt a zing run through her veins. Even now, just thinking about it gave her this fizzy, giggly feeling she hadn't had since she was young.

Did he still hold a remnant of feelings for her? If so, the days since their date that wasn't a date had been as devoid of emotion as a chalkboard. Their conversations and emails had been businesslike, almost distant.

"He's not acting like it," Kate said. "Either way, the book is a rush job, so I'll be done in a few weeks, and he'll be out of my life again."

"And you're already kind of sad about that?"

Her grandmother could read her well. Kate didn't have to say a word, just give a little nod, and Grandma leaned over to wrap her arms around her. Grandma pressed her cheek to her granddaughter's, and the soft scent of L'Air du Temps whispered between them. "He was a silly man to let you go in the first place, and if he's still that silly, you don't want him anyway, right?"

Kate laughed and nodded. "You're right. I don't."

"Good. That's my girl." The tea kettle whistled, and her grandmother got to her feet and began fixing two cups of tea. As she always did, Grandma Wanda used the delicate porcelain cup and saucer sets with the rose patterned bases and gold rims.

"You always use those," Kate said. "Aren't you worried the china will get broken or chipped?"

"Now, what good is my best china doing inside that dusty old hutch? It should be out here, with us and the linen napkins, celebrating."

"Celebrating?" Kate thought a minute, scanning a mental calendar. "It's an ordinary Friday at the end of March, Grandma."

"Ah, but it's also another day when the sun rose. Every morning that we wake up and see that sunshine is a reason to celebrate." As if on cue, a low rumble of thunder rolled through the air, and rain began to patter the windows.

"This is Seattle, Grandma. It's always raining, not sunny."

"But the sun comes out at the end of every storm, doesn't it?" Grandma poured some milk and sugar into matching serving dishes before adding them to the tray that held the cups. "Which means every day has a reason for using the good china."

Kate laughed. "That's logic I can't argue with."

"So, what's else is new in your world, my favorite granddaughter?" Grandma waved off Kate's attempts to help, picked up the tray and crossed to the table. The hitch in her step made the cups chatter against the saucers.

"I'm still your only granddaughter, so I can't be the favorite." It was a familiar refrain, as warm and comforting as the cookies. If there was one thing in life Kate could depend upon, it was Grandma Wanda. Maybe now she could repay at least a little of that love and support. "Nothing else is really new. Except for... this." Kate pulled a check out of her pocket and put it on the table. "That's enough for a new furnace and a plumber to fix that pipe."

Grandma hesitated for a second, staring at the numbers, then her eyes began to water. She sat down slowly, sliding the tray to the side as she did. "That's too much, Katie girl. I can't let you do that."

"You practically raised me, Grandma." And she had. Kate had spent more time here, with the plants and the cookies and the warm hugs, than she had at her own house. "You've done more for me than anyone else in my life. Now it's my turn to do something for you."

"But...that's so much money. How..." Her grandmother paused, then looked up, realization dawning on her face. "From working on Trent's book?"

"He has a very tight deadline and a budget with a lot of zeroes." Kate smiled. At least one good thing was going to come out of this crazy, torturous alliance with her ex-boyfriend. "Let me help you. I have plenty left to pay my bills."

"It's just so generous, honey. I don't know how I could ever repay you."

Kate reached for the plate and picked up another dessert. "Make more of these cookies, and we'll call it even."

To get through spending time with Trent and writing his life story, while writing herself out of it, she was going to need a lot of cookies. A lot.

Seven

KATE PULLED UP TO THE restaurant right as the skies opened up. There was no valet parking and no nearby spaces, so she ended up pulling into one of the last spots in the lot. She leaned over to look in her back seat—

And no umbrella. No raincoat. They were back in her apartment beside the door, drying off after her walk to Grandma's earlier today. The time had been tight when Kate had gotten home, so she'd hurried to get ready, and left in a rush. Without any raingear. Again.

The only thing in the backseat was the fleece jacket she'd borrowed from Trent after they'd gone to the bowling alley. As soon as she had gotten into her car that night, she'd tossed it in the back, because having the scent of him against her skin made her think about him altogether way too much. Even now, just seeing the pale-green soft fabric, she remembered the feel of his hand on hers, the tender way he'd draped the jacket over her. Protective and sweet.

She tried not to inhale as she slid her arms into the jacket, tried not catch his cologne or remember his touch. She failed.

Kate hurried across the parking lot, hunching into the jacket to protect her hair and dress from the rain, then ducked into the hotel entrance. The lobby opened up to a Twenties' themed bar and restaurant, already teeming with attendees for the party. Kate tugged the fleece jacket off, shook the worst of the water onto the carpet, then draped it over her arm.

The crowd in the restaurant seemed to move as a unit, with conversation and laughs flowing between the groups as easily as water running down a hill. Kate lingered on the fringes of the room, unsure and hesitant. She didn't see Loretta anywhere, or anyone else she knew. Stepping out of her comfort zone and just jumping into a conversation was akin to bungee jumping off the Space Needle—somewhere in the realm between not going to happen and never ever going to happen.

A passing waiter gave her a glass of champagne. Kate clutched it and took tiny sips, glad to have something to do with her hands. She smoothed her black dress over her hips and tried not to look out of place.

"And so I told my editor, if she wanted me to put a dog in that story, she was going to have to write him in herself," an older man with a thick white beard said to a young woman in a pale purple dress. "I'm not the kind of author who gets pushed around by my publisher. You make sure you stand your ground, miss, or the next thing you know, you'll be writing a Pomeranian into your political thriller." With that, the older man moved toward the bar, hefting his empty rocks glass in the direction of the bartender.

"Can you believe that guy?" the younger woman said as she turned toward Kate. "If I ever become that kind of diva, shoot me."

The woman, who looked to be around thirty, had a wide smile and long blond hair that she'd twisted into a messy bun on the top of her head. She thrust out her hand and gave Kate a smile. "I'm Penny Wilkins. I don't write political thrillers, and I love Pomeranians."

Kate laughed again. "Kate Winslow. I don't write political thrillers either, and I'm more of a cat person than a dog person. Either way, I think having a Pomeranian in any kind of book is a great idea."

Penny grinned. "Good. Then we can

be friends, because we agree on that." She raised her champagne glass in Kate's direction. They clinked, and each took a sip. "So, who do you write for?"

The writing question again. Kate stammered out an answer. "Oh, well, I...well, I don't publish under my own name."

"Pen name?" Penny guessed. "I get that. I should have used one when I first started. Then I wouldn't be stuck with my ex-husband's last name on all my books."

"Oh, no. No pen name, exactly. I mean, I have a women's fiction novel I've started but haven't finished yet, and that will go under my name. I am already published, sort of, because I'm...well, I'm a ghostwriter."

"Cool." Penny's face brightened, and real interest shone in her eyes, unlike the judgmental sneer Loretta had given Kate a couple of weeks ago. "So you write other people's stuff? That sounds fun."

"It can be. I love learning about people and putting the puzzle of their lives together." Kate accepted a teeny-tiny wonton from a passing waiter and popped it in her mouth. She asked Penny about her writing, which turned out to be young adult fantasy. She had five published books already, under her own name.

"That's so cool, Penny." All these years, Kate had dreamed of her own name on a book, yet had never submitted anything as herself. The dream had a nightmare on the fringes of it that held her back from finishing and selling that novel in her computer. "But weren't you worried your books might flop?"

Penny took a sip of her champagne. "Of course. I wrote them anyway." She let out a little laugh. "At first, I was terrified people would hate my books and leave bad reviews. But then I realized that not all readers are going to like my books. As long as *I* love them, that's all that matters."

"What if what I wrote is a hot mess?"

"Then you make friends with a fellow author who will gladly talk about novels." Penny grinned.

Kate liked Penny already, and the two of them exchanged business cards. Penny glanced at the subtitle under Kate's name. "So…ghostwriter. Have you written anything I'd know about?"

Kate thought of the actress and race car driver she'd worked with, both well enough known in the public. And then there was Trent, who had three hundred thousand followers on Instagram, many of them, Kate was sure, women who'd fallen for that crooked smile and shaggy haircut.

Women like her. No, she hadn't fallen for him…exactly. She'd gotten wrapped up in a spell cast by a shared dinner and a few laughs over bowling. Nothing more.

"No one I can tell you about," Kate said, because sharing any of that would create a complicated conversation. "That's all part of the deal when I ghostwrite. I'm supposed to be invisible."

"Then it's about time you were visible with your own book, Kate Winslow." Penny took her hand and tugged her across the room. "My editor's here, and I know she has some colleagues who are looking for new authors. Don't say no."

Kate's own book had been started and stopped dozens of times. Maybe Penny was right, and it was time for Kate to pursue her own dreams. She took a deep breath. "Okay, introduce me."

Penny brought Kate into the middle of a conversation between two editors and an agent. Penny knew all of them and made introductions all around. Her endorsement piqued the interest of the editors and agent, and Kate found herself telling them all about the four sisters and mother in her book. "They find a stray dog who changes all their lives," she finished.

"Is it a Pomeranian?" Penny asked with a wink, and Kate laughed. The five of them chatted books for a while longer, and Kate left the conversation with a pile of business cards and an invitation to submit.

"Gosh, thank you so much, Penny. I can't believe they all asked to see the book." Kate tucked the business cards into her pocket. A warm glow of confidence filled her chest.

Just as Penny was turning to go, Loretta came rushing in, dressed in white head to toe and with her hair up in a neat chignon. "I'm so sorry I'm late!" She bussed Penny's cheek and then Kate's. "So glad to see you two met! Penny is a darling. Am I right or am I right?"

"You're too kind, Loretta," Penny said. "Glad you could make it. Jeremy was asking about you."

Loretta rolled her eyes. "Is he talking about that dog he had to add to his book again?"

Penny nodded. "Apparently, he wants to have PETA intervene."

Everyone laughed at that, but once again, Kate had that feeling of being on the periphery. It was as if all the people in the room knew some special language or had a secret code, maybe because they were both in a club she wanted to join—published as herself, not as a race car driver or actress or heiress. Or her ex-boyfriend.

Penny and Loretta began talking about their author blogs, trading tips on increasing followers, and Kate almost added to the conversation. Loretta turned to her. "Do you have a blog, Kate? Instagram? Snapchat? You simply must if you're going to be an author today."

"Well, I have a blog...sort of. But it's not really under my name."

Loretta let out a long-suffering sigh. "I don't know how you do all this ghost stuff. I would positively die if it was me."

"Well, Kate's going to be working on her own novel," Penny said with a bright smile, "so pretty soon, we'll be reading her words of wisdom, I'm sure."

"That will be nice...when it happens," Loretta said.

With an early morning meeting with Trent on her schedule, Kate had a valid excuse to leave before Loretta's well-meaning barbs pierced the happy balloon from the conversation with Penny. She said goodbye and shrugged into the fleece jacket.

"Oh, Kate, that's a darling jacket you're wearing," Loretta said. "Although it doesn't do a thing for your pretty dress."

The backward compliment made Kate bite her tongue. "Thanks."

"Who's is it? It looks too big to be yours." Loretta leaned in close and studied the embroidered logo. "GOA. What is that?"

"It's an apparel company." With Loretta

this close, and Penny's expectant gaze, all waiting for an answer, Kate snapped out the first thing that came to mind. "It's my boyfriend's jacket."

"Well, would you look at that." Loretta flashed a grin at Penny. "Our Kate has a beau."

Kate kept yet another eye roll to herself and waved at both women as she headed out of the restaurant. What on earth had made her say she had a boyfriend?

Saturday morning.

If there was anything that said Trent was working too much, it was the fact that he was sitting in his office on yet another Saturday morning, along with a rather grumpy Sarah, who also had to come in that day to work on a couple of projects.

"I could have been bingeing something on Netflix, feet up, husband at my beck and call because I'm carrying a human in my stomach," she grumbled as he passed by her office.

"Will this ease the pain of working on the weekend?" Trent held out a box of breakfast pastries from a local bakery. "I have these and a full pot of fresh decaf coffee in the break room."

Sarah's gaze narrowed. "Did you order more flavored creamer?"

"For my favorite PR person who is working on Saturday to help pull off a perfect book launch party? Of course I did." Trent hadn't thought of it on his own—Jeremy had texted him this morning and warned there'd better be cinnamon-roll flavored creamer in the break room and a box of treats for Sarah, or the Saturday workday would be more like a concert for grumps.

For some reason, Trent couldn't seem to remember anything he had to do. He'd been distracted over the last week, increasingly so, which made no sense. Even when he'd been standing in the line at the bakery this morning, he'd debated and second-guessed his order at least a half dozen times. He'd always prided himself on being able to run in multiple directions at once, multitask while he did it, and still meet every deadline. The only thing that had been added to his schedule was the book, and the book...

Came with Kate Winslow.

He'd done his best to avoid in-person meetings with her ever since the bowling night. He'd done phone calls, emails, texts. If anything, the distance had made him think about her more, not less.

When she'd emailed him at one in the morning, he'd found himself wondering if she was up late working or lying in bed, thinking of him. When he'd seen a voicemail from her on his phone after lunch, his pulse had done a little hop. When he'd sent her a text, he'd spent an inordinate amount of time waiting for the three flashing dots that meant her reply was on the way.

"Only because you brought me those little muffins I love so much," Sarah said, "will I tell you about this great opportunity for you for tomorrow."

He groaned. "Not working again. I need to see the sun once in a while." When he'd started GOA, he'd vowed to give the employees plenty of time off to pursue their outdoor passions, to never keep anyone here from sunup to sundown, and to always build in some fun. His parents had worked themselves to death for that nursery, never taking vacations, rarely having a free weekend. Trent had told himself his company would be different—and it was, for everyone but himself.

"What would you say to a little photo op..." she held up a hand at his quick rejection of the idea, "...while you're hiking the Moulton Falls trail tomorrow?"

That cut off Trent's refusal. A hike? When was the last time he'd had time for that? And to combine it with work...the thought almost brought him to tears. That alone said he needed to get out more. "Why is this a photo op?"

"You know my friend Carissa?" Sarah waved off Trent's headshake. "Doesn't matter. She's a photographer who specializes in outdoor action shots. She's going to be there tomorrow, doing some engagement photos. The weather this week has been so great, and there's only a dusting of snow on the lower part of Bells Mountain, so it should be postcard-perfect. I asked her if she could take a few of you for the website, the book, the social media, and she said she'd love to. She's a huge fan of GOA."

"Let me guess. You offered her a deal on the new raincoats and backpacks?"

"Maybe." Sarah grinned. "We need pictures, you need to get outside because you're making all of us crazy here—"

"Me? I'm not the grumpy one." Already, the idea of a hike in the bright spring air had stirred a desire in Trent's gut. As Sarah had said, the weather had been mild for late March, which meant the view at Moulton Falls would be spectacular. It wasn't a hard hike at all and might be a nice change of pace.

Sarah rolled her eyes. "Anyway, a couple

of ponchos and a travel set is a small price to pay for both."

Trent chuckled. "Okay. Set it up."

Sarah gave him a thumbs-up and got to work.

Trent ambled down the hall of the office. "Hall' was a misnomer, since the entire space was glass and gave the illusion of being wide open. Every time he was here on a weekend, in his empty or almost-empty building, the expansive open area seemed surreal. He could see the dark, sparkling water and misty, undulating ridges outside the windows that fronted the entire floor, a different view north and south, east and west. Breathtaking, just as he'd planned it when he'd opened this space.

The employees had complained about that openness, and as he walked toward the reception area, he looked across the floor and saw Sarah, sipping her coffee while she read something. It seemed almost...wrong to be able to watch every move his employees made. The survey had said his employees thought he didn't listen to them. Trent made a quick phone call as an idea sprung to mind and left a voicemail to see if his crazy idea was even possible.

Then the elevator doors opened on the top floor, and all thought stopped in Trent's brain. Kate stepped forward, wearing a dark floral dress that nipped in at her waist and belled over her hips. She had her long hair in a messy updo and a pink tote bag over one arm. Her gaze swiveled across the lobby then landed on him. A smile broke across her face.

Now that's breathtaking. Absolutely breathtaking.

He pushed the glass door open. "Thanks for coming in on a Saturday."

"No problem. Sometimes it's easier to work without distractions and calls, like you'd have on a normal workday." She flashed him that smile again as she breezed past him and into the office.

He caught the scent of flowers and vanilla, a warm and lingering fragrance that had him following behind her like a puppy. What was happening to him? Since when did he get distracted by a woman? "Uh, my PR person is here. But that's it. Let's meet in my office. I have a great view and some comfortable furniture."

"Sounds good." Kate stopped walking, turned back, and stared at him.

"What?"

That smile again. "I don't know where your office is. It might be better if you lead the way?"

"Oh, oh. Yes. Sorry." Where was his brain today? Maybe it was all the long hours. Not the woman he'd left in his past who was seriously disrupting his present. "Do you want some coffee? Muffins?"

Kate grinned. "I think that's a rhetorical question, Trent. I love all snacks equally."

The words triggered a memory of them sitting on the floor of the common room in his dorm, studying for finals, with a junk food bonanza spread around them. On Trent's side, crackers, chips, salty treats. On Kate's, cookies and brownies and sugary decadence. She'd been so engrossed in her history books that he'd had a moment of feeling left out, so he'd snagged one of the packages of Oreos and slid it across to his side. "*Hey,*" Kate had said, "*What are you doing?*"

"*Getting your attention.*" He'd held the treat above his head, leaning back as she'd leaned forward, reaching for it. She'd tumbled into him, and they'd fallen to the floor, tangled up in each other and laughing.

"Trent?" Kate's voice dragged him back to the present day. "Are we, uh, going to your office to start working or standing here in the lobby all morning?"

"Oh, uh, yeah." He led the way down the hall that wasn't a hall, making a detour for the break room. "Better grab some before Sarah eats them all. These are her favorites."

"Sarah?" The word sounded like an innocent question, but Trent noticed Kate had stiffened beside him.

No way she was jealous. Was she? "Sarah is my PR person. She wasn't too happy about working another Saturday, so I buttered her up with some treats from the bakery on the corner."

"That little one with the pink awning? I ordered my grandmother's eightieth birthday cake from them last year. They're amazing." Kate selected one of the muffins, put it on a glass plate, then poured herself a cup of coffee in a GOA-branded mug. "No paper plates?"

He shook his head. "Can't say you're eco-friendly if you're throwing out plates and cups every day."

She leaned against the counter and took a bite of muffin and smiled. "Thanks for these."

How he wanted her to smile like that because of him. Such a crazy thought. In a few weeks, the book would be done and they would go their separate ways. He wouldn't see Kate in his break room, and he wouldn't spend his morning waiting for her to smile again.

Trent cleared his throat. "You said in your text you had some pages for me to look at?"

"Oh, yes, sorry." She dug in her bag and pulled out a file folder. "I've got fifty pages so far. Take a look and see if this is the tone and pacing you were looking for. If so, I'll email them to you for a closer edit on your end."

Trent flipped through the pages while Kate finished her breakfast. He quickly got lost in the story, eagerly skimming the paragraphs, turning to the next page, looking to see what she wrote next. "This is really, really good. I mean, it's my story, and I know every detail already, but I honestly can't wait to see what's on the next page. It's engaging and interesting and a hundred times better than what I could do."

She blushed and averted her gaze. "Thank you."

"I'm serious, Kate. You should be writing your own books. This is..." he skimmed to the bottom of the page, "...absolutely amazing. You create a picture with your words so vivid, I can see it happening as I read."

"Well, it's only because I had a good story to work with. And there's a lot of details that aren't in there—"

"Like you." Trent skimmed the rest of the pages. "You aren't mentioned at all."

"Well, I'm not exactly an integral part of your life story."

You were, he wanted to say. *You were a vital part of my life for a while.* "If it's an honest picture, then you should be in it."

"But I wasn't part of the adventures, Trent, or the idea behind GOA. I was just on the fringes of your life." She gave him a small, sad smile, then put the empty plate in the sink and gathered up her bag and coffee. "There's no sense in retreading last year or last week or the last decade. Let's get to work on the story behind this great company."

He had a feeling she was brushing him off and dismissing the subject. What was it about Kate that kept her in the shadows, instead of out in the open, as she should be? She was talented and smart, and well deserving of every accolade he could imagine. He let the topic go, though, and they settled on the sofas in his office. Kate set up a small tape recorder and powered up her laptop.

For an hour, she asked questions, and he talked. She took him through the genesis of GOA, the early days when Trent was everything from accountant to shipper, and down the path of the first designs. Her questions made him pause and think, delving deeper into the reasons behind his every decision. Her coffee grew cold as her fingers flew across the keyboard, and Trent's respect for her grew minute by minute.

A little after eleven, Sarah popped her head into his office. "I'm going to leave for the day. Before I go, I wanted to stop in and meet this famous ghostwriter."

Trent hadn't even thought about introducing them. Not because he was rude, but because he was so entranced by Kate's efficiency and intellect that everything else ceased to exist. He'd thought she was crazy-smart in college, but this ability to sift through his blathering and find the one key message amazed him. "Sorry, sorry." He got to his feet and waved between the two of them. "Kate, this is Sarah, the best PR manager in the world—"

"Stop buttering me up. I already finished the book launch party arrangements." Sarah chuckled, then stepped forward and shook hands with Kate. "So nice to meet the woman who is going to try to make this character look good on paper."

Trent shot her a glance. "Hey!"

But Kate was laughing, the sound as light as bells on a breezy day. "That's a Herculean task, but he's paying me well enough that I think I can pull it off."

Sarah grinned. "As he should."

"I'm right here, you know." Trent waved a hand in front of Sarah. "It's not good to talk bad about your boss."

Sarah stuck out her tongue, then laughed. "That's what you get for making me work on the weekends."

"What about the danishes? I thought those were compensation enough."

"The sugar high has worn off, sadly. I'm back to being grumpy." Sarah rested a hand on her belly. Her face was drawn, shadows under her eyes, and Trent vowed to give her an extra day off every week until the baby was born. Sometimes, he forgot how hard his employees worked. "Kate, leave me your card, and I'll be sure you're invited to the book launch. You're the author—you should definitely be there."

Kate shook her head. "That's all a secret. Trent's going to be the author. If I go, there'll be questions, and I don't think anyone wants those."

"You're really not going to go?" Trent said. Her reasoning was sound, but still the refusal came as a surprise.

"Once I'm done writing, my part is done, Trent. Then I'm out of your hair and onto the next project." She shuffled the pages he'd read and paper-clipped them together before tucking them back in her bag. "Thanks for the invite, Sarah. I'm sure the party will be great."

"Well, I'll save you some cake either way." Sarah turned to Trent. "I'm going to go if there's nothing else."

"That's it. Thanks, Sarah." He stopped her before she turned away. "Take Monday off, okay?"

Relief washed over her face. "Thanks. I have a million things to do before the baby comes." She pivoted toward the door, then turned back. "Don't forget the hike tomorrow. Carissa will meet you at seven at the Moulton Falls parking lot trailhead. You two can decide the best place for the photos and hike up there to do them. I think her engagement shoot is at eight, so yours will probably be afterward."

"Sounds good. Thanks, Sarah."

"You're welcome." She took a step, then stopped. "Oh, and Kate, I have some photos of Trent on his adventures that I can email you. It might prompt some conversations." She lowered her voice and winked. "I know he can be a bit hard to pry information out of."

"Still here, Sarah."

"'Course you are, workaholic." She waggled her fingers. "Have a great weekend!"

When Sarah was gone, the office seemed a hundred times more intimate and close, now that it was just Trent and Kate on the entire floor, maybe even in the entire building. A wave of nerves—insane, Trent never got nervous—washed over him, as if he was fifteen and in the same room as his crush. "Do you, uh, want some more coffee?"

"If I have any more, I'll be talking a million miles a minute." Kate glanced at her notes on her computer. "We still haven't covered your childhood and family life, so maybe we can get to that soon? I really want to understand the impact of all that on you and your decisions today."

"There's no impact." He shrugged. "I'm a different business owner from my parents. We have always moved in opposite directions."

"I think our childhoods impact us more than we think." She closed the lid of her laptop. "Thanks for the time this morning, and I'd love to stay longer, but I have somewhere to be. This deadline is going to sneak up on us pretty fast, so how about we meet tomorrow?"

He shook his head. "I have that hike tomorrow."

"I know. I heard Sarah mention it." Kate fiddled with her pen, avoiding his gaze. "How about I go with you? I mean, not, like, a huge hike, but a little one and we can talk at the same time."

He stared at her. Had the Kate he knew been switched for someone else? "You. Want to hike. With me."

"Why is that such a surprise? I'm not a total couch potato, you know. This book and deadline are important, so I'm offering to try hiking with you." She parked a fist on her hip, which canted her body to one side, making the skirt swing around her gorgeous legs. "Plus, I've heard that's a beautiful trail."

"It's also an intermediate-level hike, if we

do the entire route." Was he trying to talk her out of it? There was an easier route, one that would make for great pictures and give them both enough air to talk. "The girl I knew in college thought getting across campus was a hike."

"Maybe I've changed since then." She raised her chin as if daring him to disagree. "You have to admit, Trent, you haven't seen me in a really long time. You have no idea how much I've changed or haven't."

"True." He was basing everything he knew on a history from their early twenties. Had she changed? And why was he so interested in discovering that answer? "All right, if you're game, let's do it."

She tucked her laptop away and shut off the recorder, stowing the small machine in her bag as well. The bright pink tote seemed so unlike Kate, who had been shy and reserved in college. He'd rarely seen her wear anything other than dark colors. This Kate, in the cute dress and the pink bag, was more vibrant, more interesting, and way too tempting.

"Great. I'll meet you at the trailhead at seven-thirty." Kate glanced at her watch. "I have to go. I'm meeting my grandmother."

"You still do that?"

She nodded. "Every Saturday. We don't go as far or as long on our shopping trips as we used to, because she's getting older now and not as spry as she used to be, but yes, I still keep that weekend date with Grandma Wanda."

Once upon a time, Trent had been close to his family like that. Then he'd grown up, and his ambition and drive had taken him further and further away from that little family nursery and small-town dreams his parents had. Now their relationship was strained and his visits home rare. "I think that's really nice, KitKat."

If she heard the envy in his voice, she didn't show it. "Thanks." She dug her car keys out of her pocket. "See you tomorrow."

"I'll walk you out." Not because he needed to, or because she could possibly get lost in this wall-to-wall glass office space, but because he couldn't quite let this new Kate, the one who had volunteered to go hiking, leave yet. A hundred questions ran through his mind, but he held them back. They were working on a book, nothing more. Technically, she was his contracted employee, and mixing that with something personal would be a huge mistake.

Too soon, they reached the lobby and the elevators. He reached past her to push the button, catching another whiff of that warm, vanilla floral fragrance. "Do you need me to send anything over from our inventory? Hiking shoes? Jacket?"

"I've got it under control, Trent. And I still have your jacket in my car. I meant to bring it with me today and forgot."

"Keep it, KitKat. I'm sure it looks much better on you than on me." The elevator doors opened, Kate stepped inside and pressed the button. "See you tomorrow."

"See you soon, Trent." As the doors shut on her smile and big green eyes, Trent realized he was looking forward to this hike for more reasons than just the chance to be outdoors again. He went back to his office, his mood lighter, and with the oddest urge to burst into song.

Eight

WHAT HAD SHE BEEN THINKING?

How about I go with you? It'll be fun.

Kate paced her apartment Sunday morning while Charlie hid under the coffee table, watching her with narrowed eyes. Kate had woken up ridiculously before-sunrise early and had been a bundle of nerves ever since. She didn't go hiking or canoeing or skiing. The riskiest thing she'd ever done was play putt-putt golf on a rainy day.

She'd debated what to wear for at least an hour. Gotten dressed, changed her mind, then gotten dressed again. Her gut had been churning so much this morning, she'd barely been able to keep down a piece of toast.

"I'm not a hiker, Charlie," she said to the cat. "I'm not even a walker. I'm a writer who sits all day and tells stories. What was I thinking?"

Charlie, of course, had no answers. He kept watching her, his tail flicking against the underside of the coffee table with a steady, soft thwack sound. Kate glanced at the time and stopped pacing. If she procrastinated another minute, she'd be late.

This was what she got for taking Penny's advice, which had nothing to do with hiking and everything to do with writing. Ironic that Kate was using that hike to avoid the writing she should be doing.

She grabbed a small backpack she'd filled with a notepad, her recorder, a snack, and a couple of water bottles, then headed out the door. The weatherman had predicted a clear, sunny day with temps in the mid-fifties, and so far, Seattle had delivered with a bright blue sky and a lazy sun inching its way up from the horizon.

The Moulton Falls trailhead lot was half-filled with cars when Kate arrived. Moulton Falls was one of the few trails accessible in the winter and spring, and on such a gorgeous day, it was no surprise other people were embarking on a hike. SUVs and cross-overs with roof racks and trailer hitches—clearly people who spent a lot of time outdoors—peppered the pavement. She parked her tiny Honda sedan beside a towering dark blue, extended-size Suburban. The shadow of the SUV completely covered Kate's car, as if she'd parked next to a giant. She grabbed her bag and headed across the lot.

Trent was already there, standing by the wide road that marked the entrance to the trail. He was talking to a small group of people, his back to Kate, which gave her the opportunity to watch him and admire his ridiculously in-shape body as she crossed the parking lot. He was wearing a pair of dark brown khaki pants with more pockets than she'd ever seen on a single piece of clothing, and a dark green T-shirt. He had a black backpack slung over one shoulder, and a ballcap shading his face. He hadn't shaved this morning, which completed his man-in-the-wild look with an edge of scruffy bad boy.

Her heart began to race, and she prayed her traitorous blush didn't announce to the world how attracted she still was to Trent. "Good morning!" she said in as cheery a voice as she could manage, without a trace of nerves. She hoped.

Trent turned toward her. The smile dropped from his face when his gaze took in her outfit. "What are you wearing?"

She peeked at her jeans and sneakers. Outfit number three in her indecisive morning. Albeit, both outfits number one and two were another variation of the same combination. "Hiking clothes."

"Uh, Kate, those Chucks are a little more appropriate for hiking the mall, not the side of a mountain."

"But they're high-tops with lots of laces to keep them secure." She stuck out one pink canvas Converse. "What's wrong with these?"

"For one—" he bent down and caught her foot in his hand, and her heart did a somersault, "—no traction on the bottom. For another, thin material, which won't keep your feet warm and will instantly get soaked if it rains—"

"But the weatherman said—"

"For another, they're practically brand new, which is going to mean blisters at the end of the day." He rose and dusted off his hands. "Come with me."

She trotted behind him, trying not to feel like she'd messed up before they'd even begun, and across the parking lot to the giant Suburban that had dwarfed her little Honda. Of course that was Trent's car. Why was she surprised? He swung open the back door, revealing dozens of boxes of all sizes. Some marked *T-shirts*, others marked *PANTS*, and a set of smaller boxes with shoe sizes on them.

He shot a glance at her feet. "Size... eight?"

Not bad for a guesstimate, she had to admit. "Seven and a half. But I read online that your feet can swell when you're hiking, so maybe the eight would be best?"

He grinned. "Did you do all your hiking research through Google?"

"Well...yes. And I found this picture of these cute shoes—" she pointed to the bright-pink sneaks she'd bought last night, "—and thought they'd work great."

"What the model wears for the catalog and what works in reality..." he scanned the stack of boxes, then pulled one out and handed it to her, "...are two different things. We're hiking a mountain, and although the weather is great here in the parking lot, it'll get colder in the higher elevations. We need to be prepared for rain or snow, even if the weatherman swears there won't be any, because what happens at elevation isn't always the same as what happens below, which is why the boots are a better choice. Here, try these."

She took the box and pulled out a pair of dark brown boots. They were thick and rubbery, with heavy soles, like Trent's. "Can I ask why you have shoes and shirts in the back of your car?"

"Because you never know when a damsel in distress is going to need a pair of hiking boots." He shot her a wink, then rooted inside the box marked *PANTS* as he talked. "Actually, I did a trade show a few months ago and just haven't had time to unload the demo stuff from my car. We only had a few pairs of shoes at the show—that's a new area for us, and we were test driving them at the show. You lucked out that I had your size."

"I'm hitting the hiking lottery." Kate leaned on the back bumper, slipping into the hiking boots.

Trent tried not to notice how close she was, how a shift of a few inches would make him touch her. The heat from her body and the light scent of her perfume captivated him. His gaze kept returning to one errant curl that had escaped the ponytail, and begged for him to brush it off her cheek.

"Uh, here's some hiking pants. They'll be more comfortable than your jeans."

She arched a brow, then pointed to her feet. "Hey, Mr. Makeover, you might have wanted to tell me I was changing my pants before I put the boots on."

"Oh…yeah. Sorry." He'd been so distracted by her presence that his mind had skipped over that fact. *Focus, Trent, focus.* "Do you want a GOA shirt too?"

She glanced down at her own faded dark

blue shirt with a logo for a local cookie shop. "But this is my lucky T-shirt."

"Well, lucky or not, you should wear this under it to keep you warm." He pressed a long-sleeved Henley into her hands. "Dare I ask, why this is your lucky shirt?"

She took a breath and let the story spill out of her, talking a mile a minute. Clearly, Kate had had caffeine today too. "Ten years ago, I was at the farmer's market when I struck up a conversation with a woman who had purple hair. She turned out to be an agent, and meeting her led to my first book contract. When I met her, I was wearing the shirt, and when she made the call and said I got the job—"

"You were wearing the shirt." The story amused him and made him wonder what other tidbits he didn't know about Kate. She was so…quirky and fun, so unlike the other women he had dated over the years.

"Yup. See?" She spread her arms. The words *Life's Better with Cookies* danced across her chest. "Lucky."

He shifted closer, curious about everything from the shirt to her favorite kind of cookie. All the details he had either forgotten or not bothered to pay attention to when she'd been his. "And why do you need to be lucky today?"

"Trent?" A female voice drew his attention away from Kate. A young woman stood in front of them with a huge backpack slung over one shoulder. "I'm Carissa, the photographer. We met once before."

Kate grabbed the clothes from him and hopped off the back of the truck. "I'll go change."

Trent turned to greet the short redheaded photographer, but his gaze lingered on Kate's retreating form. What had she meant about wearing the good-luck shirt today? To protect her from bears? Encourage Trent to answer all the questions he had yet to answer? Or something else altogether?

Even as he and Carissa exchanged small talk, Trent's mind wandered back to Kate. Her silly T-shirt and the unwavering belief that it brought her luck brought him back to a funny conversation the weekend before finals. Calculus had never been his strong suit, and Trent had poured hours into studying for the exam. The complicated math equations had come easy to Kate, maybe because she had a way of seeing the whole picture, whereas he got mired in the details. They'd been sprawled on a blanket under a tree in the courtyard, books open, highlighters and pens marking and noting the things they needed to know. He'd started to stress about memorizing the equations, and Kate had stopped him.

"You've got this," she'd said. "You're smart and you have great instincts." Then she'd handed him a bright green pencil and closed his fingers over it. "If you forget that, even for an instant, pull this out."

He'd turned the pencil over in his palm. "Why green?"

"Because my father always told me that's the color of ground wires. They keep everything else from going haywire. Maybe it will help you too." She'd smiled and gone back to her studying, confident she had solved his problem. Even though he'd thought it was silly, Trent had taken the pencil with him to the exam, and when the exam had gotten tough and he'd started to sweat the answers, he'd switched to the green writing tool.

In the end, he'd scored a 91 on that test. Maybe because he'd studied. Or maybe because of Kate's grounding pencil. Whichever it had been, there was something about Kate's quiet faith in signs and superstitions that he found...endearing.

"So, does that work for you?"

Carissa's voice drew him back to the present. To business, not reminiscing. "Uh, yeah, sure."

"Great. I think the waterfall will make a great backdrop for your photo. The couple I'm working with wants their photos done on the bridge. How about I meet you at the falls when I'm done? Say, a couple of hours?"

He nodded. "Perfect. See you there."

Carissa gave him a nod, then headed across the parking lot to meet up with a young couple who were holding hands and exchanging kisses as frequently as giggles. The woman's diamond ring glinted in the sun.

Trent had never been a PDA kind of guy. But as Kate came up beside him and stood several inches away while the other couple celebrated their love, a part of him wanted to swoop her into his arms and kiss her until they were both breathless.

"I'm as ready as I'm going to be," Kate said. She smoothed a hand over her new pants. The khaki rip-stop fabric paired well with the dark blue lucky T-shirt. She'd done as he'd suggested and worn the white thermal Henley as a base layer. She looked outdoorsy and utterly adorable. "Let's get our hike on."

"One—" he grabbed a jacket out of the truck and settled it on her shoulders, resisting the urge to button it up and send the message that he was taking care of her, "—that's the dorkiest thing I've ever heard, and two, a hike is more of an experience than something you get on."

She grinned up at him and zipped the

jacket closed before swinging a backpack that Trent suspected was woefully under-packed over her shoulders. "Then let's start our experience."

Trent shrugged into his own pack, then led the way to the start of the trail, skirting the big map and a few lingering hikers who were debating which trail to take. "The trail is wide and well-used, but even in early spring, it can get a little slippery the higher we go, so watch your step."

They headed down the paved road, perfect for a first-time hiker, and an easy gradual climb up the mountain. Thick trees crowded either side, shading the trail and dropping the temperature a few degrees.

"This is gorgeous," Kate said.

"You haven't seen nothing yet. I love this trail. It's great for running too."

"You run up the mountain?"

"Well, I used to. My friend Greg and I are a tiny bit competitive, and we pretty much run anywhere we can race. The beginner loop is a handful of miles and all paved, so it's great for an out and back."

She blinked. "Okay, now you're talking Greek."

He laughed. "Go out, come back. No loops, no need for a ride at the end. The best part about running this is that the back part is all downhill."

"I hated running in high school. I can't believe you do it for fun." Kate made a face.

"Don't knock it until you try it." He put a hand behind her back, so close to touching yet not, as they made their way around a family with a couple of strollers and a wayward toddler dashing back and forth. "Running is a great stress reliever. When I can't get out and do this—" he motioned toward the mountain and the lush, green canopy above them, "—I try to at least fit in a short run."

"Well, I'm hiking today." She shrugged. "Who knows. Maybe I'll be running next."

"Are you turning into an outdoorsy girl right before my eyes?"

She laughed. "Maybe an outdoorsy-tryer? Because there's nothing I love more than snuggling up with a warm blanket, a cup of cocoa and a good book on a rainy day. That's my idea of heaven."

"Well, today you'll get to see my idea of heaven." It was the world he had wanted to share with her ever since they'd met. Dare he hope the two of them might find the common ground they had missed years ago?

Then he remembered how she'd said she often went to the working environment of the people she wrote for, not because she enjoyed it, but because it was a way to get into their heads and understand their thinking. Maybe this hike was just another cigar bar to Kate.

A few minutes into the hike as they rounded a bend, Kate stopped. "We're crossing that? Do you think it's safe?"

A little ways ahead of them sat a wooden footbridge, flanked by wooden steps on either side. Below it, the crystal waters of the Lewis River hurried along the rocks and steep banks. Budding wildflowers peeked between the stones on the bank. The water cascaded in a white rush down the rocky hill underneath the footbridge.

Trent leaned in, almost brushing her back with his hand. The temptation to touch her roared in his veins. She just looked so cute in the jacket and boots. Cute—and irresistible. "You're with me, Kate. I know every inch of this mountain. You won't get hurt. I promise."

Kate scoffed. "Last promise you made to me you broke," she said softly, then slid past him to start the trail.

"What promise was that?" He hurried to catch up to her and fell into step with Kate as they made their way up the paved road. Red alder, Big-leaf maple and Douglas firs filled the dense woods on either side.

"Let's just enjoy the hike, Trent. It's a beautiful day, and all that is in the past."

Was it? Because that past sure seemed

to be impacting the present. He watched her for a moment more, but she kept her focus on the road ahead and never even glanced at him. "This is one of those rails-to-trails projects," he explained, filling the silence between them with facts and history. "The Chelatchie Prairie Railroad still runs through here, and if we're lucky, we'll hear the train."

"Really? That's cool."

He nodded. "It's one of my favorite trails, because it's easy and beautiful. When I first started hiking, I did the Bells Mountain trail. These easy, paved roads lead to a moderate hike that's about seven miles each way, so you can get a little tougher climb in if you want, or stick to the easy path."

"Uh, are we going to do that other one today?" She bit her lower lip. "I only brought one granola bar."

Trent laughed. "Next time, we'll have a chat first about supplies. You always want to have enough for an emergency."

Next time? Where had that come from? There would be no next time. This was all part of the interview process for the book, not a date. They'd have this one hike, she'd gather some more material for the book, and that would be it.

"Noted, captain." She grinned. "As you know, I'm the girl who never remembers my raincoat or umbrella, so I'm pretty sure I'd be the first to die on the mountain."

"I wouldn't let that happen to such a great writer. Where would the world be without your books?"

Kate shot him a grin, the distance from earlier gone. Trent figured if a joke and a compliment was all it took to turn Kate's mood, he'd keep up the patter all day, merely to see that smile.

They had reached the footbridge, and as she made her way up the stone steps, Trent placed a cautious hand at her back. A metal railing guided people up the stairs, so his touch was totally unnecessary. Nevertheless, his hand ghosted along the small of her back, the touch enough to make him trip up the last step. "Sorry. Not watching where I'm going."

"Don't break a leg. We'll starve to death." She laughed, then stopped in the middle of the footbridge to take in the view of the rushing river. A dense forest on either side cast shadows over the water. The chirps of birds punctuated the roaring of the river tumbling over the rocks. "This is so gorgeous."

"We'll have to come back in early summer. It's so green and dense, it seems like you're in your own world."

She turned toward him, her eyes wide, her cheeks flushed. "It's a date."

He could tell Kate had said the words as a joke, but both of them stared at each other for a long second before Trent hurried to shift the conversation. "So, um, as we climb, you'll be able to see Mt. St. Helens and other mountains. This first part is a bit steep, but worth it. We'll get to the East Fork Bridge, and from there you'll be able to see the entire gorge."

"Okay." There was a determined set to her features as they walked off the footbridge and started up the incline. "If it's as beautiful as this section, I can't wait to get there."

"Whoa, cowboy." He tapped her shoulder to slow her pace. "We have a few miles to go. Let's take some time to enjoy the scenery."

That was twice now that he'd found an excuse to touch her, and still the urge to hold her hand, kiss her, help her over a rocky path, beat a steady drum in his head. Only a few people were on the trail, some with hiking poles, others taking a slow stroll through the woods. A couple with a Golden retriever passed them, chatting about the weather as they went. Kate and Trent settled into an easy pace, winding their way through the woods and up to the East Fork Bridge.

"So," she began as she pulled a small notebook and pen out of her backpack, "tell me about where you grew up. I only met your parents once, but need to know more than that for the book."

Oh, yeah. The book. Another reminder this wasn't a date and they weren't a couple. "Small town. Two parents. Two kids. End of story."

She rolled her eyes. "I need more than that, Trent. I have a whole book to fill and—"

Trent stopped walking. He pulled out his camera and pivoted to snap a pic. Then another. A third. "Hold on, let me get this shot."

She poked her head in front of him. "Are you seriously taking pictures while I'm interviewing you? Isn't the book more important?"

He turned and took another photo. "The photos are business too. Just because it's social media doesn't mean it's fluff."

They started climbing again, wending their way through the woods and up a little path that deviated from the main road. As they climbed, she reached for branches and stones to help herself over the climbs. She was quiet, huffing a little with the effort. Trent thought about filling the silence between them, but that would mean answering her questions about the complicated relationship with his family.

At a steep juncture, Trent turned on the slippery dirt path and put out a hand to help her navigate the loose rock and muddy embankment. "Here. Take my hand."

"This is your chance to drop me." She grinned and put her hand in his. "You know, lose the dead weight in the middle of the woods."

"I leave no writer behind." He hauled her up, and she stumbled into his chest, warm and soft and so...there. "You okay?"

Kate drew in a sharp breath and took a quick step to the side. She pretended to brush some leaves off her pants. "Yeah, yeah, sure."

About as okay as he was. Had she affected him this much when they'd dated before? "Let's...let's keep going."

"Sounds good." They started across the ridge, skirting fallen logs and jutting rock piles that cluttered the manmade trail. For a while, they hiked in silence, busy navigating until the detour took them back to the paved trail. "Did you always want to be an outdoors person, like, when you were a kid?"

"All kids like being outside, don't they?" They had covered a nice amount of ground already, and the East Fork Bridge rose ahead of them as they hiked around a bend. About time. Trent needed something to distract Kate from her dogged pursuit of his childhood memories. "Oh, look, it's the bridge."

"And the engagement photos." Kate stopped walking and watched the couple he'd seen earlier in the parking lot. Carissa stood on one end of the bridge while the man and woman kissed and laughed and posed in the center, with the vibrant, deep colors of the forest behind them and the river rushing below. The woman, a thin, tall blonde, was wearing a long white dress that caught in the breeze, swinging around her legs. Her fiancé had on a blue button-down shirt tucked into a pair of jeans. "That is so romantic."

"It's a photo." Trent grunted. Yes, the couple was laughing and touching, but that didn't mean anything about their future or the reality of their relationship. "A moment in time."

Kate shot him a sharp look. "Since when are you such a grump about love?"

Sarah had called him a grump yesterday, and now Kate. Trent thought of himself as a relatively happy person...yet, when was the last time he had been truly happy? Nothing worrying him, no stress?

The answer came to him in a flash. The night at the bowling alley.

Like the images before them, that night had been a blip of time, not any kind of indicator of where he should be or who he should be with. Besides, as much as Kate intrigued him and tempted him now, they had a business relationship. Tangling that with anything else was a surefire path to disaster.

There was also the little factor of him

breaking her heart all those years ago. The comment about the promise he'd broken told Trent their past history still stung. A smart man would steer clear of mixing business with a messy past.

Kate stood on the bridge and turned to face him, her eyes wide with wonder and a bright, giddy smile on her face. "It's sooo beautiful here. It's almost magical."

And when his heart did a little flip at the unadulterated joy in her beautiful, familiar, sweet face, Trent had to wonder just how smart he really was—or even wanted to be.

As she climbed all over Bells Mountain, with the picturesque Washington State landscape in the background, Kate's moods rushed by as fast as the East River—frustration, happiness, regret—with every minute that passed with Trent. She asked him about his childhood, starting with simple questions. "What was your favorite memory from childhood?"

"I dunno. Christmas."

"Which one? Was there a special year or memory?"

Trent shrugged. "It's Christmas. It's always good. Here, let's take this turn." And so it went, with everything from his first day in kindergarten to his relationship with his parents. A non-answer or a changed subject.

He refused to open up about his parents or his childhood, which meant she was going to have trouble finishing the book. At the same time, he found little excuses to touch her. A hand as she descended a dirt road. A touch on her back when she climbed. A quick brush when a bug landed on her sleeve. None of the touches necessary, but every single one making her heart trip.

Were they intentional? Or accidental? Should she read something into the attention or ignore it entirely?

Ignore it, she decided. Concentrate on her job.

Except, the trail was so beautiful and romantic, perfect for the engagement photo shoot she'd watched, that it was hard not to get wrapped up in the mood. To imagine Trent and her on that bridge, laughing, kissing, holding hands.

"Three years ago, I got a chance to do a cycle tour along the Camino de Santiago trail," Trent said. "It's a little over a hundred and fifty miles through the Castilian plains and El Bierzo's ancient wine valley. We stopped in this tiny town and shared some lunch with this family, who welcomed us as if we were their own. It wasn't just the scenery that was amazing—it was the people."

"What made them so special? I mean, you've had adventures all over the world."

Trent thought for a minute as he helped her past a bit of rocky terrain. "I think it was the grandmother of the family. She didn't speak a word of English, and we only knew a smattering of Spanish, but somehow, she managed to feel like she was my own grandmother. Warm and welcoming. Not to mention an excellent cook. She made this chicken that reminded me…"

When he didn't continue, she prodded some more. "Reminded you of what?"

"Of the Chick and Cheese back in college." Trent shrugged, as if it was no big deal. "Maybe that's why I had a craving for it last week. Or maybe…maybe I just wanted a taste of a great memory."

The memory of her? Or of the village in Spain? Kate didn't dare ask.

As they descended the trail, looping around to the best place for viewing the Falls, Kate stuffed her disappointment deep inside her chest. During the hike, she'd gotten part of what she'd come for—several stories about Trent's favorite adventures—but nothing about his childhood.

"We're almost done with the hike," she said as they descended the bottom half of the trail. "And I still need some more information for the book."

He paused by a thick tree stump. "Why don't I help you with the writing? You know, like when we used to study together? I'll hop on my laptop and collaborate."

She laughed. "For one, it doesn't work that way. Most of my clients want to 'help'"— she put air quotes around the last word— "and it ends up being a disaster."

"I'm not most clients."

You can say that again. She'd never been attracted to a client. Never thought about kissing or touching a client. "No, you're definitely not." She laughed. "You're more difficult."

"Me? More difficult than that race car driver?" He wagged a finger at her. "Yes, I did find out what you worked on before me. I called your agent and asked her so I could read one of the books."

"You did?" A weird sense of flattery ran through Kate at the thought of Trent reading one of her books. "Well, yes, Gerard was a difficult person to work with, but that's not why I write alone."

"And why do you write alone?"

"I've just...always done stuff by myself."

"Maybe because you grew up on your own," Trent said, and it touched her that he remembered a little bit of her past.

"True. It wasn't that my parents didn't want to be there, it was because they worked so much. Second and third shifts paid better, so most of the time, I was with my grandmother when I was young. If Grandma was busy making dinner or weeding, I was reading alone. I guess I got used to it." She shrugged but knew that all those hours spent by herself had caused her to be shier than her friends, and more given to solitary activities. Maybe it was a byproduct of her childhood, or a personality quirk. Either way, being alone had become her norm.

"And you did it in college too if I remember right."

"How so?"

"The carrels, in the library. They were like your private sanctuary."

"I did love working there. It was so much quieter than the dorm rooms, even though it was only a little wall and a few inches separating me from the person in the next one. For that time I was there, I was alone with my thoughts and my words, just in my own head like I was when I was a kid. I did my best writing then." She shook her head. "I'm rattling on and on. Maybe that's what comes from working alone too much."

"You're not rattling on, KitKat. I love hearing you talk." He cleared his throat, as if the admission had cost him something. "I mean, it's nice to get to know the person writing my life story."

"Yeah. It is." She had to look away, stare at a squirrel scrambling up a maple tree, so he wouldn't see the disappointment in her face.

Beside her, Trent kept on taking photos. He did landscape shots, selfies, but never a photo of the two of them. If anything told Kate where she stood in Trent's heart, excluding her from the photos was a clear, concrete sign.

They rounded a bend at the end of the trail, and there, in all their glory, was Moulton Falls. As waterfalls went in the state of Washington, Moulton wasn't especially tall, but still breathtaking. Twin curtains of water tumbled over the side of the ridge, spilling into a dark, deep pool. "Oh, wow. That's amazing."

Trent stood behind her, just over her shoulder, so close she caught the scent of his cologne, felt the warmth of his cheek. "I'm glad you like them. They're small but mighty."

The rush of white water stairstepped down ridges of rocks before disappearing into the depths of the ravine. She could imagine jumping in that cold water in the summer, letting the waterfall cascade over their heads, then climbing out to lie on the rocks while the sun warmed their bodies and they talked about everything and anything.

Maybe she should write fiction instead of memoirs, because her imaginary world with Trent was pretty vivid. Silly, ridiculous thoughts.

"It's so gorgeous." She snapped a picture of the falls, then shifted to the right and feigned taking another one. Instead, she angled her camera just enough to capture Trent's profile. One quick push of the button, and he was immortalized on her phone.

She was hopeless. Utterly hopeless.

Trent turned to face her. He was only a few inches away now, and with the rushing water in the background, his voice was hard to hear. She moved closer and for a second imagined him taking her in his arms and kissing her while the waterfall crashed over the rocks and the world moved on by.

"She's here," he said, nodding to a space behind Kate.

Oh, boy. Definitely hopeless. Here Kate had been thinking he was saying something romantic, and instead, Trent was pointing out the photographer. "Oh, yeah. The photo shoot."

Trent waved Carissa over, and in an instant, all the attention he'd given to Kate had disappeared. Kate's eyes burned, and disappointment sank like a lead weight to the bottom of her stomach. "I, uh, can see the parking lot from here," she said. "I'm going to go, and you two can do the photo shoot. Since I'm not part of it."

"Are you sure?" Confusion knitted Trent's brows. "You're welcome to stay."

And hear you remind me again that all your memories of us are just about the book? No thank you. "I have plenty of writing to do."

"Oh yeah, that solitude thing."

She nodded and turned away. Yep, being alone was the best choice right now, even if it sounded like the saddest thing she'd ever heard. *Work, concentrate on work,* she told herself. And maybe then she'd forget this day and the way Trent's touch had made butterflies riot inside her. She took a few steps, waving to Carissa as she passed by.

"Hey, KitKat."

Kate pivoted back to Trent, her heart leaping all over again, silly and foolish and delusional. "Yeah?"

"Let me know when you want to come up for air. Maybe we can grab some food from Chick and Cheese." The lopsided grin she knew so well spread across his face and reflected in the blue of his eyes, as bright as the sun on the falls a moment ago. "And, you know, talk about the book while we eat."

"Sounds...great." Kate hurried away before the disappointment in her eyes became something silly like tears.

Nine

TUESDAY MORNING, TRENT'S WORLD EXPLODED.

Well, not his world, exactly, but his social media. Last night, he'd finished uploading his pictures from the Moulton Falls hike to his Instagram. He'd scanned them after work on Monday, had seen landscapes, and posted the whole lot of pictures without a second thought. He'd added a few lines about the "Amazing day among such incredible beauty!" and hit Post.

This morning, he'd woken to dozens of messages on his page. Normally, he'd get a few messages asking about the hike or what GOA products he'd used. A bunch of likes, a couple of shares or retweets, because his Instagram fed into both his Facebook and Twitter. Today was different—in a bad, bad way.

I see one of the new GOA ladies' boots in

that picture. First time I've ever seen someone else on one of Trent's adventures. Who is that mystery woman?

Is the confirmed outdoor bachelor settling down?

One of my friends saw a couple doing a photoshoot at the falls this weekend. Could it have been Trent and his mystery woman?

Are you going to tell us who it is, Trent? Who's the new lady in your life?

The comments both panicked him and calmed him, which made no sense. He knew the publicity could turn on him and hurt his business. But the thought of being paired with Kate, even if only with a boot and a waterfall, sounded oddly…nice.

"Well, well," Sarah said as she stepped into his office first thing on Tuesday. She held up her phone and wiggled it back and forth, the controversial image filling her screen. "What were you up to this weekend?"

Even from his desk, Trent could see what Sarah and the rest of the internet had seen—an image of the bridge with the river rushing underneath it and Kate's ankle, pink socks and boot in the corner. He hadn't even noticed her in the shot. Maybe because it had seemed so natural to be there with her, soaking up the scenery, remarking on the birds and the trees and the other people. She'd fit in as easily as the thick carpet of ferns filling the forest floor.

He'd loved the entire trip, surprised by how well she'd taken to the hiking and how easily they'd worked together on the steeper parts. The girl who had never wanted to be a part of his world when they were younger had made it seem as if she'd always been there.

Since she'd left the park on Sunday morning, Trent hadn't talked to Kate. They'd exchanged a couple of emails when she'd asked for clarification on some of the stories he'd shared with her, but that was it. She needed solitude to work, he told himself, and that's why he was staying away.

Not because getting so close to her this weekend, and the overpowering urge to find an excuse to touch her, again and again, had left him scattered and distracted. When he'd gone to sleep that night, he'd thought about her. And when he'd woken up, he'd wondered if she had thought about him.

No wonder he hadn't paid attention to what pictures he was posting. His brain had been lost somewhere in la-la land with a relationship that would never happen again.

"Seems you created quite the buzz," Sarah said. "I can't believe how many comments you have on that one photo."

"I didn't do it on purpose. I'm deleting

that picture." He picked up his phone, but Sarah put a hand over the screen.

"Don't. Leave it."

"What? Why? The entire internet is trying to figure out who I'm dating."

"Which is great PR," Sarah said. She sat in one of the visitor's chairs and rested a hand on her belly. "Have you seen how many times that photo has been shared and retweeted? How much speculation is going on? You're a handsome, single commodity, Trent, and the social media world is all aflutter trying to find out if you're settling down."

Handsome and single? He could barely run his own company right now, never mind settle down with anything other than his accounting program. He didn't need to become the newest gossip sensation. "I was with Kate. We were talking about the book."

Why did he feel the need to defend the picture? If he and Kate had been running off and getting married—*whoa, where did that thought come from?*—it was his business, no one else's.

"Great. Glad to hear it. This—" Sarah tapped his phone "—is exactly the kind of pre-launch buzz we need. People will be scooping up copies of the book to see if you spill any secrets about your personal life."

"I'm not doing that at all," he grumbled. Which was something Kate had complained about often. She wanted more scoop, more inside information. Trent didn't have any, and even if he did, he wasn't in the mood to share with the rest of the world. He'd made his own luck in the world, had climbed mountains without any help. There were no deep dark secrets to expose. "This is exactly why I don't tell people about my personal life. One boot and a second later, I'm on the cover of *People* magazine."

Sarah laughed. "We should be so lucky to land a cover like that. Hey, if you have more boot pictures, feel free to share and keep the rumors flying."

Trent shook his head and got to his feet. "I have other stuff to worry about today. Make that go away. Please." He waved at his phone, then headed out of his office and down to the lobby, right as the elevator doors opened and two burly men stepped off. Finally, something business-related that he could concentrate on. "Just in time, guys."

On the hike, when Kate had apologized for talking so much, Trent had realized that for the first time in a long time, he'd gotten caught up in listening to her. Instead of sharing his ideas or his adventures, he'd heard Kate's memories.

When he'd tried to step in and take over with his plan, she'd reminded him he couldn't just bulldoze through with his own solutions for the book—he had to work with what made *her* comfortable. She was the one doing the work. He couldn't dictate how she did that.

The next day, after a whole lot of money and a couple of calls with the contractor he'd messaged on Saturday, Trent had a solution he hoped would create an environment that made his employees more comfortable.

As Trent led the way, the two men wheeled a large cart into the office space. Several employees stopped working and looked up at the visitors. The office, normally a hum of conversations and typing, slowed to a crawl.

"There's going to be a little noise going on here over the next few days," Trent said. "We're installing some new panels to make the workspace more conducive to the kind of environment I want at GOA."

There was a groan. Trent ignored it and gave the workers a nod. One of the men peeled back the cardboard to reveal an opaque glass panel painted with images of orca whales. A handful of others were stacked up behind it, all with different images. On such short notice, he'd only been able to get a few, but the rest would arrive in the coming days.

"These will give you some privacy and a view," Trent said. The employees gawked at the panels. Sarah sent Trent a little thumbs-up from her office. "I hope that gives you all the workspace you wanted. Either way, I think it's time we changed things up around here."

A buzz started up around the room, and for a while, no work got done as the employees watched and celebrated the change to their work area. Trent leaned against the door of his office and watched the new panels go in, one at a time filling the once-clear and open space with breathtaking images of the Pacific Northwest. The panels had cost a small fortune, but given the happy current running through the room, they were well worth the expense.

They weren't carrels in the library, but they were workspaces that would grant some solitude. Trent almost wished Kate was here to see it so he could tell her she'd been the inspiration.

Saying that would make a lot more of a wave than a boot picture. Better not to let her think he had anything other than friendly feelings for her. Right?

Jeremy strolled over and leaned against the wall beside Trent. "Never thought I'd see the day."

"What? That I'd redecorate?"

"No. That you would embrace change." Jeremy put up a hand, cutting off Trent's objection before he voiced it. "When we were a young and new business, being nimble was part of growth. You were the visionary, and you had some great ideas. But along with that, somewhere along the way, you...well, you stopped listening to the opinions of others."

"I did. And I'm sorry." Trent let out a long sigh. Woulda, coulda, shoulda. Lately, those words had become his mantra. "If I had listened to you last quarter, I would have delayed the IPO until next year and maybe not gotten the bad press we had in recent months."

"Maybe. But the fact that you don't always listen is part of what I like about you. You're a go-with-your-gut guy. I'm a lot more cautious, check-the-lane-three-times-before-merging kind of guy. Because of you, because you believed so strongly in this brand and kept on going despite how impossible it is to get a foothold in the clothing industry, GOA is going public. This company has become more than either one of us ever dreamed." Jeremy gave Trent's arm a light jab. "So listen some, but keep going with your gut, boss."

His gut hadn't been this confused in years. Trent thought of Kate's smile and the sweet sound of her laughter. Of her determination on the hike and the way he went out of his way to touch her. If things were supposed to be just business with them, why did his memory focus on everything but business? "What if my gut doesn't know what it wants?"

"It does," Jeremy said. "Sometimes we're too scared to listen. When you're ready, you'll hear whatever message is there, and knowing you, you'll jump off the cliff and dive head-first into the water."

"Maybe," Trent said. He thought of the deep dark pool beneath the falls, and how tempting it would be to take Kate there for a swim this summer. The day on the mountain had been more fun than he'd had in months, a dangerous fun that could lead him down a path he shouldn't take. "Or maybe I'm past the age where I do those kinds of things."

But Jeremy was already gone, heading to a meeting.

Trent turned back to his office and stared out at the water for a long time. Then he picked up his phone and sent a text before his gut gave him another conflicting message.

Grandma trimmed a few dead leaves off the primroses while Kate turned the pots to give them even sun exposure. It was their regular Tuesday afternoon gardening session, complete with a container of homemade wild mushroom and rice soup Kate had brought over. "So, tell me, how is it going with the boyfriend?"

"He's not my boyfriend, Grandma. He broke up with me after college, remember?"

"Well, he was immature then. Surely he's smarter now." She turned the pot this way and that, admiring the purple blooms. "These are really coming along. I'm so glad I rescued them from that nursery."

Grandma had bought a dozen dying Wanda primroses a month ago on one of her excursions with Kate. The owner of the nursery had said the plants were dried and dying and beyond saving, but Grandma had been determined, and it had paid off with a smattering of flowers and new leaves.

"I'm so surprised. I didn't think they'd make it."

"Have some faith, dear." Grandma set the pot back in place, then dusted the dirt from her hands. "You know what it takes to get something to grow? Even when it's stubbornly fighting you?"

"Is this a life lesson?"

"I'm old. Everything I say is a life lesson." Grandma used Kate's arm to help her lower herself into a cushioned folding chair in the greenhouse. "I'm so grateful the new furnace is getting installed this week. These old bones are going to love having lots of heat in the house."

"And my roof is getting patched. My landlord said he'd reimburse me because I paid for it myself. Lots of good changes around here. Or, at least, a few good changes." Kate filled the watering can and tilted it over the flowers. The gentle shower soaked into the dark earth and pooled in the drainage tray. "I'm so glad I can help you out after all you've done for me."

"Pish posh." Grandma waved that off. "I'm your grandmother. I loved spending time with you."

"You were more like my mother and father, all in one." Kate put her back to the counter and set the watering can on the floor. "I don't know what I would have done without you."

"You would have grown up just fine, that's what you would have done. You're smart, Kate, and talented and beautiful. If that boyfriend of yours is smart—"

"He's not my boyfriend—"

"—he'll realize what a prize he has in you." Grandma picked up one of the pots and turned the determined flower to face Kate. "All these little guys needed to grow is some love, my dear. Love can change everything. Even a silly boy—"

"He's not my boyfriend."

"—silly man's heart," Grandma finished. "I've seen Trent look at you, and that boy loves you."

"Grandma, that was more than fifteen years ago. His feelings have surely changed."

"Maybe so. Or maybe he just needed a little more time to mature. Like my Stanley here." She tapped the plant's plastic pot.

"Stanley?" Kate laughed at the name for the delicate purple bloom. "Well, no matter what you think, I know I have a better shot at getting Stanley there to fall in love with me than Trent." The thought saddened her, but she refused to let that show. Grandma would only worry, and if there was nothing between Kate and Trent, what was there to worry about?

"Patience, care and attention. Good things grow from that recipe." Grandma took Kate's hand and got to her feet. "Now, let's go have some soup."

"And cookies?"

"Of course. What kind of grandma would I be if I didn't bake you cookies?" She pressed a kiss to Kate's cheek, the soft scent of her fragrance and decades of memories filling the space between them.

They ate lunch and just as Kate was starting

the dishes, her phone dinged. She ignored the first text. The second. When it dinged a third time, she pulled it out of her pocket. *We need to chat ASAP. Before we meet today, I thought I should tell you I saw Trent's Instagram blowing up*, Angie had written. *Finally, All kinds of buzz. People wondering who he's dating. It's not you, right?*

The last few words hit Kate like a sucker punch. Was Trent dating someone? And why did she care? This was supposed to be a solely professional relationship.

Then Angie followed her text with a screenshot of Trent's Instagram account. It took Kate a second to look past the breathtaking scenery, the elegance of the bridge...

To her own ankle, sock, and boot in the corner of the picture. She pulled up Instagram, went to his account and read through the comments. Angie was right—speculation was running like a freight train. Surely Trent must know about this. Why had he left the photo up?

We should chat today, Kate texted Trent, four innocuous words that didn't begin to express her nervousness over being exposed as the author. That couldn't happen, right? Not from just a snippet of a picture, and a shoe at that. She started to put the phone back when she saw the little bubble of his reply, as if he'd been waiting for her to text.

I agree. Meet for coffee?

Sure. She named a coffee shop near his office and on her way to Angie's. *In about thirty minutes?*

Perfect. See you there, KitKat.

Every time he used her nickname, it made her heart trip. For that split second, they were dating again, and her world was as perfect as it could get. Then reality came rushing back and reminded her that all she was to Trent was his ghostwriter. Nothing more.

Kate kissed her grandma's cheek and promised to come back the next day and help her repot the rest of the primroses. She brushed off Grandma's questions and said everything was fine. It could be, right? This picture could be nothing. Then Kate gathered her things, hailed a cab and headed across town.

She was early for their meeting, which gave her time to grab a cup of tea and a warm cookie, then set up at a table by the window of the coffee shop. A light rain had started up, and droplets ran down the front windows in hundreds of lazy rivers.

While she was waiting, Kate opened her laptop and managed to whip out a short post on her Secret Life of a Ghost blog.

My newest project—and sorry, can't give you any deets—is with someone who is re-

ally hard to resist. Nice smile, witty remarks, and so very sweet to me. Every time we get together to work on the book, I feel like I'm on the edge of a mountain, staring down a waterfall and debating whether to jump into the dark pool below. Crazy, I know. Can you guys relate? Ever get really close to a person you were ghostwriting for?

She hit Post, then answered a few comments from the last post, and opened up the file for Trent's book. She needed so much more content, especially about his childhood. Maybe they should go see his parents, if Trent's family still lived a couple of hours away. A quick trip, gather some research. Might be worth a shot to ask him, although given his earlier reticence about his past, Kate wasn't so sure he'd agree.

She tried to write, but not a single word came to mind. Her attention strayed to the parking lot, her breath caught in her throat.

Until she saw him.

Trent had walked here, hunched into one of his GOA raincoats with the same boots he'd worn on the hike. He looked ready to whisk her away on an adventure, somewhere far from the busy city and the crowded coffee shop. He stepped inside, shook off the worst of the rain, glancing around the room as he did. His gaze came to rest on Kate, and her heart stuttered.

"Hey."

"Hey." An odd shyness came over her. They'd spent an entire morning together a couple of days ago, and had talked via email and text every day since. She'd known him for years, and yet she felt her cheeks heat and her pulse race. The picture, and the rumors swirling on the internet, had changed everything. It was as if she felt responsible for her own foot ending up in a photo. Which was insane, of course.

Trent slipped into the seat across from her. Almost every table in the coffee shop was full, and a low current of conversation ran beneath the soft jazz on the sound system. Local artists had hung paintings on the clapboard walls, watercolors and oils of scenic areas around the state. Even Moulton Falls was immortalized in a painting on the far wall, a taunting reminder of their hike.

Trent cleared his throat. "I take it you heard about the photo?"

He'd seen it too. A part of her had been hoping maybe he hadn't. That Sarah had deleted the image and the rumor mill had died down in the last fifteen minutes. "Trent, I had no idea I was in that picture, or that people—"

He put up a hand. "Hey, it's not your fault, not even a little, so don't beat yourself up. It was an accident."

"I feel bad, though," she said, then lowered her voice when she noticed how close the other customers were. The last thing either of them needed was more gossip or someone putting even more pieces together. "You have all these people questioning you now, and so much on your plate with the IPO and the book and—"

"In case you haven't noticed, I'm a big boy, and I can handle a little gossip." His hand rested beside hers on the wooden table. Not touching, but so close. "No one is going to figure out it was you."

"Which is great. Right?" Then why did she feel so disappointed? Did she really want to shoehorn herself into Trent's life? Or had a part of her expected Trent to make a public announcement, proclaiming her Girlfriend of the Year? Yet another fictional idea that was never going to be truth.

"I think so," Trent said. "Sarah says all PR is good PR, and if people are talking about the photo, it might bump up sales of the book."

"Because people will think the book will have the story exposing the truth about the woman behind the boot?" Kate laughed and sipped at her tea. "Do they think you're going to spill some kind of state secret?"

Trent broke off a piece of her cookie and popped it in his mouth. Just like old times, sharing a meal without a word. "They're going to be mighty disappointed if so."

Kate stared down into her teacup, swirling the remaining brew in a slow circle. She was not disappointed that he had just said he wasn't going to publicly claim her as his. Nope, not disappointed at all. "Speaking of state secrets, how about we take a drive up to see your parents tomorrow?"

"Tomorrow's Wednesday, right?"

She grinned. "All day."

A smile flickered on his face, and once again, another thread from the past tightened between them. "You're still using that joke?"

"Hey, if a bad joke works, I hold onto it as long as possible." She shut the lid of her laptop and pushed it aside, then crossed her hands on the table and leaned toward him. "We have two and a half weeks, Trent. I only have about half of the book done. I need a lot more material to fill it out, plus the time to write the words. So yes, tomorrow, if possible. I tried asking you questions on the hike and in person, and you were...well, vague and not very helpful. Your past is part of your present. Your parents and sister might have some pictures and memories—"

"I don't know if that's such a good idea. I haven't seen my family in a long time."

"All the more reason for a visit." She

brushed the edge of her hand against his, a featherlight touch, but it sent off sparks inside her. "If there's one thing I've learned in the last few years, it's that not every life is long. Visit and enjoy the people who love you as often as possible."

"You're right." He drummed his fingers on the table. "But tomorrow? That's a work day."

Who was this guy who put work ahead of everything else? In college, Trent had been about the adventures, and everything else—including Kate—came second. "Maybe you should take a day off, Trent. Play some hooky. You did, after all, work on Saturday and technically all Sunday morning."

He stole another bite of cookie. "Isn't driving up to Hudson Falls to see my parents another kind of working?"

"Not if your mom makes her apple cobbler." Kate shot him a grin. "Then it's just dessert."

He sat back in the chair. "Okay. You sold me with the apple cobbler. I'll pick you up tomorrow morning at eleven if that works? We'll grab some lunch on the way and have dessert with my parents."

The whole thing could have been a date, under different circumstances. Trent bringing her home to meet his parents, stopping for a romantic lunch at some roadside café...

She shook off the illusion. "Sounds perfect. If you're driving, I can take notes and—"

He scoffed. "Do you ever take a break, Kate?"

"Pot, meet kettle." She grinned. "Besides, I can't, not when I'm on deadline and working with a difficult subject."

"Me? Difficult? You must have me confused with a certain race car driver. I'm easy, flexible. Some even say nice." He got to his feet. A smile toyed with the edges of his mouth. She liked Trent's smile. Liked it a lot. "See you tomorrow, KitKat."

She nodded and watched him leave the way he'd come, ducking into the hood of his jacket as he set out in the rain. *I'm looking forward to it. More than I should.*

A few minutes later, Kate was sitting in Angie's office. The rain had stopped, and the sun was pushing its way through the gray clouds. She'd taken the time to walk to Angie's office, enjoying a second cup of tea on the way. A little trill of excitement ran through her at the thought of spending the entire day with Trent tomorrow. He wouldn't do that if he didn't enjoy her company and maybe, just maybe, Grandma was right about Trent and he just needed a little more patience, care, and attention to shift that interest in action.

Or maybe she really should switch to writing fiction. Getting involved with the man who'd broken her heart was not a smart decision. Only a fool went back for the same heartbreak a second time.

"So, how's the book going?" Angie said as soon as Kate stepped inside the room. Today, Angie's hair was a bright emerald green, the perfect complement to her black oversized T-shirt and leggings.

Kate settled into a chair opposite her agent and set her bag on the floor. "Great!"

"Wow. That's an enthusiastic response." Angie's chair squeaked as she tipped it back and rested her boots on the edge of her desk. "I thought you were having trouble with the whole past-relationship part."

Kate shrugged as if that wasn't an issue, and she hadn't thought about it, oh, a thousand times in the last couple of weeks. "Not really."

"And this whole Instagram rumor mill about the picture? Trent wasn't mad about that? Or worried your identity would be exposed?"

"It's just a boot, Angie. I'm sure no one will figure it out." Kate pulled out her notebook and a pen, in case Angie had any last-minute changes from the publisher. "I'm not going to say that us having a past together isn't a factor at all, but...we've spent a lot of time together, and he's opening up more every day, and he trusts me. That's why he's not worried about the photo. I'm about halfway done, and tomorrow we are going up to spend the day with his family."

"Sounds...almost romantic."

"Oh, it's not. Not really." Kate fiddled with the pen. It was far easier to do that than face the fact that the whole day was only a romance in Kate's mind. Hadn't Trent made it clear a dozen times that this was all business? "You said in your text that you also had the cover mockups?"

Angie nodded. "You're going to love them." She pulled up the files on her tablet, then turned the machine to face Kate. Trent's face dominated the cover. A ridge of mountains lay in the background, and a pair of hiking boots anchored the bottom corner. Beneath the words *Be True to Your Nature*, the words *by Trent MacMillan* stared back at Kate. "This publisher does a lot of memoirs. They said if you did a good job on this—and I have no doubt you will, because everything you write is fantastic—there are several others in the pipeline."

"More ghostwriting?" She'd written a dozen books for other people before, and this time, not having her name on the cover bothered her more than ever. Maybe because this whole thing with Trent had felt more like a partnership than a job. Or maybe she was reading things between them that weren't there.

"That's what you do." Angie grinned. "And you're amazing at it."

Kate traced Trent's name on the screen. When she'd been in college, she'd written his name in her notebook one time, over and over again, like a lovesick teenager. Now, his name, and only his name, would be on something they had created together. All the memories of Chick and Cheese and the bowling and the hike, under his name, not hers. "But what about...my own book someday?"

"Did you finish that novel you've been talking about for years?" Interest perked in Angie's eyes.

"No, but I was thinking about it. I met a writer the other night who wants to get together to trade pages and talk plot." Kate sat back in her chair and clutched the notebook tight. Talking about her own work seemed so risky, even with Angie. What if she failed? Then again, what if she pushed past all those roadblocks like the primroses the nursery had given up on, and became an author in her own right? "I was thinking maybe... maybe it's time I finished it."

"Hallelujah. It's past time you did that,

Kate." Angie set the tablet to the side. "Everything you write is fantastic. As soon as you finish that novel, I'll be proud to represent it."

Kate had braced herself for some reluctance, and Angie's supportive reply surprised her. "Really?"

"Of course. Now shoo." Angie waved at her. "Get out of here and go finish those books, before you're snapped up on some other memoir project. I can't wait to read that novel."

"Will do." Kate headed out of Angie's office. As she caught an Uber back to her apartment with the sun shining overhead, her mood was as light as a melody. Angie was right. Penny was right. It was time....

Time for Kate to start taking her own risks.

Ten

THE CORVETTE IDEA BACKFIRED. WHEN
Trent pulled the sleek red machine
out of the garage, a part of him hoped
Kate would be wowed by the price tag of the
car and the clear message that he was successful. It was like he was fifteen again and
trying to impress his crush. He pulled up to
the curb by her apartment, jumped out and
opened the passenger's side door.

"Cool car," she said as she hopped
inside. By the time he came around to the
driver's side and slipped behind the wheel,
Kate already had her notebook and pen out
and ready. "So, I had a list of questions—"

That was it? *Cool car*? "You know this is
a limited edition, right?"

"What is?"

"The car." Okay, now he was clearly fishing for compliments. What was wrong with

him? But his mouth kept running on, like a babbling brook of nerves. "It's a 2009 GTI Championship Edition. Only six hundred were made, a hundred in each color."

"Cool." She flipped pages in her notebook and scribbled something in the margins. "Your parents still own the nursery, right?"

"You're not impressed by the car?"

Kate glanced up. "It's a cool car, way cooler than my Honda, which is also a 2009, but definitely not a championship edition." She shrugged. "I don't know, I guess cars never really impress me. I care about who's driving the car more than about what's under the hood."

That made him pause and realize that it was silly to think a car was the answer to making Kate swoon at his feet. Besides, why did he want to make her swoon anyway? There was no swooning in a business deal, and that was all this was.

The social media firestorm was still simmering, and although Trent was tempted to take the picture down, Sarah had cautioned against it. She said removing the photo would create more questions and speculation than leaving it there. He checked the comments every once in a while to see if anyone had put it together, but so far, all he saw was rumors about him sneaking away with a famous actress or celebrity. Laughable thought, given Trent's ridiculously busy schedule.

Except, here he was, taking a day off to visit his parents with Kate, something he couldn't find time for before. Before Kate had come back into his life.

"What you said about the car is a good answer." And, if he was honest with himself, the exact answer he'd wanted to hear. Sure, he'd love it if Kate fainted at the sight of his expensive car, but he'd known far too many women—and men—who'd never seen past the Corvette's pedigree. Keeping things professional meant the car was a means to get to their meeting, nothing more.

"But...if you can open her up when we get to the highway, I'd love to see how fast this thing goes." Kate grinned and slipped her seatbelt into the lock.

"You've got it." He shifted into first gear and pulled away from the curb, the car's engine a low, patient growl as Trent navigated the side streets that led to Route 5. As soon as they hit the highway—nearly empty in the middle of a workday—Trent floored it, and the anxious Vette lurched forward, roaring down the road, the engine rumbling loud and happy.

Kate braced a hand on the roof and laughed. "Oh, my! That's incredible! So fast!"

"Scary?" He flicked a glance in her direction. Excitement lit her face.

Kate nodded. "A little."

"Just wanted you to see what she could do." Trent slowed the car until it hit the speed limit, because the last thing he needed was a speeding ticket or an accident. Most days, the Corvette sat in garage under a tarp, so the momentary burst of speed must have been just as much of a shock to the engine as it had been to Kate.

Okay, so maybe she was impressed by the Vette, and maybe this whole thing was a little more than just business to him too.

"Can I ask you something?" she said.

"Sure."

"Why do you have a car that's too fast to drive? I mean, what's the sense in that?" She glanced around at the leather interior, the pristine dash and intricate stitching. Every inch of the car had been meticulously maintained, giving it that just-out-of-the-showroom look, even more than a decade after it had come out of the factory. "I mean, it's not to impress girls or anything, right?"

"No. Of course not." Had he said that too fast? Trent rested his wrist on the top of the steering wheel and shot Kate a quick glance. "Well, maybe a little. Did it work?"

She laughed again. "Maybe a little."

They cruised down the highway, the

Corvette like a leashed dog straining to take off. The tires ate up the pavement, and the engine grumbled, yearning to explode again. "Remember that car I had in college?"

"Oh, that beat-up Saturn? It was, like, five colors. Rust, gray, green, red, and I think a little black."

His first car, bought with the small salary he'd earned at the nursery. It had cost him more in repairs than what he'd paid for it, but it had gotten him around during college. That car had definitely not been one that had impressed any girls. "Remember how it broke down on Route 5 that night we were coming back from that concert?"

"That was a great night. We had those awful seats—"

"At the very back of the stadium, with a pole right in front of us." Their memories braided together, as if they were there again, in the dark stadium with thousands of other people, anticipating the moment their favorite band hit the stage. Trent had saved for weeks to buy the tickets as a surprise for Kate's birthday. "I really thought partially obstructed view meant a tall guy in front of us or something."

"The view was fine, really, if you kind of craned your neck." She did just that, and the exaggerated gawking made Trent laugh. "The music was fabulous either way. Oh, and remember how I spilled my soda *and* popcorn on the floor during the first song? My shoes were sticky and crunchy for, like, a week."

They'd had a fabulous night, despite the bad seats and the ruined snack. Trent had wanted to do so much more for her birthday—a fancy dinner, maybe a limo to and from the concert—but in those days, his budget had been drive-thru fast food and partially obstructed seats. "It was fun until my car broke down, a mile from our exit."

"Those things happen. I was more impressed that you walked all the way to the gas station to get a tow truck," she said softly. "It was dark, and you left the only flashlight you had with me."

"I didn't want you to be scared." He shrugged, as if it had been no big deal to leave her in the car while he'd gone to get help on that cold winter night, in a too-thin jacket that had barely kept him warm. They'd been out in the middle of nowhere, far from any kind of cell tower, so he'd had to run for help. He'd never told Kate about the dozens of horror film plots that had made him take that mile at a run pace, just so he'd get back even sooner. "I'm just glad it was only a mile. I was worried about you the whole time."

"You were worried? That's so sweet." A smile curved across her face. "I mean, yeah, it was dark and cold, and my cell phone couldn't get a signal. I had that little cheap flip phone that barely worked. But I wasn't really scared."

He glanced over at her. Every time he thought he knew Kate, she surprised him. He liked that. A lot. "You weren't? Why?"

She averted her gaze and smoothed her hand over the lined paper in her lap. "I knew you'd take care of me, Trent. I...well, I trusted you."

She'd trusted him, and then he'd broken her heart a month later by ending their relationship. At the time, he'd thought they were too different to be happy together. Right now, he was having trouble seeing what those differences were. "I'm sorry, Kate."

"Don't apologize. It was still the best birthday present I ever got."

He scoffed. "We had terrible seats, and we broke down on the way home."

"But it was fun, Trent. An adventure."

A tractor trailer truck passed them, the wind tunnel effect making the Vette shimmy a little. "I thought you hated adventures."

"I don't hate them. I just..." She turned to look out the window at the passing landscape of houses and businesses as they rode through a small town on their way north. Kate was quiet for a moment. "I don't like doing things I'm not good at."

"The only way to get good at them is to do them, you know."

"I know, but...it's never been that simple for me." He didn't speak, just waited for her to continue. He could see the words on the tip of her tongue, the story waiting to be shared. So he kept driving, giving Kate time and space.

"My parents worked a lot when I was a kid, you know?" she finally said.

He remembered Kate sharing a little about her family when they'd been dating. By the time Kate had gone to college, her parents had relocated to new jobs in California until they'd retired. As a twenty-something, he hadn't thought about how tough it would be navigating the world without that support system nearby. "I can't imagine that. It seems like I was always around my family."

"I had my grandmother, thank goodness. And it's not that my parents didn't love me. It was as if..." She thought a second. "As if they were gone so much that when the three of us were home together, which was very rare, they were so tired or so behind on housework and things like that, we hardly had fun together."

He merged into the center lane as a pickup truck with a horse trailer moved to pass them. "What do you mean?"

"My dad loved basketball when I was a

kid. The one thing we would do together on Sundays was watch the basketball game. He knew every player, every team, and it was the one thing we had in common." Her face lit up with the memory, and for a second, Trent could imagine a much-younger Kate's joy at the weekend tradition. "Because my dad was gone all the time at work, I thought I'd join a basketball team at school. And, well, since we both know I'm not coordinated enough to operate anything more complicated than a pencil, it was a disaster."

Trent vowed that if he ever became a father—and that was a big if, considering he wasn't even thinking about settling down yet—he would be there for his kids all the time. "Your dad get to see you play?"

"He took time off to come to our first game. I was so excited. I thought I'd make him proud and really do well. Instead, when the ball was passed to me..." She cringed. "I ducked, and it went straight into the other team's hands."

Trent bit back a laugh. "Oh, Kate. That's awful."

"I was so embarrassed. My dad was cool about it, and he said he'd work with me and help me practice, but he worked so much, and we only had those Sundays. Suffice to say, I never got any better. I stuck to things

I couldn't fail at, like reading and writing, instead."

"You must have tried other sports?"

She shook her head. "I'm not exactly super coordinated anyway, and that basketball experience made me even more skittish. I was awful in gym and couldn't stand that class."

He chuckled. "That's where we differ. I would have been happy to have six periods of gym and none of math and English."

"When I was in high school, I tried out for the color guard. It was like that basketball team all over again. I twirled the baton at that first halftime show, and it came down and bonked me on the head." She shrugged and smoothed her jeans. "After that, it became easier and safer to just...read or write. That was part of why I didn't want to try any of those things with you. I was so afraid I'd mess up and you'd...well, you wouldn't want to take me with you again."

"So avoid making any mistakes in the first place." Trent sighed. "I never knew that. I should have put that together years ago."

A small diner came into view. Trent flipped on his directional, pulled off the highway and into the parking lot. The building was shaped like an airport hangar and had a giant propeller over the entrance of The Destination Diner. He parked and shut off the engine. "I'm sorry, Kate. I should have asked, or should have made you feel more comfortable about hiking and canoeing."

"It's not all your fault. I never shared, either. I wasn't as confident then as I am now, and I was much more risk-averse. Like you said before, we were young, and I guess we didn't really know what we wanted."

He wanted to ask if now she knew what she wanted, but he was afraid of the answer. What if it was "any man other than you?" After all, he had let her down, and then broken up with her. Far better to keep the distance between them before he did something foolish like fall for Kate all over again. "So, the sign on the door says they have the best burgers in the state of Washington. Want to test that theory?"

She grinned. "Of course."

They headed inside and grabbed two seats in a bright red booth. Every laminate table was printed with a different topographical map. Everything, from the salt shakers to the clock on the wall, was airplane-themed or airplane-shaped. Even the waitresses wore old-fashioned flight attendant uniforms with pointy hats.

They ordered burgers, fries, and sodas. While they waited, the conversation turned to simpler things—the décor of the restaurant, the weather, the lack of traffic on a weekday.

They left past history behind them, which was exactly where Trent wanted it to stay.

After lunch, they only had another hour on the road before they reached his hometown. The sign for Hudson Falls sat slightly askew, a sign of the visit to come, Trent thought. The small town had barely changed in the two decades since he'd been gone. The same gas station sat on the corner, and the same diner was advertising an all-you-can-eat fish special for Friday nights.

"This is such a cute place," Kate said.

"You think so? I think it's stifling." He took a right, and before he could change his mind about this spontaneous idea of visiting his family, they were there. His parents saw the car pull into the parking lot for the nursery, and both of them came out of the greenhouse and started waving.

Great.

Kate got out the second he parked. "Mr. MacMillan! Mrs. MacMillan! So great to see you both again!"

His mother drew Kate into a car like she was a long-lost relative. "Oh, Kate! You've gotten more beautiful over the years. It feels like it's been forever since we saw you. Come in, come in. I put on some coffee and made an apple cobbler."

Kate grinned. "I was counting on that."

His father stood to the side, as if he

was lost without his wife there to serve as a buffer. "Well. You're home. It's taken long enough."

"I've been busy, Dad. The company—"

"Family always comes before business, Trent. Always." Then his father turned on his heel and headed into the house.

Trent could hear Kate and his mother laughing and chatting like old friends. Before he'd driven up here, he'd texted his mother and told her he was bringing Kate, as a FRIEND ONLY, in all caps. Given the way his mother had already drawn Kate into the family fold, it didn't seem like she'd gotten the message.

"Come on in, Trent. Have some coffee and cobbler." His mother pressed a kiss to his cheek, as if he was still a little boy, then grabbed his hand and hauled him into the sunny yellow space. Kate was already at the table, snapping green beans and tossing them into a colander. She'd plopped into the middle of his family as if she'd always been there.

"What are you doing?" Trent whispered.

"Helping with dinner." Kate grinned. "So, Mrs. MacMillan, how is the nursery going? It looks like it's doubled in size since I was last here."

"Oh, call me Anne, please. And yes, we've expanded a little. Now that Marla is working full-time, she suggested we add a garden design section. You'd be amazed how many people want her to come up with a plan for the petunias." She turned to her husband. "Robert, why don't you show Trent the new greenhouse? I bet he'd love to see the seedlings."

"Oh, can I go too?" Kate asked. "My grandmother and I have a little greenhouse where we plant a few things. Vegetables and primroses, mostly. She loves plants and taught me everything she knows."

"Of course!" Anne tugged the apron over her head and draped it over a chair. "Let's all go."

"Oh yes, let's," Trent muttered under his breath. This was exactly what he was trying to avoid—a family reunion that drew Kate in like a moth to a flame. "We really can't stay long."

Kate shot him a glance. Okay, yes, he'd promised to stay a while so she could get background on him, but already his family was grating on his nerves and he was regretting agreeing to the trip.

"Nonsense. We're starting dinner. You have to stay for that. I'm making a roast with baked potatoes. One of your favorite dinners if I remember right, Trent."

"Mom..." He sighed. Okay, so that was a good way to entice him into staying. His mother's roast was unsurpassed. "You're not playing fair."

Her smile overtook her face. "Of course I'm not playing fair,. That's what mothers do best. Now, go ahead with your father. I'll show Kate around, and we'll catch up."

Trent didn't miss the subtle attempt to leave him alone with his father. The two of them had never really gotten along, and a single walk through the greenhouse wasn't going to change that. But Trent loved his mother, and for her, he would try to talk to Dad.

Trent jogged up to his father, who hadn't waited for anyone before heading into the greenhouse. "Hey, Dad. So you changed a lot of things?"

"Just added some things. You don't need to change much about plants. Light, water, fertilizer. The formula is the same now as it was a hundred years ago."

Trent bit back his impatience. "How's business going?"

"It's fine. We're still open, aren't we?"

His father's bark of a sentence almost made Trent head back into the house and give up. But he remembered the smile on his mother's face, and if there was one person in this family Trent couldn't bear to disappoint, it was her. So he tried another tact. "And the garden design part? Marla must love that.

She was always sketching when she was a kid."

"Fancy-shmancy gardens nowadays. I'm a simple man. I don't need a plan for the petunias."

Trent burst out laughing. He knew his father hadn't meant it as a joke, but the repetition of his mother's words, only in a grumpier tone, struck him funny.

His father stopped walking and turned to face his son. "Why didn't you ever come back here and run the business like you promised you would?"

It was a promise Trent had made before college. Before Machu Picchu. Before GOA. He'd hoped that having his own success would earn his father's praise and admiration, not more recrimination. "Dad, we've been through this. I have a company in Seattle. It's going really well. In fact, we're going pub—"

"I see a man's word still doesn't mean anything around here."

Trent shook his head. "Just because I went out on my own doesn't mean I didn't care about this business or you or—"

"The promise you made." His father's posture tightened. "Doesn't matter. It's too late anyway. You've got your fancy company to run now."

His father's disapproval grated on Trent.

"That company is successful, Dad. I'm happy there. Why can't you support that?"

His father pushed a shopping cart back into place, then worked on straightening the watering cans so they all faced the same way. "This is a family business, Trent. You're part of the family. You said you were going to get your degree and come back here. Our family built this business together, but you...you washed your hands of all of us."

They'd had this argument every single time Trent had come home, and every time, it had ended with an impasse. His father couldn't understand Trent's desire to pursue his own dreams, and Trent couldn't understand why his father wanted him to contort himself into his parents' dream. "Just because I didn't want to work in the nursery doesn't mean I didn't want anything to do with my family."

His father scoffed. "Sure looks like that. You never come home. It's not like we live in another country, Trent. We're two hours away."

"You don't come to visit me any more than I visit you."

"You know we can't leave the business." Dad began sorting the terra cotta pots, putting the like-sized ones back together on the correct shelves. "It's family-run, which means the family has to be here. That's part and parcel of self-employment."

Trent drew in a deep breath and opted to change the subject before they retread ground that would only lead to another argument. "So, tell me about what's new here. I'm sure some things have changed in the stock and services."

His father waved a vague hand at the greenhouse. "You can see it for yourself. You don't need me to show you anything. You know the way out." Then Robert turned on his heel and stalked out of the greenhouse, past a gaping Kate and disapproving Anne.

Another happy family reunion in the books.

Eleven

K ATE TRIED NOT TO NOTICE how distant
and moody Trent was at dinner. His
sister Marla came by as they were
eating dessert, and her warm and effusive
nature made Kate feel even more welcome.
Three years younger, Marla had a few curves
from having two kids, and a no-nonsense,
easygoing look with her jeans and ponytail.

Marla teased her older brother about
how cover-model gorgeous his outdoor photos looked. "Do you bring a hair and makeup
team with you? 'Hold on, let me vogue this
pose?'"

Trent rolled his eyes. "I just naturally
look good. Some people, on the other hand..."

Marla propped her fists on her hips and
feigned outrage. "I'm a mom. I can sit you
in time out with one hand while I'm making
lasagna with the other. Don't mess with me."

The whole family laughed, and Trent drew his sister into a conciliatory hug. "You're still the best little sister ever. Love what you're doing with the business, by the way."

Marla shrugged. "Just expanding into new territory."

"With all those frou-frou people who want shag carpeting on the patio." Trent's father shook his head. "Whatever happened to just planting a garden? Why does everyone have to have twenty kinds of pavers and decorative flags stuck in the ground?"

"Because it makes us money and makes the world more beautiful, Dad." Marla patted his chest and gave him a grin. "I guarantee when I'm done with your patio, you'll be sitting outside, drinking white wine and watching the sunset."

Trent's father scoffed. "Frou-frou drinks for a frou-frou patio." But he gave his daughter an indulgent smile as he left the kitchen, heading to the living room to watch the NASCAR races. Instead of staying with his family, Trent said something about needing fresh air.

Kate wandered into the living room. Cars zoomed past each other on the oval track at a dizzying pace. "Thanks for having us at your house, Mr. MacMillan."

Trent's father nodded. "You're always

welcome. Though I'm not sure my son always wants to be here."

She perched on the edge of the chair. His father's profile was so like Trent's, only a little older, with salt-and-pepper hair and a heavier build. "Trent loves it here. He really does."

Robert scoffed. "Seems to me he wants to leave the second he gets here."

"Maybe..." She hesitated then decided to say the words anyway. "Maybe he's struggling with connecting with you. I know my mom and I argued a lot because we were such different people. My grandmother is like my best friend, but my mom is more organized and data-focused than I am. But on Sunday afternoons, we used to watch movies together. All kinds of old horror classics. It was the one thing we had in common and the one thing that bonded us. Maybe that's what Trent needs to have?"

"We used to have a lot in common," Robert said. "Then he moved off to the city, and things changed."

"Deep down inside, Mr. MacMillan," Kate said as she got to her feet, "I think Trent is the same person he used to be. It's just going to take a little digging to get to that person."

Kate left Robert to watch the race while she headed for the kitchen, where Marla and Anne were putting food away and doing dishes.

"So, are you and my brother dating?" Marla asked.

"No, no. We're just...friends." Although they were something more than that, weren't they? Whatever that was, Kate couldn't define it. She wondered where Trent had gone outside and why he was so removed from his parents, who seemed like lovely people and clearly loved him, and vice versa. "I'm helping him with his book, and we came up here so I could get some more background on him."

"I don't care what the reason is, I'm glad you're back in Trent's life," Anne said. "You're good for him, Kate."

"Me?" She scoffed. "I don't see how."

"He was more grounded when he was dating you. You are, in fact, the only girl he ever brought home to meet the family, and considering he's brought you home twice now..." Anne shrugged. "I don't know. It seems like a lot more than just friends to me."

Dare Kate hope his mother was right? No, that would be too risky. Kate would end up doing something foolish, like falling in love with Trent again. She already knew how it would end—with him walking away, certain they were too different to be together. "So, tell me some stories. Any cute or funny stories about Trent as a kid would really help flesh out the book."

His mother ran water into the sink and squirted in some dish soap. "Trent was always my adventurous one. He walked before he was a year old. We bought him a bike for his fourth birthday, and wouldn't you know, he had mastered it and wanted the training wheels off within a couple of weeks."

"That's pretty young, isn't it?" Kate made a note on her pad. "I think I was still scared of riding a bike when I was in middle school. But then again, I'm not athletic like he is."

Marla smiled. "You and I are the same. I'm the one who thinks through a decision seventy-five times before I make it. Trent just...wings it."

"Terrifying to do, isn't it?" Kate had always been so cautious, so afraid to mess up or take a risk. Where had that gotten her?

"I think I have some pictures," Anne said. "The dishes can soak. Let's go through the photo albums and thoroughly embarrass Trent."

Marla grinned. "He hates it when Mom drags out the pictures of him as a little boy."

"All the more reason to do it," Anne said. She hurried into the next room and came back with a pile of leather-bound albums. She set them on the kitchen table, and the three of them sat down. Anne turned the pages of the first one, opening to a picture of a bright and happy baby Trent.

For a second, Kate imagined what it would be like if that was their baby. If they had worked out all those years ago and gotten married, would their child have the same eyes and head of blond hair? "He was adorable."

"He was, but such a handful. Busy as a bee, every day of his life." Anne turned a couple more pages, showing pictures of Trent's first steps and first birthday. As she did, she talked about his bright, inquisitive nature, and how he had explored every corner of the house from the time he could crawl.

Kate scribbled notes, took pictures of the photos with her phone to remember them for later and listened as Anne and Marla took turns talking about a young Trent. It was so clear they loved him deeply, and that his had been a happy childhood. "When did he go to work in the nursery?"

"When he was about ten, we opened our doors. Marla was only seven, but the two of them started out sweeping, setting things up. Easy tasks." Anne turned another page, showing the family standing around a Christmas tree. "When he was thirteen, he started working over the summers, helping with sales and tending. He seemed to take to the business like a duck to water, and we always thought..." His mother's voice trailed off. She flipped the book closed. "We're just glad he's been so successful and happy with his own thing."

Marla scoffed. "Most of us are happy for him."

Anna's lips pinched. "Trent's father always hoped the whole family would work here. He's a little more..."

"Stubborn," Marla finished. "They both are. I swear, watching them is like watching two bulls in a china shop."

"They'll figure it out," Anne said. "Did Trent ever tell you about the time we all went fishing? He was, oh, fifteen, and he caught the biggest fish of all of us. I have a picture of it somewhere." She flipped through some pages and talked as she recounted the story of the family vacation.

Kate listened and took copious notes, learning lots of anecdotes about Trent and seeing another side of him. A more open side, family-oriented, committed. It surprised her, maybe because she'd always seen him as the loner who hiked mountains and cycled across countrysides. The extra stories would really round out the book. In the back of her mind, she was already seeing how the pieces could fit together.

"Honey, why don't you check on Trent?" Anne said as the dishwater drained and the day drew to a close. They'd gone through all the photos and talked for what seemed like forever. "Marla and I can finish up." She gave Kate a good-natured shooing out the back door.

Kate found Trent wandering among the dwarf pine trees. He looked like a giant among the tiny green triangles. He trailed a hand along their pointy tops, taking his time meandering down the aisles. "You left kind of abruptly after dessert. Everything okay?"

"I told you this was a bad idea." Trent shook his head. "I don't want my family or my childhood in the book."

His parents were nice, even if his father seemed grouchy and standoffish. That didn't mean Trent shouldn't include that part of his history. "This place and these people are an integral part of you, like it or not. You can't write a book and call it the unvarnished truth if you're leaving out a major part of that very truth."

"It's my life story. I can say what I want to, and I just want to focus on the business."

"How is that being true to your nature, Trent?" She waved at the plants and the shrubbery that filled the acres of the nursery. "This is part of your nature, like it or not, and it should be part of the book. Since I don't have enough material to finish writing,

I accepted your mother's offer to let us stay overnight—"

"What?"

"And help them with their big sale tomorrow." Let Trent be annoyed; Kate didn't care. She liked his family and wanted to repay them, even in a tiny way, for their kindness today. "It's a lot of work for three people, and your mom said you used to help all the time when you were young. I don't know how good I'll be on a cash register, but I do know plants."

"You want to stay. Here. Overnight."

It wasn't a question. She raised her chin, daring him to disagree. "Yes, I do. We can help your family, and then head back to Seattle. I got a lot of stories from your mom and saw some pictures from your childhood, but I'd love to fill in some of the gaps while I have access to your family and hear all about the little boy who took his training wheels off when he was four. There's nothing at GOA that can't exist without you for a few more hours."

Amusement lit his eyes as he considered her stern words. "What if I say no?"

She held up his car keys and dangled them in front of him. "Well, Trent MacMillan, I'm going to make that impossible." Then she tossed him a grin and headed back into the house.

From the outside, the lights glowed golden and soft. The MacMillan family moved about inside, sharing some after-dinner coffee and more conversation. Trent stayed on the outside, watching and not joining, until the air grew too cold.

Cars were lined up before the nursery opened. From the second they unlocked the doors, the MacMillans and Kate were insanely busy with sales. "Wow, is it always this crazy?" Kate asked as she hurried to restock the seed starter kits. "I've barely had time to grab a drink of water."

Trent chuckled. "I think by the time spring comes, people are so ready to get their hands in their dirt that this sale is a big deal. We're also one of the bigger nurseries in the area, and my parents carry a lot of plants people can't necessarily find at the smaller places."

She straightened the mini greenhouses, trying to hurry, which sent one tumbling toward the floor. Trent reached out, catching it at the last second. "Thanks."

He set it on her stack. "We make a good team."

"We do," she said, holding his gaze with a smile.

He wanted to linger with her, to tell her more about spring planting and garden clubs and all kinds of things that would keep this nursery conversation going, but his mother called him over to help carry out an order, and Kate hurried to do a price check on a garden fountain.

It took Trent some time to get back in the groove, which meant his impatient father sent him more than one annoyed glare. By mid-afternoon, the crowds had died down, and the family began straightening up the chaos created by the busy sale day.

His father was at the back of the nursery, struggling to lift a big bag of soil, part of a tower of potting soil that had been knocked over by a rambunctious kid earlier. Trent saw the strain in his muscles, the hunch in his back. When had his father gotten so old? It seemed like Robert had aged thirty years, not ten, since Trent had last been home. He hurried over and before his father could object, lifted the opposite end. "Let me help you with that."

"I've got it."

"I'm sure you do, Dad." Trent didn't let go. Together, they swung the big, heavy bags into a neat pile against the fence.

When they were done, his father wiped the sweat from his brow.

"Thanks."

"It was a nice busy day today. Seemed busier than the last few sales."

His father stopped walking and turned to face him. "When was the last time you were here for an annuals sale? Ten years ago? Twelve?"

It had to have been at least that long. Trent had let the busyness of college and then GOA keep him away from Hudson Falls. How could he do that? He knew firsthand how consuming a business could be, and yet he'd somehow gone around thinking his was more important than the one run by his aging parents. "I'm sorry. I should have come up more often."

"Yeah." His father opened his mouth as if he wanted to say more, then shook his head. Trent turned to walk away but stopped when he heard his father call his name. Just like that, Trent's frustration dissipated.

"Help me with this shelving unit, will you?"

The shelving was thick, heavy metal, and after Trent had seen his father struggling with the bags of potting soil, there was no question of not helping. This was also his father's way of apologizing, through working together. Trent could hold on to his resentments, or he could set them down and pick up the shelving instead. "Where are we going with it?"

"Your mother wants to bring in one of those fancy wicker patio sets. Suggested selling, or marketing, whatever Marla is calling it."

"I think that's a great idea. But what if..." Trent spun a slow circle, "...we move the two white shelving units over here and put them into a T-shape? The patio set can go between them, sort of like a little room. We can use the shelves to display all those little last-minute decorative things people like. The plant pots, those lanterns, maybe even some of those...what are they?" Trent pointed at a small set of figurines.

"Your mother calls them gnomes. I think they're trolls."

Trent laughed. "Okay, so some plant pots and trolls. With the warmer weather, everyone is going to be looking for new things to spruce up their gardens. We can even put up some photos of Marla's designs on the shelves."

His father thought about that. "It'll seem like the customers are on their own patio."

"Exactly. And if they can see it as their own, maybe they will want to replicate it at home. More business for Marla, and for you."

"Smart thinking, Trent."

It was the first compliment his father had given him in a long while, and it warmed Trent's heart. Like a typical man, he coughed away the emotion and muttered a simple "Thanks, Dad."

"Well, let's move this thing." The two of them lifted the heavy metal unit and began to duck-walk it across the nursery. His father peeked around one side of it as they staggered to the other side of the nursery. "Remember that camping trip we went on with the Boy Scouts when you were, what, fourteen? Fifteen?"

"The one where we got caught in the rainstorm in the mountains? We almost got washed down the side of Liberty Bell Mountain." So close to the Canadian border, even a summer night got chilly. When the skies had started rumbling, several of the dads and their sons had turned back and went home, but a few hardy souls, like Trent and his father, had stuck it out.

"You know what I liked about that trip?"

"Not the rain, that was for sure," Trent said. It had been the kind of cold, stinging rain that hurt your face and seeped into your bones. Trent had been tempted to go back home too, but his dad had said they should try sticking it out, because eventually the storm would move on and the sun would come back out.

His father snorted. "Definitely not that. I liked the way you and I figured out what to do. Together. The whole group was worried because it was so windy, and once it got dark, we needed to have some kind of safe shelter solution against the weather. It could have been disastrous, but you and I built off each other's ideas and created that shelter."

The memory of the two of them working together, hurrying before the storm intensified, came rushing back to Trent. "It was really cool. We used that felled tree and some homemade thatching. And we made a bed on the floor of it with pine needles and leaves." Everyone in the troop had stayed warm and safe that night, and when the storm had abated, they'd awoken to a spectacular morning and a long, wonderful day spent fishing.

"It was a good trip," the two of them said at the same time. "Well, what do you know. Maybe we do have a few things in common," Trent said.

"Maybe." Dad stepped back and assessed the new area. He cleared his throat, once again coughing away the momentary emotions. "This looks good."

"Yeah. Marla's going to love it. It was a great idea, Dad."

"Wasn't mine. It was yours. I just built off it, like I did on that camping trip. You're smart and creative, and that's part of why I liked about having you around, Trent," his father said. "I was so looking forward to when you came home from college and started working here full-time. I wanted to see what we could do with this place, where the two of us could take it. Instead, you went off on your own."

Trent sighed. Just when they seemed to have found common ground, the two of them circled back to the same argument. "Dad, why are we having this argument again?"

"Because..." His father held up a plant that had overgrown its pot. Roots twined their way out of the base, then knotted into a circle under the pot. "Just because you can't see the roots of who you are doesn't mean they aren't there."

Kate watched Trent and his father work together, rearranging some outdoor furniture into a home-like setting on one side of the nursery. They seemed to be getting along, even talking. Until they didn't. Robert went off one way, Trent another.

"Those two men," Anne said with a sigh. "I hope they work things out someday."

"I think it's just that they're too similar," Kate said. "That can make it hard to see each other's viewpoint."

"Well, if you talk to my son," Anne said softly, "tell him that his father might be as gruff as a grizzly bear, but he loves and misses his son something fierce."

"I will, I promise."

His mother gave Kate a quick hug. "After all the hours we spent together, you're practically family."

The words warmed Kate's heart and set off a longing deep in her chest for this whole thing with Trent and his family to last longer than a couple of days. What would it be like to truly be a part of his family? To come up here on the weekends and spend time together with everyone?

Silly fantasy thoughts. None of that was going to happen. Wishing and hoping for things that would never be didn't make them real.

Trent strolled over and handed her an icy glass of water. "What do you say we play a little hooky?"

"Oh, thank you for the water." She took a long drink. Her legs and arms ached from being so active all day, but it also felt good to not be behind the computer. She'd spent most of her time with Trent's mother and sister, hearing everything from the story of his first steps to the day he'd skipped school in first grade to go see a neighbor's puppies. "What do you mean by playing hooky? Because if it involves lifting dirt or plants, no way. I'm pooped from today."

He laughed. "Just an easy hike. There's a short trail at the end of my street. I'd like to show it to you and I'll tell you all about my first hike on it while we climb."

"Sure. That sounds fun." She put a hand to her forehead. "Wait, maybe I should check myself for a fever."

"Why?"

"I think I've caught some kind of outdoors bug." When he rolled his eyes, she grinned. "Yet another bad joke."

"You do seem to have an awful lot of those." But he laughed as he said it, and the mood between them lightened. Trent called out to his mother that they'd be back in an hour, then Kate and Trent set out down the street.

His neighborhood backed up to part of the Cascade Mountains, a breathtaking view, even from street level. Snow-capped mountains rose in little white triangles above them, one after the other, as far as the eye could see. A small dirt path wound behind the houses and into the ridges. Thick groups of trees marched up the slope, their roots poking above the worn earth.

"Lots of loose gravel here, so watch your step." Trent took her hand, guiding her past the first slippery slope. His touch was warm, comforting, and made her feel, even in this small space, safe and secure. As soon as they were on solid ground, Trent released her hand.

Kate told herself not to care. This was an excursion for research, not to be alone. Except why did Trent keep getting close and moving far away? "So, uh, did you hike this trail a lot when you were young?"

"It's the first hike I ever did. My friends and I would come here to play, but we never ventured very far. Then, when I was nine, I got it in my head that I wanted to see how high I could climb. I set out on Saturday morning and got all the way to that ridge." He pointed to an outcropping so high above them, she could barely see it against the dark mountain side.

This was the Trent she had been looking for in all these interviews she'd done with him. The headstrong, brave, strong man who had reached the top when no one else thought he could. "Wow. That's really high. Weren't you scared?"

"I was too dumb to be scared." He grinned. "I set out with almost nothing. A water bottle and some cookies my mom made. I told her I was going to the bottom of the ridge to play with my friends like I always did, but instead, I kept going. I didn't even have a jacket. It was cold as heck up there, and that's when I started to get scared."

"Sounds like my kind of hiking prep." Kate grinned. "So, what happened?"

"My dad found me. I had asked him about hiking that trail one time, and he said he used to climb all the way to the top when he was younger and not so busy with the nursery. He warned me not to go alone, that someday he'd take me, but he never found the time. I guess when I took off that sunny Saturday, he figured out I was going to do the same—I never was a kid who liked to listen to rules—and he set out to find me."

She could see that in Trent's father, and in Trent himself. The stubbornness, the courage, the deep love neither of them showed on the outside. "That's wonderful. It shows you both think a lot alike."

Trent scoffed. "I don't know about that. We have the same interests in sports and the outdoors, and when I was young, we did stuff together whenever he wasn't working. After that day on the mountain, my dad insisted I join the Boy Scouts, so I'd learn to always be prepared. He went on some of the camping trips with me, and it was one of the few times we got along. Maybe it was because we were both outdoors, doing something we loved. In the nursery, we butted heads all the time, but when we were putting up a tent or building a fire, we got along like best friends."

"Deep down, your dad sounds a lot like

you." When the two of them had been standing together earlier, they were almost mirror reflections with the same stance, sandy-brown hair and piercing blue eyes.

Trent scoffed. "He'd say the opposite."

"You're wrong, Trent. Maybe he doesn't say it to you, but he does to other people," she said. "When I talked to your dad, everything he said was so full of pride. He told me he couldn't believe how much further you went than he did. That you had bigger dreams and you didn't let anything stop you. Sort of like on that hike."

Trent stepped up onto a high rocky ledge. A couple of pebbles skittered past them. He turned, put out his hand and hoisted Kate onto the same ledge. "He has never said that to me. All he talks about is how I disappointed him."

"Because you didn't come back to work in the nursery?" She glanced back, decided that was a bad decision because everything looked so far away and the world below so small. If she concentrated on Trent, and only Trent, the hike was almost…fun.

"I guess it was always assumed," Trent said. He moved through some brush and between two towering trees. "I'd go to college, and then take over for him when he retired. I had told him a hundred times that I didn't want to be chained down to one location, one small business for the rest of my life."

"And yet, aren't you sort of that way now? You love your company, like your dad loves his, and because of that, you've devoted your life to it." He held out a reusable water bottle, and she took a long drink before continuing. "I don't think your dad feels chained down, any more than you do. He loves his work, and when you love your work, it's not a burden."

Trent thought about that for a moment. "I've never looked at it like that. To me, the nursery was suffocating. Like living in a tiny house with eleven other people. This town, my life, all of it felt that way. It's why I come to places like this." He spread his hand, indicating the beautiful vista ahead of them. A small lake punctuated the lush valley below them, its dark waters still and deep. Tall pine trees dotted the landscape, a stark, rich green against the rocky face of the mountain. "Out here, there are no constraints. No deadlines. No phone calls or appointments or demands for my time."

"I'm going to go out on a limb here, though, and argue that maybe, just maybe, that's what your dad feels when he's puttering around in the greenhouse?" She bent down and cupped the leaves of a seedling a few inches high, struggling to reach its own patch of sunlight among the towering trees and expanding ferns. She thought of the tomato plant Grandma Wanda had given her, the plant that tried so hard despite impossible odds. "A seed is like its own little world. Like *Horton Hears a Who*, you know?"

He chuckled. "So gardening is like Dr. Seuss?"

"What I mean is that when you plant a seed, it's almost so tiny you can't see it. But it's in there, and it's determined to become something more. In a greenhouse, that seed is almost entirely dependent on you to feed it, water it, make sure the sunlight hits it at just the right time and angle. A million things can go wrong, but a million things can also go right." Now she was sounding like her grandmother, but that was okay. Grandma Wanda was full of wonderful wisdom. "You love and live in a broad world, Trent, full of mountains and lakes. Your father's world is smaller, but just as big and just as important to him. You reach the top of a mountain and feel a huge sense of accomplishment. He takes a seed and turns it from something like this—" she pointed to the seedling, then rose and pressed a hand to the bark of the maple tree beside them, "—to this, and it's just as big of a deal to him."

Sort of like when an author wrote a book under someone else's name. Kate had put the same loving care and attention into her ghostwritten books as Loretta and Penny put into their own books. Just because her name wasn't on the cover didn't make the work mean less. It was simply a different route for the seeds of her words to climb out of nothing.

"I never thought of it that way," Trent said.

She shrugged. "Maybe it's time you saw things from his perspective. Your book is about being true to your nature, and just like this seedling, your father is part of that nature, part of your nature. That's why I need the backstory, the fertilizer and water and sunlight, that brought you from there to here." Kate chuckled. "Okay, that was totally corny and overdone, but you get the point."

"I do." A smile curved across his face and he shook his head. "You are brilliant, KitKat."

"Well, I don't know about that." She looked away, suddenly shy and unsure.

"I do." He shifted closer to her, so close the heat from his body mingled with hers. He reached up and cupped her cheek, his thumb brushing a lazy curve across her skin. Every nerve ending inside her roared to attention. Her heart thudded in her chest, so hard and loud, she was sure people could hear it for miles.

"You are brilliant," he said again, softer

this time, "and breathtaking and captivating." He shifted closer, so close his lips nearly brushed hers, and Kate's breath caught just as Trent leaned in and—

"Hey! Are you Trent MacMillan?"

Trent jumped back and released Kate, the moment over before it even began. Disappointment rushed through her, and she turned away so he wouldn't see the reflection in her eyes.

"Oh, hey," he said to the couple behind them. "Yes, I'm Trent."

"I thought so." The guy stepped forward, his eyes wide. He had a rainbow beanie over his dreadlocks and a GOA branded backpack slung over one shoulder. "Dude, I have, like, all GOA stuff. It's the coolest."

"That's great. Thanks."

"Yeah, like, we hike a lot. Not, like, crazy hikes like you do, man, but we get outdoors in our apparel." The kid grinned. "Get it?"

Trent smiled back. "Yup. Clever."

"Like, I totally dreamed about running into you on a hike someday," the kid with the dreads went on. His partner just stared at Trent, like he was a movie star on the street. "And here you are. Isn't that wild?"

"Totally," Trent said. He exchanged a little more small talk and took a selfie with the hikers. Kate shifted away, embarrassed she'd thought he was going to kiss her, but given how quickly Trent had moved away, she had to have had the wrong impression. Her hopes had rushed ahead of her reality.

"We, uh, have to get going," Trent said after picture number ten with the couple.

"Nice to meet you. And if you email me, I'll send you a coupon for the online store."

"Whoa! Cool, dude! That's, like, so awesome. I'm going to tell everyone what a cool guy you are." The kid shook Trent's hand, then waved goodbye. As he and his girlfriend walked away, the guy was already whipping out his phone to post the picture on his social media.

"We should get going," Trent said. "We need to drive back today, and it's getting late."

"Yeah," Kate said as they started to walk away. She glanced back at the space where Trent had almost—almost—kissed her, and told herself she was glad, not heartbroken. "Totally."

Twelve

THE TWO-HOUR DRIVE BACK TO Seattle was nearly silent, except for the clacking of keys and the occasional question. As soon as Kate and Trent got back to the nursery to get in the car, she'd pulled out her laptop and gone to work on the book, telling him she wanted to work on it while everything was fresh in her memory.

Which gave Trent altogether too much time to think.

He'd almost kissed her on the mountain, a moment when he'd stopped thinking about what was smart. His brain had ignored the complications of getting involved with someone who was technically working for him. She was his biographer, essentially, and mixing a relationship with the book could only spell disaster.

At least that's what he'd told himself

when they'd hiked back down the mountain. It was easier to believe that than deal with the attraction he still felt for her. Even now, looking over at her and watching her type away, working hard on the story of his life, he realized how amazing she was.

"I had a question about college," Kate said, oblivious to his meandering, sentimental thoughts. "I know you struggled in high school and the first two years of college—"

"Because all I wanted to do was be outdoors, not stuck in a room with thirty other people studying *Great Expectations.*"

"Well, I hated that book too. I think everyone does. But I love the rest of Dickens' works, and I'm sure there's at least one other one you would have liked." She grinned. "But when you graduated from college, you graduated with honors. What made the difference that last year or so?"

He rested his wrist on the top of the steering wheel. The Corvette glided along the highway, hugging the curves like a close friend. "You want the truth?"

"Well, the book is called *Be True to Your Nature,* so...yeah."

They passed the diner where they'd stopped for lunch. It was closed now, clearly just a breakfast and lunch place, the parking lot empty, and a single light burning over the door. The thought made him sad, because he would have liked to stop there again with Kate, if only to have that memory a second time. "It was you, Kate."

"Me? What did I do?"

"You worked so hard, and you were so dedicated to studying. It rubbed off on me." He shrugged as if it hadn't been a big deal. In reality, her work habits had encouraged him to do the same. Once he'd applied himself, Trent had realized how hard work paid off, which had translated into better grades and, eventually, better work habits.

Her eyes were wide with surprise. "I...I had no idea I was an influence on you."

He chuckled. "You were more than that. You were that little dose of honesty I clearly needed. Do you remember that test we had on *To Kill a Mockingbird*?"

"I remember it was an excuse for a date." The shock yielded to laughter and teasing, the side of Kate he liked best. "I think you asked me out to dinner because you wanted my notes."

"I wanted much more than that." He'd wanted to know the girl who had loved that book, who had argued with the professor with a confident vehemence he'd never heard in anyone before. "You were so smart in that class, Kate. In all your classes."

She dipped her head. Her cheeks flushed. "Thanks."

"We were studying, and you could tell I hadn't really read the book." That fact had been obvious in the first few minutes, when she'd mentioned a passage. He'd stared at her with a blank look and realized skimming the summary of the book wasn't going to be enough to pass.

"I said reading the CliffsNotes doesn't actually count."

He laughed. "And you were right. I wasn't much of a reader in school—too much fun to be had outside to be stuck indoors reading a book—but you refused to help me study until I read the book. 'It will change your mind about novels,' you said."

"I did say that. But I'm biased. It's one of my favorite books ever."

"So I went home and read it that weekend, cover to cover." He'd stayed up late into the night to finish, as hooked on the story as he'd been on Kate in those days. He'd skipped a canoeing trip just to get through the last few chapters. "I didn't do it because you told me to. I did it to impress you."

She closed the lid of the laptop and rested her arms on top. "Why did you want to impress me?"

"Because you were—and still are—beautiful and smart and way out of my league."

"Says the man whose multimillion-dollar company is going public in a couple of months." Kate shook her head. "And whose book is going to be published worldwide. I'm just a ghostwriter who lives in a tiny apartment with a cat."

"Money doesn't make anyone impressive," Trent said. "It just seems like it does."

"Well, I'm pretty sure the electric company would argue with that theory. They kinda like me to pay them on time."

Why didn't Kate see herself the way he saw her? She was incredibly smart and devastatingly beautiful. She'd done something he couldn't do—write a book—many times over. In the pages he had read so far, she'd managed to create something that both sounded like Trent and made Trent seem human, real. "When we were studying for the test, you asked me to pick my favorite part of the book. I told you it was when Atticus Finch says, 'I wanted you to see what real courage was' to Scout. I said I loved it because it was such a great life lesson about taking risks and getting out of your comfort zone. Do you remember what you said to me?"

She shook her head. Her green eyes watched him, fascinated, as if he were a movie with a cliffhanger. He'd never known anyone else who gave someone such complete attention.

"You said to me that real courage is about not avoiding what you are truly capable of, what you have been gifted with. You said I was smart, too smart to be goofing off in school and wasting my education, and then basically I should man up and start paying attention in school. You pushed me, Kate, to try harder, to be better, though inside I sometimes resisted—"

"And took off on a bike ride or paddle instead of going to class—"

"Leaving you behind."

"Yeah." The single word was soft and sad. "But that's all in the past."

"Is it?"

"It has to be, Trent." She flipped open her laptop again and rested her hands on the keyboard. "Let's just finish the book."

She wanted to change the conversation, to move it out of thorny, muddy territory and into something easier. Just as she hadn't let him slack in school, he wasn't going to let this go that easily.

Trent flicked on the directional and merged toward the exit for Seattle. Their road trip was almost at an end, which would mean they'd go their separate ways again. Trent wasn't quite ready for the moment to end. "I took me a while to really buckle down, but once I did, I noticed my grades went up, and I became more engaged in school. I even read more books."

She typed a sentence or two. "Authors love people who read books."

He knew she'd said the words as a joke, but hearing "love" from Kate's lips stirred something inside Trent. Something he chose to ignore for now. "I think that work ethic you sort of kicked into place for me is part of what made me so successful with GOA. Ever since college, I've been more focused on learning and reading, and being the best I can be at my job."

"That's awesome," she said. Her fingers flew across the keyboard. "That's such a great quote for the book."

He put a hand over hers, and she stopped typing. "I was saying it to thank you, Kate, not to fill a chapter or create some blurb in the book."

"Oh. Well, I..." That blush appeared again in her cheeks. "You're welcome, Trent. It was really no big deal."

"Maybe to you. But it made a big difference for me." He pulled his hand back and focused again on the road. Every other minute, it seemed he was wrapping himself up with Kate again.

So many parts of his life, though, were interwoven with her, or memories of her. She'd taught him to appreciate books, to dig deeper into the text and unearth the lesson the author had scattered among the words.

She'd been the one person who had believed in him without doubt or reservation, a cheerleader at a time when he'd really needed one.

But none of that would be in the book, at Kate's insistence. It seemed wrong, somehow, to erase the lines that underscored so much of his life.

"Oh, look, we're at my house already." Kate closed the lid of the laptop and tucked it in her bag. "I should get inside and get to work. I have so much to write and not much time to do it."

"Let me help you. Not write, but, like, get you all the takeout from Chick and Cheese you can eat." He flashed a smile at her. "You concentrate on the book, and I'll take care of everything else."

"Don't you have a business that needs you?"

He did, but right now, nothing else seemed as important as her and extending this warm feeling from the two days they'd spent together. This was all good for the book, he told himself, as if that was the real reason he wanted to linger in her presence. "Like you said, there's nothing at GOA that can't exist without me for a few more hours. Or days."

"You'd really do that for me?"

He nodded. "It's the least I can do, considering you're doing the hard part."

Her gaze narrowed, but amusement lit her face. "This wouldn't be your way of sucking up to me just to make sure I make you look like a superhero in the book?"

"Well, if that happens..." He flexed his biceps and shot her a crooked smile. "Seriously, I want to help, Kate."

"All the takeout I can eat? Hmm...that's a really good offer." She tapped her lip, as if she was giving it serious consideration, then her green eyes met his. "How do you feel about cats?"

Charlie, the traitor, took to Trent from the second he walked inside the apartment. Trent bent down, rubbed behind Charlie's ears, and the cat immediately fell in love, twining himself in and out of Trent's legs with a loving purr. "I think I've made a friend."

"Charlie hates everyone other than me. Did you slip him some chicken or something?"

Trent laughed. "No. I had some kittens around my house for a little while when I was a kid. I forgot all about that story until now."

"So maybe I'm not the only one who loves animals?" She flipped open her laptop, pressed the power button and poised her fingers over the keyboard. "Tell me all about the kittens."

"It was no big deal, really. I think I was maybe six or seven. I'm not sure because it was a long time ago. We had a stray cat living under the house, in the crawlspace under the porch. My dad tried everything to get her out, and she wouldn't leave. Turned out she had a bunch of kittens with her. I used to climb under there and feed her until she trusted me enough to get her and the kittens out from under there and into homes. I would have kept one, but my mom is really allergic to cats and dogs, hence no pets for me as a kid."

"That's so sweet of you to do for the kittens." She typed quickly. "That is totally going in the book."

He groaned. "You're going to make me sound like a softie."

"Anyone who crawls under a porch to take care of some kittens *is* a softie. The best kind of softie." Her voice had gotten all sweet and tender and was betraying her as badly as the cat. Geez. Could she get any more obvious about how she felt? This entire day had been one softie moment after another, from the way she'd seen him help his father, to the security of his hand helping her up an embankment. And then, that almost kiss...

Kate shook her head and refocused on

the book. *Priorities, Kate, priorities.* He was a client, and she had a job to do. Maybe after that was completed...

Maybe. To be honest, she was afraid of having her heart broken a second time. Once was enough.

"I'm going to shut up now," Trent said, "and go get some coffee or something, before you turn my hard-earned reputation as a hard-edged cliff climber into a marshmallow." He thumbed toward the kitchen. "Do you want me to brew some for you? Or go out and get it?"

"Coffee sounds amazing. If I have enough, I'll stay up all night and finish your book."

"Sounds like a plan," Trent called over his shoulder as he headed for the kitchen. There were a few muttered curses and the sound of cabinets being opened and closed, but within a few minutes, she heard the sound of the percolator and caught the promising scent of rich, dark caffeine.

After the couple of days with his parents, the words poured out of Kate, on the long car ride back and now in her apartment. Stories his mother and sister had shared as they'd done the dishes, observations she'd made while she'd watched Trent working the sale at the nursery, and a sense of the setting of the town where he'd grown up and its im-

pact on him. She moved on to the growth of
GOA, likening it to climbing a mountain and
including several stories about Trent's adventures in the outdoors.

The only thing missing from the book
was Kate herself. There was no mention of
them meeting in college, no mention of her
working the annuals sale. She painted a
picture of the Trent she knew, the man she
had once been in love with, filling him in with
bright colors and subtle details.

"One sugar and lots of cream, right?"
Trent called from the kitchen.

He remembered how she took her coffee?
Why did her heart melt at that realization? It
was nothing, Kate told herself. Nothing at all.
But when he brought her a perfectly sweet-
ened and lightened mug, Kate's eyes burned
a little.

"Okay, so you have a full pot of coffee but
no food in your fridge. I'm going to run by the
office, check on a couple of things, and come
back with dinner. Sound good?"

Sounded like a wonderful thing for him
to do. The kind of thing a boyfriend would do.
Kate nodded. "I appreciate it."

"No, I appreciate what you are doing.
You're turning my life into something people
will want to read." He shot her a grin, then
headed out of the apartment.

Kate sighed. Charlie, no longer spoiled

by Trent, curled up by Kate's feet and tucked his head into his chest. "What am I going to do with him, Charlie?"

The cat flicked his tail.

"I can't fall for him again. That would be crazy." She glanced at the file on her computer, then at the stack of notes she had. "I guess the best thing to do would be to finish this book and be done with the whole thing once and for all."

Writing those final words would stop this torture of seeing Trent, getting close to him, and losing herself in his world. She wanted—no, needed—to go back to her quiet, predictable life of soup with Grandma, plants on Saturdays, and books about people she wasn't in love with.

Kate took a long gulp of coffee, then started typing. She shoved her emotions to the side, in a compartment in the back of her mind, and worked her way through the notes. From time to time, she'd add a little story or another detail to other pages, fleshing it out as she went along, like an oil painting with layers of colors.

When her doorbell rang, it startled Kate out of her writing frenzy. She jerked to her feet, making Charlie meow in complaint about the sudden movement, then hurried to the door. Trent stood on the other side, a little damp from the quick shower a moment before and holding a big bag. "Trent."

"You sound surprised to see me. I don't have a key, so I had to ring the bell. I said I'd bring dinner." He held up a bag. "And something else." From behind his back, he produced a bouquet of white daisies.

"Daisies?" She took the bouquet and inhaled the light, soft fragrance. What a sweet gesture. So thoughtful. "I love them. But why…"

"You were working so hard. I wanted to thank you." As he stepped into her apartment, he leaned down and lowered his voice, the words warm against her neck, "And it never hurts, if you ask me, to make my ghostwriter happy just before she finishes your book."

Kate's face heated. Was this a romantic move? More than something professional? And did she want that? "I'll, uh, go put these in a vase." She hurried off to the kitchen.

Why did she keep falling for him? They were supposed to just be colleagues working on a project together. Why couldn't she keep that concept locked in her mind? She kept getting swept away by vistas and coffees and daisies.

"I can get that if you need to get back to work."

Trent's voice behind her made Kate draw in a sharp breath. She bit her lip and blinked, praying her eyes wouldn't betray her. "Thanks. I have one more chapter to go."

"Wow, really?"

"Yeah. Seeing your parents gave me lots of inspiration. Why don't you set up for dinner, and I'll take a break then?" Anything to get her out of the kitchen right now and give her a second to compose herself.

"Sure thing." Trent spun a slow circle in her kitchen. "Plates are...here?"

Kate nodded. She couldn't trust her voice or herself. "I'll be right back." Then she dashed into her bathroom, turned on the faucet, and took a solid minute to wrestle her emotions back into place. She touched up her makeup, brushed her hair and smoothed a wrinkle out of her shirt—all to present a ghostwriter who wasn't emotionally involved. Not because she cared whether Trent found her beautiful.

You are brilliant and breathtaking and captivating.

Had he really meant all of that? Or were they just words strung together to keep the writer happy? Verbal versions of the daisies?

Doesn't matter, she told herself. She had a job to do, and once it was finished, she could throw out the daisies, clean out these memories and move forward. Even the thought of doing that made her choke up again, which meant another minute of erasing any trace of her emotions.

When she came out of the bathroom, she saw that Trent had set up her table, with napkins and silverware and the vase of daisies in the middle. It all screamed "evening at home between a couple," and right now, Kate couldn't...she just couldn't. "I'm going to eat at my desk. Sorry. I just really want to get the book done."

"Sure." He scooped some food onto a plate, grabbed a fork and some napkins and set all of it on the space beside her computer. "Do you mind if I hang around? If you're going to be done tonight, I'd love to see how it turns out."

"Yeah. No problem." She sat at her desk, leaving the food untouched. Her appetite had deserted her somewhere between the daisies and the words *make my ghostwriter happy*. Charlie plodded over to the tabled winding himself around Trent's legs in a blatant attempt at begging for chicken.

"You know I'm a sucker for a needy face, don't you?" Trent said, his voice low and friendly. "Okay. Just one bite. Don't tell your mom."

Despite all her pretty little resolutions a moment earlier, Kate smiled, and her heart softened. She drew in a deep breath, then set to work on the last pages. The only thing standing between her and the end of everything with Trent. Again.

Thirteen

T RENT ATE, DID THE DISHES, answered some emails on his phone, watched a couple of movies, and marveled at Kate's dedication and work ethic. She had her hair back in a ponytail that exposed the easy curves of her neck. The T-shirt and yoga pants she'd changed into when she'd gotten home urged him to touch her, as if she was a soft place to fall. And the single-minded focus in her face only made him crave her attention more. When she was writing, Kate seemed to block out everything else in the room, focusing only on the words on the screen.

A few hours later, Kate let out a little whoop and pushed back from her desk. "Done."

"Really? That's pretty amazing."

"Thanks." Her cheeks flushed. "It's only words."

"If you ask me, it's a lot more than that. All that creating and thinking and writing. It's like your hands were on fire. Just amazing. So…can I read it?"

"Of course you can. It's your story. I need you to look it over for any inconsistencies or mistakes." She clicked on the screen, and the printer beside her computer whirred to life. "I'll print out a copy for you. I think it's easier to see what's missing when you're looking at the printed page."

"And you go eat." He nudged the untouched plate of food toward her. "I can't have my ghostwriter starving to death before the book is published."

Something flickered in her eyes, but she pushed a smile to her face, then grabbed her plate. "You're right. Thanks."

The printer spat out the pages, and Trent grabbed the stack. He dropped into Kate's desk chair and started to read. From the first sentence, he was hooked, and barely heard Kate heating up her food before sitting on the sofa to finally eat.

Maybe I was born an adventurer, or maybe living under the shade of the Cascade Mountains ignited that flame in my heart. I grew up an ordinary kid in an ordinary small town, with ordinary parents who own a small nursery. My mother was hearth and home, apple cobbler and warm hugs at the end of the day. My father was the one who had the love for the outdoors and a passion for anything green and vibrant. His bedtime stories were about climbing mountains and sleeping under the stars. So it was little wonder that I decided to do my first solo hike when I was ten, with a water bottle and a granola bar, and not a whole lot of preplanning.

It was as if he was listening to a tape of himself speaking as he read. The way she described the deep chasms that sliced into the side of the mountain as if the gods had cleaved the world in two. The rich, deep greens of the forest floor and the steady, imposing strength of the towering trees. The way the air he breathed on a climb filled not just his lungs, but his soul. It was poetic and beautiful and compelling.

Trent turned page after page, so attuned to Kate's words that he barely heard the soft murmur of the television or noticed her cat weaving in and out of the chair legs, seeking attention. He devoured his own story, like watching a movie unfold. He knew the plot, the details, the ending, but the way the story was told kept him glued to the seat.

Finally, a little after two in the morning, he finished the last page and set the manuscript in a neat pile on the corner of her desk. It was his life, captured in beautiful prose and true in every sense of the word except for the gaping hole where Kate should have been. She'd talked about how he had decided in the beginning of senior year to buckle down and apply himself in school, instead of telling the true story about how she had nudged him to be his best self. When the story about writing the book came up, she made it sound like comparing his life story to the mountains he loved to climb was all his idea.

He glanced over at the couch. The TV was playing, lights flickering across Kate's peaceful, still face. She'd curled up on the arm of her sofa, her dinner only half eaten, and fallen asleep. She looked so beautiful, so tranquil, and a part of him wanted to curl up on the couch beside her.

He crossed to the coffee table, but as he reached for her plate, Kate stirred and woke up. "What time is it?" Her voice was sleepy and soft.

"A little after two in the morning."

She rubbed the sleep out of her eyes and sat up. "Oh, wow. I can't believe I fell asleep."

"You've been working really hard lately. You were typing like a madwoman over there for hours."

"It's always like that at the end of a book. Sort of like rappelling down a mountain, only without the dangerous part." Kate drew her knees to her chest and hugged them. Her feet were bare, bright-red toenails peeking out from beneath the wide-leg yoga pants. "Did you read the book?"

"No." Her face fell. He dropped onto the sofa beside her and put a hand on her arm. "I *devoured* it, Kate. It was...amazing. Maybe the best book I've ever read, and not because it's my life story. Starting a company isn't always the most exciting thing, but you... you made it compelling and emotional and a hundred other things I don't have the words for. You are an incredible, amazing, talented writer, Kate. I'd call you more adjectives, but I'd need a thesaurus."

That adorable blush filled her cheeks. "Thanks. That is, after all, what you were paying me to do."

"Speaking of which..." He reached into his pocket for the slim piece of paper he'd held onto for hours. "When I ran out for dinner, I stopped by the office and had my CFO cut the check for the second half of the advance. He's mailing your agent her cut, but this is for you."

She took the check, then stared at him. "Why are you giving me this? Normally, the client just sends the check to Angie and then she pays me."

"I couldn't wait any longer."

"To hand me thousands of dollars?" Kate chuckled. "I'm not going to complain about that, but really, Angie sends me my part of the fee right away."

"I couldn't wait to fire you, essentially." He shifted over to the coffee table, close enough that their knees could almost touch. "Because if you're no longer working for me, we can go on a proper date."

Kate's mouth opened. Closed. She blinked. "Maybe I'm still a bit sleepy and not with it, but did you just...ask me out?"

"I do believe I did. And I don't mean a dinner in a diner. You deserve more than that, Kate. Something special. So let's get dressed up and go out for dinner tomorrow—" he glanced at the clock, "—technically, tonight for dinner. After you get some sleep and I stop by the office for a little while. I'll pick you up at seven, and we'll go somewhere fancy and delicious."

A smile blossomed on her face, as bright as sunshine after a storm. "That sounds wonderful, Trent."

"Then it's a date, and I mean that. It's a date." All those hours he'd spent watching her work, then reading the amazing story she'd put together, had quadrupled his respect for her and reminded him of how empty his life had been without Kate. The story he'd read didn't make sense without her, and it had taken all those pages before he'd understood that fact. He got to his feet and grabbed his car keys off the table. "I'll let you get some sleep, Kate. Before I go, I just want to say thank you."

"For what?"

"For creating something amazing with your words. You are a truly gifted writer. And I can't wait to see what happens next." He wanted to kiss her, wanted that more than anything, but no. It would wait. Kate deserved a special night, a moment as beautiful as she was, and Trent intended to deliver.

"You are singing to my primroses." Grandma parked a fist on her hip. "What happened?"

Kate giggled, actually giggled, like a high schooler in love. "I finished writing Trent's book and when I was done, he said—" she took in a deep breath, "—that he wants to date me."

"It's about time that silly man saw what a prize you are." Grandma patted her cheek. "You look happy, my dear. I'm glad to see that."

"I am happy." As she said the words, she realized they were true. Reconnecting with Trent, spending all that time hiking and at his parents' house—all of it had been fun. They'd flirted and joked, talked and confessed. And tonight, they had a date planned.

She didn't care where they went or what they ate—all she knew was that she was going to be with Trent as his girlfriend, not his ghostwriter. That thought made her as giddy as she had been in college before that first dinner at Chick and Cheese.

"Sometimes," Grandma said as she picked up one of the seedlings that was growing too tall for the starter pot, "all it takes is some time to make something grow from nothing. Maybe you two needed those years apart to appreciate each other now."

"Maybe so." Kate pressed a kiss to her grandmother's cheek. "I've got to go get ready for my date. I'll be back on Saturday, and we'll hit the farmer's market. It's supposed to be a lovely day, so a few of the vendors will be there. And, I'm going to treat you to lunch, wherever you want to go. Don't you dare say no, because I'm doing it anyway."

"You are the best granddaughter anyone could ever have." Grandma hugged her tight. "And you tell that boy I'm glad he finally smartened up."

Kate was still laughing as she climbed in her car. The skies opened up, and she looked around the Honda for her raincoat—of course, not here again—but Trent's jacket was, and Kate slipped it on just to have the scent of him nearby. She hummed as she drove, doing a mental inventory of her dresses. Maybe the black one. No, the blue, because it would offset the green of her eyes and the brown in her hair. Like the sky on a sunny day.

Just as she pulled into her apartment parking lot, her phone rang. Kate's agent's profile picture lit up the screen. "Hey, Angie, what's up?"

"Can you come in right now? I have some...news for you."

"Sure. What about?"

"It's better if we talk in person. See you in a few."

Hmm. That was unlike Angie to be so vague and so insistent on an in-person meeting rather than a quick heads-up on the phone. Kate turned the car around and headed across town. The skies had turned gloomy, and the temperature had dropped several degrees while she'd been at Grandma's. The weatherman had forecasted a storm moving in, with wind and up to four inches of snow. If she was lucky, the storm would hang on the coast and not hit Seattle before the weekend, or before her date to-night.

But as she parked and went into Angie's office, an angry wind snapped at the fleece jacket and chased up her spine. Kate drew the oversized coat tighter to her body and hurried inside to Angie's office, where the air was warm. "What's up?"

Angie's face was lined and serious. She gestured toward the chair across from her. "You're going to want to sit down for this."

Kate sank down, and a heaviness settled in her gut. "Uh-oh. That doesn't sound good."

"It's not." Angie picked up her tablet and clicked on the screen, swiping to get to a specific app. "Do you know Loretta Wildwood?"

"Yeah, sure. We went to college together, and I've run into her a few times this month. She invited me to that networking event, where I met Penny. The other writer who's going to critique with me."

"Well, it seems Loretta was determined to blow your cover and—" Angie handed the tablet over, "—she has."

There, in bright color and a bold headline, right under a picture of a smiling Loretta, was Kate's face beside Trent's. The words screamed back at Kate, harsh and blaring: *Ghostwriter is Author of Former Boyfriend's Book*

Her worst nightmare, right there on the screen. Her identity public, and her relationship with Trent made public at the same time. The article implied there was still some feelings between them and that her emotions had shaped the words she'd written, making Trent look better than he was. Kate's emotions had shaped her writing, but she would never paint a picture of anything other than the truth. "This isn't happening. This can't be happening."

But it was. The look on Angie's face was enough to tell Kate the enormity of Loretta's public outing. "Keep reading," Angie said. "It doesn't get better, unfortunately."

Kate dropped her attention back to the blog post. *It's always interesting the things you learn when you research a character,* Loretta had written, *and for my newest book (available in stores in November! Order your copy today!) I based one of my characters on my friend, Kate Winslow. She and I went to the same college, and while I became a real author, she became a ghostwriter.*

Kate bristled. Loretta's condescending attitude was infuriating. "Just because my name isn't on the book doesn't mean I'm not a real author."

"I know." Angie sighed. "We both know that. Loretta, though, had some kind of point to prove."

I came across a blog by a ghostwriter, called The Secret Life of a Ghost, and was using that for my research, when lo and behold, I read a little tidbit about networking at an author event and how that had been so much fun for the ghostwriter. She talked about working in a coffee shop and eating chocolate chunk cookies, and I thought...I know a ghost-writer who went to that party and who likes chocolate chunk cookies...could it be?

So I did my sleuthing (as all good mystery authors should) and found this picture. Right by the mention of cookies and parties, Loretta had posted the photo Kate had shared of the waterfall at Moulton State Park. *And I also found this one, by another former college friend (and Kate's old boyfriend), Trent MacMillan, who owns that sporting goods company. I follow him, because, you know, he's an old friend.*

"I don't think Loretta ever said two words to Trent." Kate shook her head and scrolled down, seeing that the story did indeed, as Angie had promised, get worse. Loretta had found Trent's Instagram picture with the boot in it, then mentioned seeing Kate in a GOA jacket.

But the final clue that solved the mystery was this!!! Loretta had made the exclamation points bold and had even added a bright red arrow pointing to another photo. In an instant, Kate recognized it from twenty-four hours ago—had it really only been a day?—up on Mt. Cascade, with Trent and his mountain fan—

And Kate standing off to the side. She hadn't stepped into the picture, but the girlfriend of the dreadlocks kid must have kept the zoom angled wide enough to capture Kate too.

"Maybe the clients won't figure it out?" Kate said, but her voice was high and tenuous.

Before Angie shook her head, Kate knew the horse had already escaped the barn, and it was too late to think they could keep the secret. "Loretta is pretty well known, and you know how things spread on social media. I already have a call from Gerard, wanting to make sure no one is going to put together that you wrote his book, and three other people's messages on my voicemail."

"This is going to ruin my career." Kate's body began to shake, and flashes of heat and cold ran through her. All these years, she had worked hard to be circumspect and to not disclose the identity of her clients. One blog post from Loretta, and all that was gone. "What am I going to do?"

She thought of Trent's company, which needed stability and good publicity ahead of the IPO. How hard he had worked to build GOA from the ground up. And maybe a little selfishly, she thought of the two of them, how they'd reconnected and just now had started to build something special. All of that was at risk of disappearing because of this one moment.

"What about the NDA?" Kate asked.

"Like, could Trent sue me?" Would he sue her? She'd like to think not, but this exposure could seriously damage his company and his reputation. Those kinds of stakes could change...everything.

"We'll worry about that when we get to it, if we get to it," Angie said. "I think we can make a pretty valid case that you didn't do anything that exposed the connection."

"Still..." Kate buried her face in her hands. "This is a disaster. It will destroy my career, at the very least."

"Well, maybe you should look at it as an opportunity," Angie said as she gently took the tablet back and turned off the screen. "You could finally send me those chapters of your novel and see where that goes."

Hadn't she procrastinated on finishing her novel long enough? All those hikes and the day working at the nursery and the chances she had taken in the last few weeks had done one thing—it had taught Kate that she was stronger and more capable than she had ever believed. "I did make enough money from finishing Trent's book to cover my bills for a few months." Finishing that novel, without the parachute of another ghostwriting contract, was still a risk, but if not now, when? She was tired of waiting for her life to be everything she dreamed of. Tired of being the one on the sidelines, not the one in the middle of the conversations. "All right. I'll send you what I have as soon as I get home. If you think it's good—"

"Of course it will be. You're an amazing writer."

"Then I'll finish it." Kate glanced at the now-dark tablet sitting on Angie's desk. Nerves and regrets rolled in her stomach, an angry storm that left her nauseated and scared, despite her brave statement a minute ago. There would be fallout yet to come from Loretta's blog post, which meant this wasn't over. Not by a long shot. There was still a possibility Loretta wouldn't figure out the identity of the other authors Kate had ghosted for, but it didn't matter.

This earthquake in the middle of her career, Trent's company, and their relationship had thrown them all into a deep cavern. Somehow she needed to find a way to climb out and fix what had happened.

Fourteen

I F THERE WAS ONE THING Trent loved about social media, it was how quickly news could spread. If there was one thing he hated…

It was how quickly news could spread.

Sarah had stormed into his office first thing that morning, showing him a stream of connections from some author's blog—an author who claimed to be his friend from college, but he didn't remember her at all—to another author's Twitter feed, to another and another, until an online tabloid got ahold of the story about Kate being the real author behind his book. The tabloid blasted it across their homepage, calling Trent a fraud. In a matter of hours, the entire thing had gone viral and was undoubtedly making its way into the feeds and inboxes of his investors. As they were wont to do to up ratings and readers, the tabloid turned the story into a doubting taunt about the irony of a title with the word *True*, because Trent was lying about writing the book. They peppered the article with lots of questions about what else Trent might be lying about. Like his profits. His sales. His future.

The worst kind of rumors any company could have just before it went public. This had the makings of an epic disaster.

His stomach knotted. He'd spent so much time with Kate, had opened his heart and past, and paid her to write to keep this confidential. Had she betrayed him? The thought that she could have done this on purpose—either for her own career or for money or for some other reason—drove a fist into the nausea churning in his gut.

"We have to do something, Trent," Sarah said. Dark shadows dusted the space under her eyes, and her lips were set in a grim line. Everything Trent needed to know about the cost of this story was written all over Sarah's face. "We can't afford bad publicity. Not now."

"I know. I know. I'll figure something out."

"The irony is that you can't be honest and tell everyone you used a ghostwriter. If you do, then people are going to doubt the authenticity of the book, especially because there is a proven previous relationship between you and Kate," she said. "You've built this company on a premise of being a hundred percent open about your life, your adventures, your struggles."

"That was about hiking and cycling tours, Sarah. Not writing. People shouldn't be surprised I had help with writing the book. This—" he waved around the office, "—is my specialty, not words."

Sarah worried her bottom lip, something she only did when she was nervous. "That's not going to be enough. This is a major blow to the company, the book, everything. There are going to be questions and doubts for years to come, so we need to do damage control right now. We'll figure out something you can say to minimize this story. But before I work on some kind of a statement…"

"What?" he prompted.

Sarah shifted her weight and averted her gaze. "Do you think there's any possibility that Kate sold the story about the ghostwriting to maybe make some extra money? I mean, I know you trust her, but some of those tabloids pay an awful lot for gossip and rumors."

"Kate would never." Would she? He hadn't seen her in almost fifteen years, and he had to admit, the irony of being paired with his ex-girlfriend as his writer was an awfully convenient event. Had Kate somehow arranged to be the writer for his book? He thought of the woman he had once known and the one he had met again last month. Sure, she lived rather cheaply, in a one-bedroom apartment that could use an update or ten, but nothing about Kate gave him the sense that she was a mercenary person.

"I only met her once, but I frankly can't see her doing that either. Still, you never know with people." Sarah shrugged. "Either way, I think you should issue a public statement, maybe with that magazine that's doing the profile in a couple of weeks. That gives us time to see if this dies down before we make any kind of big response. If we do issue a statement in the interview, it should take care of any lingering doubts anyone might be having. Their magazine has a lot more prestige in the marketplace than that...trash on the internet, so hopefully that mitigates some of the damage."

"Which magazine?" Trent felt like he was running in seven hundred directions, trying to get ready for the book launch, the IPO, and now dealing with this.

"*Outdoor Fun.* Remember the one Carissa took the pictures for? Just reiterate the company line, that everything was written by you and not a ghostwriter. We'll paint Kate as an editor or something. You have a sit-down with them scheduled in a couple of weeks, and we can use that as an opportunity to get your message out."

He glanced at the story on his computer screen. Just while they'd been talking, another ten comments had been posted, and email notifications were popping up like weasels on his home screen. "What do we do until then? This thing seems to be spreading pretty fast."

"Talk to Kate. Make sure she's not part of it. If she isn't, then maybe send out a joint statement on social media."

Doing that would expose Kate as a ghostwriter, which Trent had to think wasn't good for her business. Albeit, she was already exposed, and that information was hurting *his* business. How did he choose which to save? What was fair?

Maybe there was a way to help them both, but if there was, Trent couldn't see his way to that answer.

"I'll think about it. Thanks, Sarah."

He paced his office for a long time after Sarah left, thinking and strategizing. Working his way through one direction and another, turning the problem every direction he could think. As the rest of the office began to filter out and head home, Trent grabbed his coat and headed out the door. A storm had been brewing all afternoon, and the wind whipped around him as he crossed the parking lot. Snowflakes spattered his cheeks, his hair, and coated his windshield with a pale white curtain.

His cell rang twice while he was driving. Both times, Kate trying to reach him, but he let her calls go to voicemail until he figured out what to do about this disaster and he could tamp down the anger in his chest. If he talked to her right now, he was afraid his temper would explode. So far, the media didn't have his private cell number, but Trent was sure it was only a matter of time before he got those calls too. Sarah was right. He needed some kind of party line statement.

The storm had started picking up, snow falling heavier and thicker now, as Trent pulled into her building's lot. He ducked inside the building, then took the stairs two at a time. When he knocked on her door and she opened it, he realized what time it was.

If none of this had happened, he would have been picking Kate up for a date. They would have laughed and kissed, like they had in the old days. Now, that was ruined, maybe forever. And maybe on purpose by her.

"Obviously, I'm not here for dinner," he said, his voice cold and harsh.

"Obviously." She drew in a deep breath. "Why don't we go somewhere and talk about what happened? I tried to call you several times, but you didn't answer."

He swallowed hard and, once again,

stood across from this beautiful, incredible woman and broke her heart, ending them before they could become anything. "We're aren't going out to dinner. We're definitely not going out together in public. We need to have a serious talk about how this happened and who leaked the information, Kate." As soon as he said the words, her face fell and Trent wished he could take them back.

"Let's get the conversation over with then. You might as well come in before someone sees you on my doorstep and thinks you're actually involved with me." She opened the door, and he crossed to the couch. Kate sat in the chair at her desk, a clear division between them.

Trent hesitated, clasping his hands together and wishing the carpet would give him some kind of answer. He got the first, most important, and most painful question out of the way first. Like ripping off a bandage—maybe if he did it quickly, the words wouldn't sting so much. "Did you give this Loretta woman some kind of inside scoop?"

Kate bristled. "You know me, Trent. Why would I do that?"

"She figured it out somehow. No one in my company, besides my CFO and Sarah, knew about this book arrangement."

"I went to college with Loretta," she explained. "We were in writing classes together and a critique group after school, so I'm sure she saw us together when we were dating. I ran into her a month or so ago, and she took this crazy interest in my ghostwriting. I had no idea she would put all that together. Then she saw me wearing your jacket, and I kinda said it was...my boyfriend's."

"What? Why would you say that?"

"I was caught off guard and I didn't say it was yours. It was just a GOA jacket I could have gotten anywhere."

"Then how did she figure this out?"

"If someone follows both you on Instagram and me on my blog, they could notice the similar pictures from our hike at the falls. You had the one with my boot, and I had a more generic one of the landscape. I didn't put your face up there or your name, though, and I never would have connected that boot to me. But she's a mystery writer and followed all those breadcrumbs..."

"Right back to me and my company." Trent sighed. Charlie the Cat wove his way between Trent's legs, begging for an ear rub. Trent gave the cat a little attention and relaxed his stance. Kate had been just as affected by this story as he had been, and they needed to be on the same team. "I believe you. I'm sorry I questioned you at all. You're right, I do know you and you're not the kind of person who would sell me out, or anyone else for that matter."

"The story is out there, and I can't erase it. I wish I could." She slipped off the sandals and set them side by side on the floor.

For some reason, the sight of Kate's heels sitting there, not to be worn tonight, filled him with a deep sadness. If this media firestorm hadn't happened, he would have been taking her out to dinner, watching her laugh, hearing her sweet voice, and maybe kissing her goodnight. Now...

"I think the best thing to do is to put as much distance between us and that story as possible," he said. "I'll make an announcement that I did work with you on my book, but only as an editor. All the words are mine."

"Okay."

"And..." he drew in a breath, "I think it's best if we don't see each other for several weeks. The last thing we need is people putting us together and thinking we are hiding something else."

The sorrow in her face nearly undid him. Trent told himself he was doing what was best—for the company, for himself, and for Kate. They were still two different people, and they were still on two different trajectories.

"So, I'll call you in a few weeks, okay?"

Kate got to her feet, her spine straight

and her demeanor cold and distant. "I don't think that's a good idea. At some point, Trent, you have to stop hovering on the shore and just dive in. Until you do that, I think our business is concluded, don't you?" Then she crossed the room, opened the door, and waited for him to leave.

Trent stepped out into an angry squall and climbed in his car. He sat there for a long time while a storm raged around him and he wondered why making the right decision made him feel so terrible.

Fifteen

THE NEXT MORNING, KATE PACKED up
Charlie, her laptop, and some clothes
and headed to Grandma Wanda's.
Losing everything had spurred her to finally take some action in another direction.
Grandma took one look at Kate's face, drew
her into a tight, warm hug, and whispered
the magic words, "I made cookies. Let's go eat
as many as possible."

As the snow fell outside and the world
dealt with slushy streets and chilly days,
Kate ignored the internet and her social media. Let her calls go to voicemail. Instead, she
plugged in her laptop, opened up the file for
her novel and started to write. She had nothing else to risk by doing this—her ghostwriting career was toast for the time being—so it
gave her a courage she had never had before
to write and submit. Angie had read the first

few chapters and sent back one word: AMAZ-ING! Then a second email that had said FIN-ISH IT!

The encouragement lit a fire under Kate, and she immersed herself in words and story, the characters and their world becoming as real as her own. The love of writing that she'd had when she'd been younger returned, as if some switch had been flipped in her brain, and all the "writer's block" she'd had for years disappeared. She wrote all day and long into the night, taking advantage of the quiet and peace at her grandmother's house.

On the third afternoon, Penny texted and asked Kate if she wanted to talk shop and grab a glass of wine. Kate met her at a cozy bar downtown, and over the course of the next couple of hours, the two of them exchanged pages and opinions.

"So," Penny said, setting Kate's printed pages to the side. "Now that we're done, let's talk about the elephant on the internet that we haven't mentioned. I heard what Loretta did. That was wrong, in case I haven't said so."

"Actually, it's okay." Kate ran a finger along the rim of her wine glass. Two raspberries sat at the base of the delicate flute of sparkling Moscato. "I may never ghostwrite again, but it did force me to start working on my novel. And that may never have happened if not for Loretta."

"Well, that is a good way to look at it, because the novel is terrific," Penny said. "I can't wait to see how it ends. I'm really hooked on those sisters and their mom. It's such a...warm story. Feels like they're my own family, you know?"

Kate beamed. "I'm so glad to hear that. And I really loved your suspense novel. That chapter had me on the edge of my seat."

"We make good critique partners." Penny clinked glasses with Kate. "I hope I get to talk words with you a lot more often, Kate."

"Me too." She gathered up her pages and laid down some cash for the tab. "It was good to get out—not just out of the house, but out of my comfort zone. I think that's all I've done for the last two months—things that scare me."

"And I'm sure it's made you a better writer." Penny finished her last sip of chardonnay. "Speaking of things that affect your writing...have you heard from Trent?"

Kate filled Penny in on everything that had happened in the days since Loretta's expose blog. Considering the whole thing had become a public conversation, she didn't see the sense in not talking about it. "I told him I don't want to see him again. I mean, I do, but not if he wants to stand on the sidelines of our relationship."

Penny covered her mouth and bit back a giggle. "I'm sorry, I don't mean to laugh, but from everything you've told me about him, it seems like you were the one who did that before. Now you're the risk-taker and he's the scared one?"

It did seem like the tables had turned. Maybe once she'd started doing the things Trent liked to do, he had lost his argument about why a relationship between them would never work. Maybe Penny was right and this had nothing to do with the blog post and more to do with Trent being scared of what that meant for the future.

"It doesn't matter." Kate got to her feet and grabbed her purse. "We're over."

Penny put a hand on hers. "Maybe you are, maybe you aren't. You still have a few chapters to write in your own story, and the ending is still up in the air. Could it be the same with Trent?"

Kate tucked her pages into her bag. "Sometimes, Penny, you have to know when to stop trying to make the story work."

Greg pounded out the miles beside Trent, the two of them not talking as Trent struggled to keep up with Greg's long legs. Trent was happy with the silence, if only because it gave him time to puzzle out the Kate situation and relieve the stress of the last week. The calls to GOA's offices had been nonstop. The backlash on social media had been swift and strong, a critical whip for the first few days. Then attention began to die down, and Sarah's efforts to promote more positive aspects of GOA's environmental and charitable efforts began to change the tide.

There'd be more to do once the book came out, but he'd worry about that then. For now, there was the nagging question of whether he had been wrong to mistrust Kate. She'd made it clear she didn't want to hear from him, and thus far, she hadn't responded to any of his emails or texts. She'd done the minor revisions he'd requested, but had sent them back through her agent, putting as much distance between them as she could.

Trent told himself it was all for the better, and kept on running. Maybe one of these days the run would quiet all the thoughts in his brain.

As they rounded the bend that marked the halfway point of their run, Greg slowed his pace. "This is our fifth run in as many days. Are you training for a race or avoiding something?"

"Is it that obvious?"

Greg arched a brow in answer.

Trent stopped running and bent over, drawing in deep breaths. "I can't keep up with you, man. You're killing me."

"I don't mind walking for a bit." Greg waited for Trent to straighten, then the two of them headed down the path. "I wanted to thank you for the drum set you got Dana for her birthday. Or rather, not thank you." He pressed his hands to his ears. "Next thing we're getting her is lessons."

Trent chuckled at the image of Greg's eight-year-old daughter banging on the drumset. "I'm the godfather. I'm supposed to buy toys that annoy the parents and make the kid happy."

"Excellent job on that." Greg grinned. "When she was six, she wanted a pony. I'm glad she didn't tell you about that one."

"I would have gotten one." Trent winked. "She is the cutest kid, so it's hard to say no."

"I agree. I would hang the moon on her wall if she asked me to. Last Christmas, she wanted this miniature pony toy. It was on her list to Santa, and she wanted it to have real horse hair. Do you know, I spent weeks looking online and in antique shops and hobby shops, trying to find one?"

"Really? That's so...sentimental of you." Trent gave his friend a shoulder jab. "Nah, seriously, that's sweet."

"I didn't find one until Christmas Eve. I was driving home from work, I was exhausted, and I just wanted to get home. I saw this one shop I'd never noticed before, and it was still open. At the last second, I decided to stop in, and what do you know? They had the exact thing Dana had asked for. I bought it, wrapped it up, and made her Christmas morning."

Trent would like to think he would be that kind of dad when he had kids. He realized that for the first time, his mind had thought the word "when," not 'if.' A future, where he was married and settled down and had a family? Maybe not such an impossibility with someone like...Kate? Either way, it was a thought for way down the road.

"My point, and I had one in telling you about the Christmas pony, is if she's worth it, you go the extra mile." Greg put up his hands in a don't-shoot-the-messenger move. "I read about the whole thing with Kate and your book and the company in some online magazine. The internet trolls are saying she wrote a biased piece and it isn't the truth. But I've heard you talk about Kate a couple of times on long runs, and she doesn't sound like the kind of woman who would lie. She sounds like the kind who knows you pretty darn well and would shoot it to you straight, like Virginia does with me. I also get the feeling she's the kind of woman who's worth going all the way to Montlake Terrace."

Trent thought back and realized Kate's name had come up in some of those long-run conversations with Greg. All these years, Trent had thought he'd moved on, forgotten her, but she'd clearly lingered in his mind all along. "I could go to Timbuktu and it wouldn't matter. I think she hates me right now."

"Then maybe you have to go farther," Greg said, breaking into a jog again. "And faster, you slowpoke turtle!"

Trent sucked in a breath and ran after Greg, pounding the pavement until his lungs hurt and his mind stopped replaying his last conversation with Kate and the hurt that had been in her eyes. Once again, he'd broken her heart.

With Penny's advice in mind, Kate went back to work on her novel over the next few days. She'd talk the story through with her grandmother from time to time and read some passages aloud as they sat out on the porch at night, looking for the Big Dipper and eating whatever batch of cookies was fresh from the oven.

Grandma raved about every chapter like

it was the next *War and Peace*, of course. Kate reminded herself that this was her grandmother, who would rave about Kate's grocery list, but either way, there just seemed to be something wonderful happening with this story. Even Kate could feel it as she wrote.

Trent called and texted, but Kate ignored him. At least once a day, he asked if they could talk, but she never replied. She'd already fallen for him twice and had had her heart broken both times. Only a fool went back for a third strike.

All of it was compounded by the guilt she felt about what had happened. She hadn't been the one to expose the truth, but maybe if she hadn't talked to Loretta or hadn't worn his jacket...

Trent was undoubtedly still angry about what had happened, and Kate wasn't sure she could hear that at the same time she was nursing a broken heart.

The writing helped her block out that pain and the memories of him. Every once in a while, she'd pull up the picture of the falls and allow her heart a moment to mourn. Then she'd click the photo away and go back to her fictional world that didn't have a ghostwriter, a Loretta, or a Trent darkening the pages.

She blocked out the rest of the world too,

avoiding social media, her blog, her emails. Kate kept her head down and kept working on the book. As page after page poured out of her, her self-confidence grew, and the words flowed even faster. She helped Grandma turn over the soil and fertilize the garden, getting it ready for the spring planting. She made lots of soups, typing while the ingredients simmered or tea brewed in the delicate china cups Grandma loved so much. The weather began to abate as March began to edge toward April, and Kate set a little time aside every day to visit the garden and greenhouse.

"Thank you for everything," Grandma said. Today, the two of them were working together, transplanting a trio of red geraniums bursting out of their pots. "But you've been with me for over two weeks now. I love having you here, but maybe you should go back to your own life."

"Charlie's here, you're here, and my laptop's here. I have everything I need." Okay, so maybe Grandma had a point and Kate was hiding from the things she didn't want to face, but it was all for a good cause—her grandmother and her novel.

"You have everything...except for the man you're in love with."

"I'm not in love with him, Grandma." It was amazing how easily the lie slipped from her mouth and how believable the words sounded. "I just...got swept up in believing we had something real this time. I should have been more cautious."

Grandma's hand covered hers. "Love is about risk. Caution has no place in the equation."

Kate scoffed. "I did that once. Not going to do it again."

Grandma lowered herself into the wooden chair beside the potting table. She set the geraniums aside and began selecting some of the hardier cucumber plants that would go in the garden soon. "Did you know Grandpa Jack and I broke up once?"

"Really? No, I never heard that." Her grandfather had been a charming, witty man who'd adored her grandmother. Every time he'd looked at her, it was as if he'd been watching a rainbow in the sky. They'd met as teenagers and had married straight out of high school. When Kate was six, he'd died, and it had taken decades for Grandma to get over the loss of her best friend.

"Your grandfather was a stubborn man, for all his charms." Grandma's eyes watered at the memory of her late husband. He'd been tall and dashing, with a full head of hair and pale green eyes that had always seemed to sparkle. "When we met, I was sixteen and he was seventeen. My father wasn't going to let his little girl leave with an older man—"

at that, Grandma laughed a little, "—so we sat on my front porch most evenings, sipping lemonade and playing cards."

"That sounds perfect, if you ask me."

"Those are some of my favorite memories, I must say. You learn what a man is made of when you can't go off fadiddling around alone with him. Jack was happy just to be with me. Didn't matter what we were doing."

"People on Mars could see how much he loved you, Grandma."

"And I loved him just as much. I thought we were going to get married, soon as I graduated high school, but then your grandpa got this foolish idea the day he turned eighteen. He decided he was going to see the world with his cousin and just leave me to pine away at home."

"What did you do?"

"I told him to go right on ahead and see the world." Grandma raised her chin, and even all these years later, Kate could see the strength and defiance in her face. "I wasn't going to wait on him to realize I was the best woman he was ever going to meet. Then I took my lemonade, went back in the house and shut off the porch light, leaving that silly man in the dark."

Kate laughed. "How did he take it?"

"I told you, he's a stubborn man. I kept my back to that door, just waiting for him to knock and apologize and say of course he knew I was the best woman he'd ever met. Instead, that silly man went off to see the world."

"He did? I didn't know that." Kate didn't remember her grandfather ever talking about traveling when he was young. As far as she knew, he'd gotten married, gotten a job at Boeing as an engine repairman and had eventually worked his way up to management.

"Well, that's because he didn't get very far. Jack and his cousin set out the next morning. They made it all the way to Denver before he came to his senses. He turned that car around and came right back to Seattle. His cousin had been sleeping, and when he woke up, they were heading west. Oh, his cousin was as mad as a hornet at that, but Jack said he kept on driving until he got back to my front porch. He knocked on my door, and my father answered and gave him a good yelling at for breaking my heart."

"Poor Grandpa Jack." Kate giggled. "I bet he deserved it."

"Of course he did. But as soon as my dad was done yelling, Jack said, 'Sir, you're right about everything you just said. I was a fool, but now I'm back, and I'd like to ask for your daughter's hand in marriage.' My father said to him, 'Why would I let my daughter marry a fool?' And you know what your Grandpa Jack said?"

Kate shook her head.

"'Because this fool knows that she isn't just the best woman in Seattle, she's the best woman in the whole wide world.'" Grandma's smile stretched ear to ear. She swiped away a tear before it could fall. "Oh, how I miss that man."

"Well, I wish he was here to give Trent a stern, what'd you call it? Yelling at." Kate sighed. "I don't think he's going to come around."

Grandma waggled her fingers in the direction of the vegetable seedlings. "Bring me that tomato plant. That one I made you take home a few weeks ago."

Kate did as her grandmother asked, placing the pot in her hands. "I didn't think you noticed I brought him back."

"Him." Grandma chuckled. "See? I'm rubbing off on you. Look at how good he's doing."

"Well, he finally got his own pot. I'm sure that helped the plant grow." She fingered the thick green stalks and serrated leaves that spread in triplicate from the end of each stem.

"Exactly. Branching out on his own helped this little guy be the best he could be." Grandma set the pot on the wooden table and clasped one of Kate's hands in both her own. "Just like you did this past month."

"All I did was work on my novel."

"You did so much more than that. You took a job that meant risking your heart again. You went on adventures—"

"We didn't exactly climb Mt. Everest."

"—and you braved a terrible storm from that awful blog," Grandma went on undeterred, "while deciding to tell the story you were meant to tell. When you did all that, you had no idea what was waiting for you, or what weeds you'd encounter, but you did it anyway."

"Writing Trent's book was my job. I needed the money and..." Kate let out a long breath. "You're right. I could have turned it down and taken a different job. When that blog came out, I could have quit writing."

"Instead, here you are, working on that lovely novel and taking a chance with your talent."

"And hiding out from the world, and Trent." She had become a hermit of sorts, only venturing out to see Penny and trade pages. The writing had been part work, part excuse to avoid everything.

"You're simply giving that silly man an opportunity to realize you are the best woman in the world." Grandma gave Kate's hands a little squeeze. "It's all in how you look at things. If you keep looking for clouds, that's all you're going to see."

Once again, her grandmother had just the right wisdom at just the right time, and in a moment when Kate hadn't even realized how much she needed the support. Kate gathered her grandmother in a tight hug. "I love you so much, Grandma. Thank you, for always being there for me."

"You don't have to thank me, sweetheart." Grandma drew back and gave Kate a smile. This time, when a tear escaped, she didn't brush it away. "I do it for the soup."

Sixteen

T RENT ALMOST WORE A HOLE in the carpet of his office, pacing back and forth in front of the windows. The magazine interview was later today, and he'd rehearsed the statement Sarah had given him at least a dozen times.

"You look like a polar bear who's been in the zoo too long," Jeremy said from his seat on the leather sofa. He'd come in earlier with the charts and projections for the company. Everything looked to be on track, despite a slight dip after the terrible press from the blog post. "Will you quit pacing?"

Trent dropped into his desk chair. "I'm just worried about this interview. If I say the wrong thing, I could mess up everything." As much as Trent had hoped the whole thing would just go away, it hadn't. People were still talking about the controversy behind who had really written his book.

Jeremy leaned back in the visitor's chair and crossed one leg over his knee. "You need to stop that."

"What, worrying about messing up the company? That's all I do, Jeremy."

"No, that's all *I* should do. You're the vision, Trent. Your instincts brought us to where we are today. You've taken risks I never would have. Made decisions that made my heart stop. Not everything worked out, of course, but by and large, because you jumped off mountains, GOA has become a force to be reckoned with. So don't worry about the company. I'll do enough of that for the both of us." He held up the spreadsheets and reports he'd been analyzing earlier. "Just go on taking those risks and living outside those neat little boxes the rest of the world has."

"Kate said something very similar to me," Trent said. It seemed like a million years since she had stood in his conference room, looking beautiful and fierce. Every single day, he had tried to reach Kate, but she wasn't responding. He'd sent flowers to her apartment that had gone undelivered, because she'd never answered the door. He'd texted and emailed, called and left messages. Nothing.

"Well, if you ask me, Kate knows you

pretty well. I read the book, and it's like she peeked inside your skull. I've known you for fifteen years, and even I learned a few things. She did an excellent job."

Trent had thought so too, but it was good to see Jeremy agreeing. Sarah had also looked at the pages and told him last week that she thought the book was amazing. "Kate did a fabulous job writing the book. I shouldn't be taking credit for it." Sarah had helped him craft a statement that clarified Trent was the sole author of *Be True to Your Nature* and reiterating that Kate had merely served in an advisory role for structuring the content.

Since that day, Trent had printed out the book and read it three times, and every time, the guilt about that statement haunted him a little more. None of it was true, just as his memoir was less than truthful. Jeremy and Sarah might think it was a realistic portrait of Trent, but he knew the truth—that there was a hole in his history and a falseness in his byline.

"Well, do what you think is best for the company." Jeremy got to his feet and clapped Trent on the shoulder. "You always do."

"Yeah, sure. I'll try." The problem? For the first time in his life, Trent didn't know what to do. He stared at the statement on his desk until the words blurred. Beside it sat the printed manuscript, with his name beneath the title. He felt lost and alone, like he had gone too far to figure out his way back to the right thing.

Trent picked up his phone and dialed a number he hadn't called in so long, he wasn't sure the other end would answer. It rang three times, and then the strident voice of his father boomed through the speaker. "Hey, Dad."

"Trent. It's a surprise to hear your voice."

Meaning for years, Trent had let months go by between contacting or seeing his family. Not because he didn't care, but because he let work get in the way of what was important. Guilt washed over him. "I was just calling to see how the nursery was doing."

"Good. That sale is always a great kickoff to the season. I'm glad the weather finally broke and it's getting warmer out during the day. People will be wanting to do some planting now. Marla's got a lot of new design clients, so it looks to be a busy spring for us."

When had his relationship with his father become one of small talk about the weather and gardens? All those years Trent had stayed away, determined to carve out his own path, had come at the cost of the relationship with his family. When he'd been back home with Kate, she'd been the bridge between them all, the one who had made it easier for him to connect. Maybe it was time he did some of that work on his own.

"Is that all you wanted?" his dad asked. "I have some things to do."

It would be so easy to hang up, end the call, and go back to the frosty impasse he'd had for too long with his father. "Not yet," Trent said. "I wanted to ask you something. Do you remember that time you rescued me when I got stuck on Mt. Cascade?"

His father chuckled. "Of course I do. You scared me so badly that day. I was afraid a bear would get you before I could get there."

"I never asked you...how did you find me? I mean, how did you know where to go?"

His father paused for a long time. In the background, Trent could hear the sound of passing cars, which meant Dad was probably outside the nursery. "At first, I wasn't sure. Like I said, I was so scared and worried that I went off in five different directions. I was calling you and looking for you and panicking more every second."

Trent had no children of his own, but he could imagine the terror in his father's heart when he'd realized his son was gone. Young Trent had no concept of those repercussions, but adult Trent did. "I had no idea, Dad. I'm sorry."

"It's okay. Kids will do that to you." His father chuckled. His tone eased as he spoke, as if the memory had knocked down a few of the bricks in the wall between them. "You gave me a lot of scares over the years, but I figure it was payback for all the times I scared my own parents by riding my bike too fast or climbing something I shouldn't."

"Mom has always said you and I are more alike than not," Trent said. "I guess I never really thought about what we had in common."

"I think when you hit eighteen, you start looking for the ways you're not like your father. It's part of growing up and spreading your own wings."

Those wings had brought Trent far from the family business, and far from the people who loved him. He'd used the excuse of the business to be too busy to go home, too busy to call, too busy to send a card. With each excuse, the wall between Trent and his family had gotten taller and thicker and more impossible to climb. That had to change going forward.

"I'm sorry. I..." Trent fiddled with the papers on his desk. "I guess I spread my wings so far, I wasn't sure how to come back home."

The noises on the other end of the phone changed, and Trent could picture his father heading to the back of the nursery, to the plants he loved and spent his days tending.

"That's the kind of kid you are, Trent. It's part of why you have this big, international, going-to-be-on-the-stock-market company, and I have a little nursery in Hudson Falls. You fly farther and higher than I do, but that's okay. I'm proud of you for what you've done and how far you've gone."

Never had his father said those words. His father was a stoic man, stingy with praise, flush with criticism. The compliment was unexpected and rushed over Trent, making his eyes water. "Thank you, Dad. That means more than I can tell you."

"Shoulda said it sooner." His father cleared his throat. "I guess in my eyes, you're still that little boy stuck on the mountain, scared and hungry and stubborn."

That made Trent smile. He'd been called that more than once in his life. "Stubborn? Who, me?"

His father chuckled again. "Yet another trait you get from me. Your mother is the one who tempers that in me. She's the one who stops me when I'm going off course, reels me back when I get lost. She did it that day you went missing."

"She did? I didn't know that." It made sense, given the relationship his parents had. They loved each other deeply, and his mother's soft, gentle way dulled the sharp edges of his father.

"When I was panicking looking for you, your mother told me to take a deep breath. She said no one knew you like I did, because we are so alike in many ways. I was stubborn, and I argued with her, but she won, like she usually does. Little tip, son. If a woman who loves you tells you something, chances are it's true. When I stopped arguing with your mother, I stood there and inhaled and started thinking about where I would go if it was me. I remembered there was one little vista where you could see into the Skagit Valley. It was spring when you made that climb, and the tulips are blooming then. The valley is incredible at that time of year."

Trent could still see the lush carpet of red, yellow, pink flowers, running for what seemed like miles along the rich earth of the river's delta. "It was stunning. I'd never seen anything like it."

"It's the first climb I ever took with my dad. Did I ever tell you that? Anyway, I climbed up there and found you, shivering and starving."

When his father had crested the little ridge Trent had been sitting on, the relief had been almost overpowering. Trent had run to his father, hugged his legs, and tried not to cry. "And then I wouldn't leave."

"You said you wanted to watch the sunset fall over the valley. Stubborn." But this time when his father said the word, it was edged with love and admiration.

Trent sat back in his chair and closed his eyes. These were the parts he'd forgotten, the memories he'd pushed to the side with all those excuses that had kept him away from home. His throat got thick and his eyes stung as the vivid memory played in his mind. "Instead of yelling at me, you took off your jacket, and you put it over my shoulders. Then you sat down beside me. We sat there for so long, watching the sunset."

"It was all kinds of purples and oranges. Amazing."

The weather that day hadn't been much different from the weather right now, and up on the mountain, the temperature would be even lower. Yet Trent couldn't remember his father ever complaining, not once, while they'd sat on the hard, chilly stones and waited for the sun to descend. "Weren't you cold, Dad?"

"How could I be cold, Trent? I was with my son watching one of the most spectacular sunsets in the world. It could have been ten degrees below zero and I wouldn't have cared. I knew right then that this was a moment I would maybe never have again, and I was going to hold on to it with all my strength." Emotion pitched the syllables in his father's words a note or two higher. "In the years you've been gone, Trent, that's been the moment in my mind. It is the truest, sweetest memory I have. There was nothing but the sun and the tulips, and you and I."

Trent paused a long time, because if he said anything, he would start to cry. It had to be the tumult of these last few weeks, or maybe just the simple words, *I'm proud of you.*

"I wish we could go back there, Dad." Trent sighed. He traced over the statement on his desk, the words he was going to have to say very soon. "I've got some hard decisions to make, and I'm not sure which way to go."

"Then take a breath, Trent. Pull it into your chest and hold it there, and think about the things that matter most. The moments you want to hold on to with everything you have. When you have to make a choice to go right or left, always go in the direction of the things that matter most."

Trent considered those words for a moment. The manuscript sat on his desk, waiting for him to approve it for the publisher so they could print it and launch his life story. An incomplete story. He couldn't change that, but he could change the next moment and maybe give his dad more than a sunset to hold on to. "Say Dad, do you think it would be okay if I came home for dinner on Sunday?"

There was a long silence, so long that Trent worried his father would tell him no. Then he heard Dad take a breath and a sob catch in his throat. "That would be more than okay, Trent. And maybe after we eat, we could go watch the sunset over the valley?"

"I'd love that, Dad." He cleared his throat and swiped away the emotion in his eyes. "I'd love that a lot."

An hour later, Trent sat in his conference room with Sarah on one side and the reporter from *Outdoor Fun* on the other. Trent was sure the reporter, a thin guy in his twenties with dark-rimmed glasses, had no idea what kind of turmoil he'd gone through in the last couple of weeks. He set a tape recorder between them, preparing to do the interview that meant the future for his company, and all Trent could think about was Kate.

"So, Mr. MacMillan, I would like to start with talking about the book." On the table beside the recorder, the reporter had a printed copy of the tabloid story about the ghostwriting. "This article says Ms. Winslow was your ghostwriter. That you, in fact, didn't write any of the words in that book."

The statement Sarah had prepared, polished and memorized in his head was ready to go. *Ms. Winslow served as an editorial consultant only. I wrote every word in Be True to Your Nature. I'm a hundred percent the author of my memoir, and Ms. Winslow was merely a go-to for advice on structure and grammar.*

Sarah gave Trent a questioning look. She nodded toward the statement, printed and sitting by Trent's elbow. A couple of sentences, that would be all it took to set the company to rights again and get things moving in a positive direction. A couple of sentences, and the book would launch without a hitch and the IPO would go smoothly. A couple of sentences, and he could erase the publicity road bump caused by the tabloid article.

Even though the printout with the reporter was facing away from him, Trent could see Kate's face in the picture the fan had taken on the mountain. She was standing to the side, watching Trent pose with the couple they'd met on Mt. Cascade. Her gaze was intent, and a half smile played on her lips. She looked like…

Well, like she was proud of him. And like she loved him.

The book was heading to the publisher later today. The complete story of Trent MacMillan's rise to fame and fortune, the back cover copy said. The truth about how a small-town kid took a hike up Machu Picchu and before he knew it, became the owner of a multi-million-dollar company.

"Mr. MacMillan? About the book? I just want to verify that you wrote *Be True to Your Nature.*"

"No, I didn't." The words slipped out, almost under his breath. Sarah gasped. Out of the corner of his eye, he could see her pointing toward the statement, her face full of panic. His main focus, though, lingered on Kate's face, on the honest emotion in her eyes. "Kate Winslow wrote every last word."

"Wait...you're saying that tabloid story is true?" The reporter leaned closer, his eyes wide behind the owlish glasses.

"More or less, yes." Trent flipped the prepared statement over. He wasn't going to need that. "I have known Kate Winslow since college. We dated for about a year and broke up shortly after graduation."

"So that rumor is true? You two did date?" The reporter scribbled notes, as if he couldn't wait to get this exclusive down fast enough.

"We did. And because of that, there was some understandable history between us. In fact, when I found out she was the ghostwriter for my book, I initially said no," Trent said. "But then I realized no one will know me like

Kate knows me. Plus, she's a phenomenal writer, and I knew she would do a great job."

"So you hired her even though you two had a past history?"

He nodded. "I hadn't seen her in almost fifteen years, not until she was standing in this very room a few weeks ago." He could still see her curves, silhouetted against the view outside the window. That determined set of her jaw and the sparkle of interest in her eyes. "She and I started working together on the book that night."

"And you weren't dating during the writing of the book?" When Trent shook his head, the reporter plowed forward. "Then why was she reported to be seen wearing your jacket?"

"It was raining the night we had our meeting, and she forgot her raincoat." He chuckled, remembering how Kate had been swamped by his jacket yet had looked so cute in it, he would have given her every piece of his wardrobe. "She forgets her raincoat all the time. It's sort of...adorable."

Sarah's brow arched, but she didn't say anything.

"And was it Kate Winslow's foot in that picture from the hike?"

"Yes, it was. I took her along with me to sort of see my world and to talk some more. She was never much of an adventurer back in college, but she took this in stride. She surprised me."

Had she changed that much since college? Or had he changed? It seemed like they got along better now, understood each other better, and that she was more open to being a part of his world. Even if it cost her everything.

The reporter leaned back and gave Trent a grin. "Seems you have more than just professional feelings for her?"

That wasn't a question Trent was going to answer, not to a nosy reporter from *Outdoor Fun.* Trent tapped the reporter's notepad. "I want to make sure that when you write this article, you give all credit for the book to Kate. Mention how brilliant she is, what an incredible writer she is, and how she took my box of Post-It Notes and scribblings and turned it into something...well, something pretty amazing."

The reporter nodded as he wrote all those words down. The recorder whirred in the background. "So you're pleased with how the book turned out?"

"I've read it several times, and it's kept me captivated, even though it's my life story, which I know pretty well." He grinned. "She has this way of weaving suspense and emotion into everything from climbing a mountain to rescuing sea turtles."

The reporter glanced up. "There's a story about rescuing sea turtles in there?"

"No. But there should be." Trent got to his feet. "Call me or email me if you have any other questions. Sarah can provide you with an excerpt from the book. Just make sure you get the author's name right. K-A-T-E W-I-N-S-L-O-W. That's the only name that should be after the word *by*."

He left the conference room and headed for his office.

Sarah stopped him in the hall, a little out of breath from hurrying after him. "What... what was that?"

"A little bit of the truth."

"You know this could be disastrous, right? We needed to keep the image of the company pristine, and this whole social media firestorm is only going to get worse now."

Trent considered her words. Sarah had worked for him for a long time, and he trusted her guidance. Almost every time. What had Jeremy said? That it was Trent's gut instincts that had brought them all this far. He was going to trust those instincts again right now, just as he had with the reporter. "The day I got the idea for this company, I was standing on the top of Machu Picchu and looking out over the ruins of the Incan civilization. I saw a world that stairstepped up the side of that mountain in Peru, one level after another, until they reached the pinnacle."

"And you saw trash, and that gave you the idea of the eco-friendly outdoor apparel company. I know the story, Trent. I wrote the company brochure."

Everyone knew the story of the genesis of GOA. Even Trent had thought he knew every detail, but it turned out he had forgotten a thing or two. "I was thinking about that day this morning when I woke up. I was flipping through some of my pictures from then, because the publisher wants to include them in the book. And you know what I saw?"

Sarah sighed. "I give up. What?"

"People who got to the top because of each other. There wasn't one Incan who decided, 'hey, I'm going to take this spot on the apex of the mountain.'" He could see the excavated site before him in his mind, rows and rows of stone remains, built one above the other. "There was layer after layer of homes and buildings, built by people who worked together for the common good. More than a hundred sets of stairs, over a hundred and fifty buildings, all created by the Incan people together. No one stamped their name on it. No one took sole credit. It was a team effort, just like GOA."

"What does that have to do with the book?"

"I wouldn't be here, with this company as successful as it is, without you and Jeremy and the dozens of other people whose hard work has helped build GOA. And I wouldn't have the book that I have without the hard work of Kate." He shoved his hands in his pockets and shrugged. "She was the one who built all the structure and filled it in with walls and roofs that I could set the next layer on. She was the one who created all those steps that took my scraps of paper and turned them into a mountain. My taking credit for that would be wrong."

A look of understanding dawned in Sarah's eyes. "And not true to your nature."

"Exactly."

Sarah let out a long breath, still holding a little worry in her features. "Okay. I'm not sure it's going to work, but I trust your instincts, Trent."

"And it's about time I did too." He said goodbye to Sarah, then grabbed his jacket and headed out the door into a bright, crisp day with a sweet hint of spring in the air.

Seventeen

KATE PERCHED ON THE EDGE of the
sofa, her stomach in knots, waiting. The slight rustling of paper was
the only sound in the room. She'd worn her
lucky T-shirt, because she figured she needed all the luck she could get today. When the
last page was turned, Kate leaned forward.
"Well?"

Angie set the printed pages on the end
table beside her. "It needs work."

"I figured that. But is it...good?"

"No." Angie drew in a breath, and a
second later, just before Kate fell apart with
disappointment, the serious tone in her voice
yielded to bright notes. "It's incredible. I loved
the relationship between the sisters and their
mother. It made me tear up several times."

"I'm glad." She'd worked so hard on those
pages, drawing on the emotional connection

with Grandma Wanda as inspiration. "Not that I made you cry, but because that's exactly what I was going for with those pages."

"You should *want* to make me cry, and make every reader cry," Angie said. "That's what creates memorable, compelling books that people remember and share and recommend. I'll put together some thoughts about revisions and send them to you. Once those are done, I have a few editors in mind already who would love this book."

"That sounds awesome." Kate had to restrain herself to keep from bouncing with joy. All the time she'd been writing, she wasn't sure how the book would turn out, or if she really had what it took to produce a novel worth publishing. Penny and Grandma had only read snippets, but Angie had seen the entire book and loved it. "I'll make whatever changes you ask for."

Angie picked up the printed manuscript and leafed through the pages. "I can tell that when you wrote this, you went with your instincts, rather than some predestined plot. You took risks with what you were writing, and too many authors don't do that because they're so afraid to step outside the box. There were a couple of times the book went left when I expected it go right, and that was awesome."

"It was?"

"You have good instincts for story, Kate. That's what has made you such a success as a ghostwriter. So when you see my suggestions, take them as just that, suggestions. Trust what your gut says about which changes to make and which changes won't work. I have no doubt you'll make this even better."

"Thank you. I'm so excited you liked it, and I can't wait to see it in print." She got to her feet and slung her tote bag over her shoulder. "I'm going to go home and get right to work."

"Before you go..." Angie grabbed her tablet, pulled up a page and turned it toward Kate. "I assume you've seen this interview?"

Below the online article for *Outdoor Fun*, Trent's picture stared back at her, familiar and painful. She recognized Moulton Falls behind him and the poses Carissa had set up for the photo shoot that day. The memory shredded Kate's heart, and she tore her gaze away. "No. I...I've avoided anything to do with that project."

"Well, this one you shouldn't avoid." Angie slid the tablet over to Kate. "I highly suggest you read this."

Was it going to be another speculative piece that trashed her as a writer? Or the public statement Trent had promised to make relegating her to the role of editor and consultant? Kate settled back in her chair and at first, only skimmed the article. Her jaded view began to slowly soften as the words filtered through. *Kate Winslow is the sole author... Incredible writer... Knew exactly what questions to ask and how to capture my truth... Couldn't have done it without her expertise... Team effort, with Kate pulling most of the weight... Took my scattered notes and turned them into a story I couldn't put down.*

Kate raised her gaze to Angie's. "He said all this?"

Angie nodded. "He made it very clear that the book is your work, not his. The reporter says that later in the story."

"But I thought..." Kate shook her head. This didn't make sense. It wasn't what they had agreed to say, and not what Trent had planned. "I'm just the ghostwriter."

Angie grinned. "Not anymore. This ghost is out in full view of the public now."

Great. No client would ever trust her with a nondisclosure agreement again. "That'll ruin my chances of ever working on another project."

"Actually, it's had the opposite effect." Angie motioned toward her desk and a stack of pink call notes sitting beside her keyboard. "My phone hasn't stopped ringing with people looking to work with you. I've got several emails to return, and a bunch of voicemails to answer."

"That all happened in the last couple of weeks? Why didn't you tell me?"

"Because I knew it would distract you from what you needed to be doing—working on your own book. Ghostwriting can be a side business, but really, you've put your dreams on hold long enough. This"—she hefted the manuscript Kate had worked so hard to write over the couple of weeks—"is amazing. Your voice is beautiful, and your story is rich and emotional. I want to see this on a bookshelf, not languishing in your computer."

Kate laughed. "Okay. I get it. I'll go home, make some revisions and start another book. You happy?"

"Delighted. I can't wait for the world to see how Kate Winslow creates a *fiction* story the reader just can't put down."

The echo of Trent's words in the article caused an ache in Kate's chest. She'd ignored his calls and texts for weeks. Had he been trying to tell her he was going to tell the world she was the real author? Or had this story been just another publicity move? "I'm just so surprised Trent changed his story. I wonder why he did it."

"You can ask him yourself in a minute." Angie cleared her throat. "He wanted to meet with me to discuss the book and asked if there was a time anywhere close to when you would be here. Apparently, he's been trying to reach you for a while."

"I've been ignoring him." Her landlord had turned away several flower deliveries from her building, and Kate had sent every call to voicemail. She'd deleted the messages before she'd listened to them and had a stack of unread text messages from Trent. The only email she had responded to was his short list of corrections—sending the revised book back to him indirectly.

"Maybe," Angie said gently, "maybe it's time you stopped being a ghost there too."

Before Kate could answer, there was a knock at Angie's door. The sound startled Kate. Her pulse raced, and she fought the urge to bolt before her heart got broken a third time.

"I can send him away or ask him to come back later. What do you want to do?"

Kate glanced at the tablet, at the selfless act Trent had done, saving her career over his company, over himself. He'd come clean with the truth, no matter what it cost him, because of her. The least she could do was thank him. "Let him in."

Angie crossed to the door and opened it. "Trent, hi. Nice to see you. Kate's already here."

Kate's heart stopped. She half expected

Trent to turn around and leave. Instead, she heard the familiar notes of his deep voice.

"Good. I was hoping to speak to her." He skirted past Angie and stopped in the center of the office, quiet, almost shy. His hair was a little long and brushed across his brows, almost blocking his piercing blue eyes. He had on the same fleece jacket he had given her, over a white Henley like the one she'd worn the day of the hike. She wanted to curl into him and never leave. "Hey."

"Hey." She got to her feet, praying he wouldn't see how much she was shaking. Kate stood ten feet away from him, but it felt like ten thousand. "I saw the article."

From behind Trent, Angie looked at Kate with a question on her face. When Kate nodded, Angie sent her a thumbs-up, then slipped out of her office, leaving Kate and Trent alone for the first time in weeks.

The space seemed too small and too big at the same time, and Kate wanted to both dash from the room and stay right where she was. She elected to stay, because she wasn't sure her legs could carry her if she moved.

"Before you say anything, I want to share something with you," Trent said.

"Okay." She hoped it wasn't another article or social media post. She couldn't handle any more of those.

He took a step forward. "Did you know

that Ridley sea turtles, both the Kemp and the Olive Ridley, are the only turtle species that do mass synchronized nestings?"

She stared at him. Was he really talking about sea turtles? Where was this going? "Um yes. I think so."

"The larger populations of Olive Ridleys in places like India have always done this, re-searchers think," Trent went on as he closed the distance between them a little more. A smile played at the edges of his lips. "In French Guiana, the populations of the Olive Ridleys began to drop drastically, like, by ninety percent, so low that researchers con-sidered putting them on a watch list. Until ten years ago."

She took another step closer. She was captivated, utterly captivated, by the story. "What happened ten years ago?"

"The researchers had attached those things to their backs—"

"Transponders."

"—and had been watching them for years." Now Trent was inches away from her, so close she could feel the warmth of his body between them. "All of a sudden, they re-alized the French Guiana turtles began doing the same thing, as if some of the other ones had migrated and spread the word, or there was some kind of survival instinct that made them band together. They started synchronizing their nesting, all coming out of the sea on the same night to lay their eggs. Within ten years, the population of Olive Ridleys in French Guiana had tripled."

The scent of his cologne lured her even closer. He was a few inches taller than her, just enough that she had to look up to see the amusement in his eyes, the slight shadow of stubble on his chin. All the things she loved about his face were so close. "What do Olive Ridley turtles have to do with anything?"

"Without each other, they wouldn't have survived." He took Kate's hands in his larger, warm grip, and her heart did a little leap. His thumbs skated over the ridges of her knuckles. "I wouldn't have made it through that book or the last few weeks without you, Kate."

"All I did was write the words."

"You helped me focus, to find what was important, and most of all, you helped bring me home." His blue eyes met hers, as deep and dark as the ocean. "I'd forgotten what was important until you came back into my life and reminded me."

She didn't dare ask the question, but if she didn't, she'd die of curiosity. "And what is that?"

"Love," Trent said softly, and hope exploded inside Kate. "That's what's important. Love for my company, the work that I do."

The hope in her chest shriveled. She managed to eke out a few words. "Oh, yeah, that's important."

"Love for my family."

"That's important too." Why was he torturing her like this? Just to talk about the company? She wanted to leave, to end this painful moment right now. "Trent, I should go—"

But he held on to her hands, held on to her gaze. "And love for the people who bring out the best in me." He smiled that crooked smile she had fallen in love with in the hallway of the English building. "Or rather, person."

She didn't dare ask who he meant. Too much of her heart was counting on the answer to hear someone else's name. "That's good, Trent."

He craned his neck until she was looking into his eyes again. "You stopped answering my calls."

"I thought you were mad at me." She shrugged, and cursed the tears that burned at the back of her eyes. Why had he come here? Why was he holding her hands and talking about love and turtles and the book? "For the blog post and for all those clues Loretta put together."

He brushed away a tendril of hair that had fallen against her cheek. "You were being true to your nature, and just being you. Who could be mad at that?"

"Well...some people."

"I'm not one of those people." The fleecy edge of the jacket tickled along her fingers and tempted her to curve into the softness. "I read the book you wrote three times. No, four."

"You did? Why?"

"Because I kept looking for what was missing."

She thought back over the pages she'd written, the notes she'd taken, the stories he had told her. "I think I got everything, Trent. Your childhood, the nursery, the hike—"

"What was missing was *you*, KitKat. Our history. Your impact on me. And your name on the cover."

Why did he have to keep mentioning that? Her name and her involvement in this book was what had started all the problems in the first place. She shook her head and broke away. "That's not how it works, Trent."

"Says who?" He came around her, standing between her and the view outside Angie's window. "I called the publisher and told them I wasn't going to publish the book, not the way it was."

"Is there something wrong with the text? I can change—"

"There's nothing wrong with the text,

Kate. The book is perfect. It's the cover that needs to be changed. In fact"—he reached into his pocket and pulled out a folded sheet of paper—"I had them send me a mockup of the new cover."

Trent's image was gone. In place of his face, the photo she'd taken that day was there, with Trent's silhouette on one side and the mountains and the waterfall and the beauty of Washington State on the other. And at the bottom of the cover, the words *By Kate Winslow and Trent MacMillan.*

"I figured your name should be first, since you did all the hard work. All I did was talk your head off." He grinned.

"Where did you get my picture? I never posted that anywhere."

"You showed it to my mom when we were visiting. You were telling her and Marla about our hike to the falls, and my mom asked you for a copy of the picture. She showed it to me last week and I realized that was the perfect image for the cover. Because it was yours."

Kate had forgotten all about that. She'd been flipping through the pictures with them after dinner, talking about the hike, and his mom had asked for a copy. "I had no idea she showed it to you. That is so sweet of you to use it on the cover, Trent, and my name... I'm..." She let out a little laugh. "Speechless."

Now that photo, a quick snap she'd taken because she didn't want to forget that day with Trent, was going to be immortalized on the cover of the book, right above her name. The gesture touched her heart and made tears rush to her eyes.

"It's a small thing to try to begin to make up for the big things, KitKat. When we were young, I broke up with you because you were scared to do the things I wanted to do. But I was the one who was truly scared of how hard I fell for you, and how much you meant to me so quickly. I was too dumb and stupid to know what to do with a love like that, so I let you go."

She understood that, because she'd been afraid of so many things for so long. Maybe Grandma Wanda had been right, and college simply hadn't been the time for Trent and Kate to be a forever couple. "My grandmother said that maybe our hearts needed a little more time to mature. Like a plant in the greenhouse." Kate laughed. "Then again, she compares everything in life to plants."

"I know I needed more time to mature and figure out what's important. Like my family, and you." He cupped her jaw with his hands, so gentle, so easy, she thought she might melt right there. "I loved you then, Kate, and I love you now."

Her heart soared, and every cloud that had loomed in her thoughts over the last few weeks disappeared. "Because of you, I took risks, Trent. Did things I never imagined I'd do. Like...fall in love again. Oh, Trent, I love you too."

A smile burst across his face, lighting his eyes. He leaned in and kissed her, a slow, sweet kiss that was like a melody, skating across her lips, treasuring every moment. She curved into his chest, into the softness of the jacket and the strength that had always been Trent. She didn't say anything, because there were no words that could possibly be as sweet as that moment.

Epilogue

THE PARTY WAS IN FULL swing, with dozens of guests filling the newly re-designed space behind Trent's house. In the space of a few weeks, the plain grassy lawn had been transformed into an oasis with several seating areas, a cozy firepit, and dozens of flowering plants. The sun was just starting to set, and tiny white lights strung between the trellis and the stone patio blinked on, casting a gauzy light over the festivities.

"It looks beautiful, as do you, KitKat." Trent's arm stole around Kate's waist. She had on a pale yellow dress that offset the green in her eyes and long brunette curls that cascaded down her back. For the millionth time, Trent thought he was a very, very lucky man to have such an incredible woman in his life. "You and my sister came up with a fantastic design."

"Marla's so talented. All my grandma and I did was plant." Kate waved at her grandmother, who was holding up a small pot of primroses and explaining the plant to Trent's father. "Thanks for including her. She loved being a part of the gardening."

"Your grandma is awesome." He'd always loved Kate's grandmother, and in the last few weeks, he'd spent a lot of time helping her with her garden and having long talks about the future. "She said she's glad I smartened up."

Kate laughed. "You did indeed. Oh, look, my parents are here! I didn't even know they were coming. I'm going to go say hello."

Trent waved at the older couple, who'd actually been in Seattle for a couple of days. He'd flown them in early, and put them up in a hotel close to Kate's apartment. The whole surprise had been orchestrated without a hitch. "Before you go," he said, "can I ask you something?"

"Sure."

"On the hike, you said you wore your lucky shirt on purpose. Why?" That dark blue shirt from the cookie shop that she'd worn every time she had a momentous occasion. He was darned glad she'd worn it the day he'd woken up and realized he would be a fool to let her go.

"Well, one because I was half afraid I would break my neck climbing up a mountain, and two..." Her cheeks flushed. "I was hoping you'd fall in love with me again. And you did, so it worked. See? Lucky."

"I'd say I'm far luckier than that shirt." He pressed a kiss to her temple. "Go say hi to your folks. I'll be over in a minute."

Kate dashed across the lawn. Her father swept her up into a hug and the three of them started chatting, clearly overjoyed to be together. Across the way, Kate's grandmother waved to her daughter and son-in-law while she was chatting with Trent's parents and sister. His family had closed the nursery for a couple of days to come down to Seattle, stay with Trent, and help him put the finishing touches on the yard. He and his father had been outside until late last night, weeding and trimming and talking. The long, quiet moments with his father had been as wonderful as that sunset all those years ago.

Sarah was sitting at one of the tables, her sleepy baby in her lap. She'd been out on maternity leave for the past few weeks, and seeing her now, so happy and in her element as a mom, made Trent glad he'd worked out a work-at-home option for Sarah to stay at

GOA and still be home with her new daughter.

Jeremy ambled over. "Those new employees are working out great, boss."

Trent had hired a couple of managers to fill the gaps, which meant Trent didn't have to work weekends or miss his daily run with Greg. That part was both good and bad, because Greg always pushed him to run faster, a healthy competition Trent secretly enjoyed. There'd be time now to hike and bike, and take Kate on trips. "I'm glad. Are the employees happy with the new schedules?"

"Yup. That new flex-time plan means everyone gets to get outdoors more often," Jeremy said. "It's making for some very motivated and productive employees. The last employee survey didn't have a single complaint."

"Great. Profits are up, the IPO is looking good, and my life is finally in order." Trent glanced around the yard. Huge posters of the book cover were mounted on poles in the corners of the yard, and dozens of copies were stacked on the tables as gifts for everyone he'd invited. The party was meant to be for the book's unveiling, but Trent had one more thing he wanted to reveal, now that all his employees were here.

"I've got to go give a quick speech," he said to Jeremy. "Go enjoy the party. You work hard, and you deserve more time off."

Jeremy laughed. "I'm not going to argue with that."

Trent crossed to the makeshift stage he'd had workers install beside the patio. He flipped on the microphone, and conversation ebbed to a stop. "Thank you everyone for being here. It means so much to me to celebrate the success of Get Outdoors Apparel as well as the fabulous book Kate wrote, with the people who mean the most to me."

Kate stood on the edge of the patio, beaming at him with so much love in her eyes, it made his heart ache, in a good way. She clapped and whooped. Their families cheered.

"Profits are up fifteen percent this quarter, and Jeremy is predicting a really strong holiday season. I owe it all to you, my loyal and wonderful team. Which is why we're changing the company slogan to..." Trent did a little drum roll against the mike, then he pulled a small cord and a banner unfurled across the stone wall. *True to Our Nature* was written beneath the company logo. "We're changing the *your* to *our* because it's only because of all of us, working together, building on each other's successes and strengths, that we are here today."

There was a large swell of applause and cheers. The photographers Sarah had invited snapped some pictures. Trent didn't pay attention to any of that. He had one more important thing to do tonight, something that had waited far too long.

"The most important member of my team, the one who made all of this possible because of her wisdom and patience and amazingness, is Kate." He crossed the patio and took her hand, hauling her up to the front of the group with him. "She is the rock I stand on, the one I can count on to always be honest and true. Because she loves me, and I love her."

There were more whoops and applause. Kate blushed and whispered, "I do love you."

Every time she said those words, his heart filled so much, he was sure it would burst with joy. "And because I want you to always be prepared for anything, Kate, I've filled this backpack with everything you need for survival." He handed her a branded bright-pink bag he'd special-ordered just for Kate. "In there, you'll find granola bars and water bottles and flashlight."

She laughed. "I don't plan on taking off to parts unknown by myself. I've gotten more adventurous, but not *that* adventurous."

"We're going to have lots of adventures together in our future too." He gave her a quick, sweet kiss. "There's no custom backpack for me, because I have everything I need for my survival right here." Then Trent pulled a velvet box out of his pocket, dropped to one knee and flipped the lid back. "That's you, Kate. Will you marry me?"

Kate gasped. Tears sprung to her eyes, and she nodded. "Yes, Trent, yes."

"Those are the only words I wanted to hear." He slipped the round-cut diamond on her left hand, then pulled her to him. As Trent kissed his wife-to-be, there were champagne bottles being uncorked and congratulations being shouted, but the only thing he could see was the woman he loved and the long, happy life that lay on the trail ahead of them.

The End

Guacamole Grilled Chicken Club

Kate, the heroine of *In Other Words, Love*, has to work long hours to finish ghostwriting Trent's memoir. To show his appreciation and support, he promises to bring her unlimited takeout from their favorite restaurant, Chick and Cheese. She especially loves their Guacamole Grilled Chicken Club sandwich. Our version is perfect for a busy day. Make it for yourself, or someone you love!

Prep Time: 5 minutes
Cook Time: 15 minutes
Serves: 4

Ingredients

- 4 boneless, skinless chicken breast filets (about 1 pound total)
- Salt and black pepper, to taste
- 4 Ciabatta rolls, sliced horizontally, buttered and toasted
- 1/4 cup Chipotle mayonnaise, recipe below
- 4 green leaf lettuce leaves
- 8 slices bacon, cooked crisp
- 1 cup guacamole
- 1/4 cup Cojita Mexican cheese, crumbled

CHIPOTLE MAYONNAISE

- 1/4 cup mayonnaise
- 1/2 teaspoon peppers in adobo, pureed

Preparation

1. Preheat grill.
2. Season chicken with salt and pepper and grill over medium for 5 to 8 minutes on each side or until cooked through.
3. Spread chipotle mayonnaise on bottom half of each roll and top with lettuce, chicken breast, bacon, guacamole and crumbled cheese.
4. Close each sandwich with top half of roll and serve.

Thanks so much for reading
In Other Words, Love. We hope you enjoyed it!

You might like these other books
from Hallmark Publishing:

Country Hearts
The Story of Us
Love By Chance
The Secret Ingredient
Beach Wedding Weekend
Love on Location
Sunrise Cabin

For information about our new releases and
exclusive offers, sign up for
our free newsletter at
hallmarkchannel.com/hallmark-
publishing-newsletter

You can also connect with us here:

Facebook.com/HallmarkPublishing

Twitter.com/HallmarkPublish

About The Author

When she's not writing books, *New York Times* and *USA Today* bestselling author Shirley Jump competes in triathlons, mostly because all that training lets her justify mid-day naps and a second slice of chocolate cake. She's published more than sixty books in twenty-four languages, although she's too geographically challenged to find any of those countries on a map.

Turn the page for a sneak peek of

CORY MARTIN

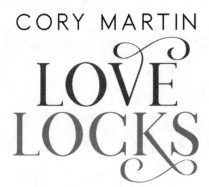

Based on the Hallmark Hall of Fame Movie
Story by John Tinker and Neal Dobrofsky & Tippi Dobrofsky
Teleplay by Teena Booth and John Tinker

Chapter One

A Time and a Place

IN YOUNG LOVE, THERE ARE rarely specific
dates. When you are in that all-consumed
state, love has no number. Love is your
first kiss in seventh grade outside the gym –
sweaty palms, blue jeans, and curled hair. It
is the boy who left you heartbroken the summer before senior year just as you made the
varsity soccer team, and the wondering what
happened to the guy you met on a family vacation to Hawaii.

Love is a marker of moments passing
and standing still. It is a time and a place.
And that is where this story begins...

Twenty years ago. Paris.

It was late fall, or early winter. The leaves
were gone, but the sun still shone, and two
Americans rode the streets on bicycles.

Lindsey and Jack met at the Sorbonne.
She was an art student; he was a student of
life with a major in business.

Lindsey had moved to the City of Lights
in September to study art at the univer-
sity as an exchange student. Jack, though an

American, had lived in Europe for most of his life. His father, a hotelier and restaurateur, showed Jack the world through his businesses. While Jack was studying the economy in class, he was learning it firsthand at his father's latest hotel in Paris.

Though it may have seemed as if they came from two separate worlds, they were more similar than many would believe. They both worked hard—she at painting, he at pleasing his father. Jack had plans to own his own hotel one day. Each had dreams of the future where life was grand, yet they also understood the importance of the moment. As twenty-somethings, they lived young and carefree.

The contents of their bike baskets jiggled along the cobblestone streets. The colors in her paint box shook with every pedal stroke, and the baguette peeking out of his picnic basket bobbed up and down. They spent many days on their bikes, weaving in and out of the hidden parts of Paris.

"Let's stop here," Jack said as they approached the Place Du Tertre, a square at the heart of the Montmartre quarter where a penniless Picasso had once lived. Lindsey happily obliged. It was one of her favorite places to paint.

She appreciated small ways Jack supported her, like this—choosing to picnic in a spot she loved. He understood her, despite not being an artist himself.

As they leaned their bikes against a lamppost and locked them up, Jack pointed to a man painting portraits with a cat beside him.

"We should get one done," Jack said.

"A portrait? Really?" She viewed this kind of painting as a cheesy tourist attraction meant to sucker men into buying things for women. Plus, where would they hang it? His place or hers?

"It'll be fun." Jack grabbed her hand and gently guided her toward the man's easel. "You need something to remember Paris by once you go back to New York."

"But I'll have you." Lindsey didn't need a generic painting to remember her time with Jack.

"How much?" Jack asked the artist.

The artist looked at them. "Thirty francs, but if you hold my cat, I give you a discount."

How could she say no to a man and his cat? She looked at Jack and smiled, then turned to the artist. "We'll do it."

Jack handed the man the money and pulled his red knit hat off his head. Lindsey fluffed his brown hair to make him present-able, then grabbed the gray-and-white cat and placed it between them as they sat close on a small chair. Jack leaned over and kissed her windblown cheek.

"That kiss. That is, what do you call it? The... the... essence of the two of you. That is what I shall capture." The artist made rounded strokes as though sketching the shapes of their heads in black charcoal against a pre-painted backdrop of the Eiffel Tower.

Though she knew the painting wouldn't end up in a museum one day, Lindsey felt her heart lift with happiness. She reached over and squeezed Jack's hand. This moment she would remember forever, regardless of whether the sketch captured anything at all. It would be a reminder that life could never be fully planned. If she'd arranged every detail of the day, they wouldn't be getting a painting done right now.

Lindsey had come to Paris to learn how to paint, not with technical skills but with the kind of passion she felt every time she entered the Louvre. She hadn't come to fall in love or find "the one." She was young and looking to a future where she might one day have her pieces hanging in a gallery. She'd come to Paris with a mission. Nobody would interrupt her process. She was strictly there to perfect her craft. However, the first time she'd seen Jack's blue eyes, she'd known she was in trouble.

After the first two weeks with Jack, her vision of the future had changed. And now, she couldn't imagine life without him.

Her time at the Sorbonne was nearly over, and she and Jack had discussed their future. After he finished school, he would come to New York. She needed to know what it would be like if he was part of her world—

not in this fairytale land, as Paris often felt like to her, but New York City. She knew everything about him, and she wanted Jack to see the other part of her world.

A small piece of her feared that, like all great things in life, their relationship would eventually come to an end, but another part looked excitedly toward the future. For now, she was content that they would have this sketch to remind them of their time together in Paris.

"Should I be smiling or should I be brooding?" Jack asked, interrupting Lindsey's train of thought.

"Smile, of course," Lindsey said. "I love your smile."

"This one?" Jack grinned as wide as he could. He looked cartoonish. Lindsey giggled.

The artist interrupted their moment of playfulness. "Um, no, *monsieur*. My cat is Cheshire cat. You? Please, smile like a young man."

Lindsey and Jack burst out laughing, then looked at each other and turned to the artist with the biggest grins they could each muster.

The artist shook his head, then continued painting. Ten minutes later, he finished the piece.

"Okay, lovebirds. I am done. You take this and enjoy your day together. And you," he said as he turned to Jack, "don't forget— a woman that you can make smile like that is a woman you keep." Jack's face suddenly became serious as the artist handed him the finished painting. For just a moment, Lindsey thought she caught a bit of fear in his eyes.

No. She was imagining things, perhaps because of her own fears about whether their connection would last.

Lindsey took the painting from Jack's hands and studied it. Their faces were nearly caricature-like, and the background with the Eiffel Tower was terrifically touristy, but Lindsey loved it. "It's beautiful," she said and thanked him for his work.

"Maybe I see you two again sometime," the artist said.

"Maybe," Lindsey whispered as they walked off.

As Jack unlocked the bikes, Lindsey stopped him. "Why'd you get so serious back there?"

"What do you mean? I did?" Jack sounded defensive.

Lindsey paused. Maybe she shouldn't ask the question on her mind. But she had to know. "Are you sure that guy didn't freak you out when he mentioned you should keep me?"

"What? That's crazy. Of course I'm going to keep you," Jack said. "So are we heading to the bridge now?"

Lindsey nodded. Today was supposed to be a special day for them.

The tradition in Paris was that couples

would write their names on a lock, place it on the metal grates of the Pont des Arts—a pedestrian bridge that connected the Instuit de France and the Palais du Louvre—and throw away the key. The bridge was the first metal thruway constructed in the city. Engineers had conceived it to resemble a suspended garden. It had become home to the fate of thousands of couples worldwide.

Lindsey and Jack planned to seal their fate on the very same bridge.

As they rode past Notre Dame Cathedral and the Louvre, she thought about the past three months. During that time, she and Jack had spent every moment—when she wasn't painting or he wasn't working with his dad—together. Outside of class, they were inseparable. Today would be their day to declare their devotion to one another.

They rode side by side through the city streets, then out to the river, and stopped halfway across the bridge. They hopped off their bikes and stood at the railing covered in locks. Lindsey placed her hand over the lock in her pocket. She'd bought it two days ago at the local hardware store before she'd even had the courage to ask Jack if he would put a lock on the bridge with her. Yesterday, she'd asked him if he would do it and he'd happily agreed. Putting the lock on the bridge was the only thing Lindsey had planned for the day, and, she supposed, for their future.

After all, that's what the lock symbolized—a love that could not be broken.

Lindsey looked at Jack's blue eyes and immediately became lost. The cool winter breeze nipped at her ears, and the crisp smell of the water from the Seine whipped by her nose. In the distance, she could see the tip-top of the Eiffel Tower. All around them, couples were fastening their locks to the bridge. Her heart ached. Moments like these made her never want to leave Paris.

"I don't want to go back to New York," she said, and then had an idea. "What if I don't? I can stay here and paint."

"Hey, we have a plan, right?" He grabbed her hand and pulled her close with a smile. "It's going to be fine."

Lindsey knew they would see each other again soon, but still, she wasn't ready to leave. "It feels like we're saying goodbye."

"It's not goodbye. It's a few months," Jack said, but Lindsey knew it wasn't that simple.

"Did you tell your father you're quitting?"

Jack's part of the plan was to quit working for his father, go to New York, and find a job there, but he'd been putting off the first step for weeks. "I will." He put his arms around Lindsey. "We'll be back together by Valentine's Day."

The thought of being back with Jack on the most romantic day of the year made everything seem okay. "Top of the Empire State Building?" Lindsey asked.

"Not quite the top of the Eiffel Tower, but it'll do," Jack answered as he took Lindsey in his arms and kissed her. The only time she had ever been to the top of the Eiffel Tower was with Jack. It was there they had shared their first kiss. She imagined that their first kiss in the States would be at the top of the Empire State Building. That way, each moment their lips met on different soil would always have a special time and a place.

She lingered in their embrace for a moment longer before gently pulling away. Lindsey took the lock from her left pocket and produced a Sharpie marker from the right. She held up the lock proudly, then wrote her name on it.

"We lock it on the bridge, and our love will last forever," she said as she handed the lock to Jack.

"Forever?" Jack said with a slight inflection as if he were asking a question. Lindsey tried to ignore it as he wrote his name. Jack held up the lock. "With this lock, I thee…"

It slipped in his gloved hands. She reached for it, but as she put her hand out, it went flying. They both scrambled to catch it, but it was no use. They watched as the symbol of their love went sailing through the air and over the railing, falling into the water with a loud splash.

🔒

Get the book! *Love Locks* is available now!